"I don't see you, I don't see you . . ."

Justine staggered down the hallway, the floor reeling beneath her feet as though she were on a ship at sea—a rough, rolling sea—instead of at home in her calm, land-locked apartment.

"Dammit," she said, as she stumbled into a wall. She was not drunk—didn't even like to drink, except maybe for the occasional glass of wine. No, a problem with her inner ear was to blame. This was vertigo, and her doctor told her to hold tight, and it should pass.

Finally she reached the doorway to her bedroom and swept past the Mountie standing there.

Mountie?

She turned ever so slowly and there he stood, the Mountie, tall and broad shouldered, attired in hat and scarlet coat and shiny boots. With his square jaw and sandy, neatly trimmed hair, he looked as though he'd just walked off a movie set.

Justine screamed, and between the shock and vertigo, she fell to her backside.

He bent over her, scrutinizing her. "May I help you?"

—From "Justine and the Mountie" by Kristen Britain

IMAGINARY FRIENDS

Also Available from DAW Books:

Mystery Date, **edited by Denise Little**
First dates—the worst possible times in your life or the opening steps on the path to a wonderful new future? What happens when someone you have never met before turns out not to be who or what he or she claims to be? It's just a date, what could go wrong? Here are seventeen encounters, from authors such as Kristine Katherine Rusch, Nancy Springer, Laura Resnick, and Jody Lynn Nye that answer these questions. From a childhood board game called "Blind Date" that seems to come shockingly true . . . to a mythological answer to Internet predators . . . to a woman cursed to see the truth about her dates when she imbibes a little wine . . . to an enchanting translator bent on avenging victims of war crimes . . . to a young man hearing a very special voice from an unplugged stereo system . . . these are just some of the tales that may lead to happily ever after—or no ever after at all. . . .

Fellowship Fantastic, **edited by Martin H. Greenberg and Kerrie Hughes**
The true strength of a story lies in its characters and in both the ties that bind them together and the events that drive them apart. Perhaps the most famous examples of this in fantasy is *The Fellowship of The Ring.* But such fellowhsips are key to many fantasy and science fiction stories. Now thirteen top tale-spinners—Nina Kiriki Hoffmann, Alan Dean Foster, Russell Davis, Alexander Potter, among others—offer their own unique looks at fellowships from: a girl who finds her best friend through a portal to another world . . . to four special families linked by blood and magical talent . . . to two youths ripped away from all they know and faced with a terrifying fate that they can only survive together . . . to a man who must pay the price for leaving his childhood comrade to face death alone. . . .

The Future We Wish We Had, **edited by Martin H. Greenberg and Rebecca Lickiss**
In the opening decade of the twenty-first century, many things that were predicted in the science fiction stories of the twentieth century have become an accepted part of everyday life, and many other possibilities have not yet been realized but hopefully will be one day. For everyone who thought that by now they'd be motoring along the skyways in a personal jet car, or who assumed we'd have established bases on the Moon and Mars, or that we would have conquered disease, slowed the aging process to a crawl, or eliminated war, social injustice, and economic inequity, here are sixteen stories of futures that might someday be ours or our children's from Esther Friesner, Sarah Hoyt, Kevin J. Anderson, Irene Radford, Dave Freer, and Dean Wesley Smith

IMAGINARY FRIENDS

**Edited by John Marco
and Martin H. Greenberg**

DAW BOOKS, INC.
DONALD A. WOLLHEIM, FOUNDER
375 Hudson Street, New York, NY 10014

**ELIZABETH R. WOLLHEIM
SHEILA E. GILBERT
PUBLISHERS**
http://www.dawbooks.com

First Printing, September 2008
1 2 3 4 5 6 7 8 9

DAW TRADEMARK REGISTERED
U.S. PAT. AND TM. OFF. AND FOREIGN COUNTRIES
—MARCA REGISTRADA
HECHO EN U.S.A.

PRINTED IN THE U.S.A.

ACKNOWLEDGMENTS

CONTENTS

INTRODUCTION

John Marco

SEVERAL years ago, while finishing up my degree in psychology, I was assigned a research paper for my class in human development. We could pick any topic we liked as long as it involved the psychology of childhood and, importantly, we could find enough research literature to support a paper. My mind went to work trying to come up with an interesting topic. Hands shot up at once as my fellow students announced what they would write about, which were mostly pedestrian, well-worn subjects like the effects of divorce on children or sibling rivalry. I sat quietly for a time, rejecting ideas as fast as they came to me, until at last inspiration arrived. I would write about imaginary friends.

I was probably calling upon my inner fantasy writer when I came up with my topic. The notion of imaginary friends has fascinated me for years. I love the idea of a friend that no one else can see or sense but who uniquely belongs to a single child, conjured out of some deep, private need. Armed with my topic, I headed to the university library to find everything I could on the subject. I combed through books and journals and online databases, expecting to find a wealth of data. Surely a topic that interested me must also interest others, right?

Wrong. All I found were a few weak research projects and oblique references to the phenomenon of imaginary friends. Certainly not enough to write a weighty paper on the subject. Dejected, I informed my professor that I would be writing about birth order instead.

But it's a funny thing about subjects that interest you. They follow you around, demanding to be heard. Rather like some of the imaginary friends in this very anthology. If I couldn't write a research paper about these ethereal playmates, then surely I could write fiction about them. Or better yet, I could helm a whole collection of stories about imaginary friends and see what kind of companions might spring from the minds of my fellow writers.

Many of us have had imaginary friends. Maybe we don't want to admit it, but if we think back to our youth, we might be able to summon a whisper of that talking lion who protected us when we were frightened or that perfect, petite little girl who was talented and fabulous and made us believe that we could be those things too. My own imaginary friend was a sandy-haired boy named Peter, who was miraculously the same exact age as me and liked all the things I liked. Peter was with me off and on for a while, and while I don't remember much about him, I remember the *sense* of him. He wasn't just my friend. He was also my secret.

The thirteen writers in this collection all tapped into that part of their brain where unseen companions lurk.

Some of these friends are the kind of heroic protectors we hope our own children might conjure. Others can hardly be described as "friends" at all. And because the imagination is boundless, these beings come in all shapes and sizes and very often aren't human at all.

From the pen of Rick Hautala comes the tale of a boy and a dragon, the kind of bittersweet story-telling that smacks of the end of summer. In Bill Fawcett's "The Big Exit," an imaginary buddy returns after years of being nearly forgotten to aid his "boy" in the desperate battlefield of war-torn Iraq. Other companions do their work quietly, such as Biff, the stuffed St. Bernard in Tim Waggoner's marvelous "Best Friends Forever," or the silent and sly "little friend" in Kristine Kathryn Rusch's startling and funny contribution.

From the dark side, Anne Bishop brings us a haunting fairy tale of a woman trapped in a tower, forced to view the world only through a mirror. In "Walking with Shadows" by Juliet McKenna, a young girl on the precipice of change summons a life-threatening cohort. And Jim Hines brings us Death himself, coming in the guise of a cartoon character to warn a mother and her son that life is both precious and fleeting.

To all the authors who contributed to this anthology, you have my thanks. Thank you for your hard work and willingness. Most of all, thank you for helping me put a punctuation mark at the end of a project that has simmered in my mind in various forms for years now.

To the readers of this book, I hope more than just enjoyment for you. Let the stories in this collection start your mind to wandering and to remembering, and maybe to recalling a friend of your own who was there when needed.

A GOOD DAY FOR DRAGONS

Rick Hautala

THE waves hissed and writhed like a nest of snakes as they washed across the sand, leaving behind dirt-flecked foam that bubbled angrily for a moment before it disappeared. The dragon walked along the beach close to the water's edge, leaving huge, round craters wherever he stepped. The holes were soon swept away by the next rush of the rising tide. The dragon's name was Benedict—Benny, for short. The boy who sat confidently astride Benny's back between his large, leathery wings was called Alfie.

The day was just about perfect . . . a good day for dragons. If it hadn't been for a very slight chill that blew in off the water, it would have been beyond compare. But now the sun was dropping low in the western sky, casting Benny and Alfie's shadow across the sand dunes like a wash of deep blue ink. The salty tang in the air was laced with adventure, but so far Benny and Alfie had been disappointed. They had spent the entire afternoon lying on the beach, enjoying the sun and sand, and taking an occasional dip in the ocean; but all day, they had been expecting the pirates to return to Mockingbird Bay. And all day, there hadn't been even the slightest hint of their ship on the horizon.

"Maybe we scared them away for good yesterday," Alfie suggested, leaning close to Benny's ear so the dragon could hear him above the gentle roar of the surf.

"I doubt it," Benny replied in a deep, booming voice that sounded like distant thunder. "They don't scare very easily."

"Neither do we."

Benny paused and turned to look out to sea. The ocean heaved with tall, white-crested swells that rippled like flame in the light of the setting late afternoon sun. Out past South Port Head, the sky and water blazed with a dazzling display of orange and yellow that blended so perfectly that it was all but impossible to tell where one ended and the other began. The setting sun shone warmly on their faces, the last traces of this near-perfect summer day. Alfie sighed as he wiped a thin sheen of sweat from his forehead with his bare forearm. His other hand rested gently on the hilt of the wooden sword he wore under his belt.

"What if they landed on the other side of the headlands?" Alfie nodded toward the huge, rounded hill that jutted out into the ocean. Waves crashed against the rocks, sending up white plumes of surf. "What if they're sneaking up behind us right now?"

In spite of the warm afternoon, a shiver rippled like an earth tremor through Benny. He belched. He did that whenever he got nervous. It was usually followed by a brief burst of flame from his nostrils, but thankfully, that didn't happen this time. Benny realized it would have been all right if it had. He was facing out to sea, and he wouldn't have burned anything except perhaps a swatch of sand and seaweed, or maybe he would have made the seawater boil and bubble a bit. When he really let loose, his breath was hot enough to turn beach sand into tiny beads of glass, which Alfie simply loved. He told Benny he took those glass beads home to his mother as gifts, and she strung them in her hair and around her neck. But Benny had never seen Alfie's mother, and he began to wonder if she existed at all.

But glass beads and burned kelp and invisible mothers were the furthest things from either of their minds.

The pirates, led by the vicious captain known as Skipper Black, had come ashore yesterday morning, shortly after sunrise. It had taken all of Benny and Alfie's bravery and skill as warriors to defend the beach. Only after a hard-fought battle that had lasted for hours and hours, when the sun was at its hottest, did the pirates finally retreat to their ship and sail away. Benny was so exhausted from the fighting that he didn't have any flames left to burn the pirate ship before it sailed out of the bay. Alfie reminded him to save some of his fiery breath if they showed up later, but yesterday afternoon had passed peacefully, as had today, and evening was drawing on.

"Should we go around the headlands and check?" Benny asked, turning his head, which was the size of a small pony, so he could look back at Alfie.

Alfie cupped his chin with his hand and was silent for a long moment as he stared out across the glittering water. The sunlight was so dazzling that it would be easy not to see the pirate ship heaving over the

waves until it was too late. Dark red clouds were closing in fast, looking like the slashes of angry claw marks
across the sky. Alfie had a far-away look in his eyes,
and Benny wondered if his friend could see better
than he could. Alfie claimed that he could, but Benny
wasn't always sure he trusted everything Alfie said.
He'd been known to exaggerate on occasion . . . like
the time he told Benny about the fairy fruit he had
stolen when he surprised a group of fairies having a
midnight picnic.

What was a little boy doing out in the woods at
midnight? Benny wanted to know. And if he had
eaten fairy fruit, he wouldn't be here today to talk
about it.

Before Alfie could answer him, they got their answer when a cannon boomed from somewhere far off
in the distance. The sound echoed within the small,
sheltered cove, so at first neither Benny nor Alfie was
sure from which direction it came.

"From the north," Alfie said, pointing in that direction, but Benny shook his scaly green head and said,
"No. From the south."

"Are you sure?"

"A dragon's ears are much sharper than his eyes,"
Benny said knowingly. "And his eyes are sharper than
an eagle's."

His shoulders and back grew rigid with tension. His
wings, which were tucked up close to his body, began
to twitch.

"What say we fly there?" Alfie said, his voice
pitched high with excitement. He was never happier
than when they were flying together . . . especially if
Benny was also breathing flames down on their ene-

mies. Yesterday and—hopefully—today it was pirates, but the day before that—and maybe the day after tomorrow—it would be Indians or aliens from outer space. It didn't matter *who* they were fighting. Whenever they were in the air, Alfie whooped and hollered and waved his arms with delight as Benny soared above the earth and breathed his fiery death upon their mortal foe *du jour*.

"I suppose we could go up and have a look around," Benny said. He knew how much Alfie loved to fly and was teasing him. "Are you sure you want to?"

Alfie nodded with excitement lighting his eyes.

"Hold on tightly, then."

Alfie clung to Benny's neck and dug his knees into the dragon's flanks as, with a few quick hops followed by several powerful strokes of his wings, the dragon became airborne. The ground receded at a rapid, dizzying rate. The higher up into the sky they went, the stronger the wind blew in their faces. Alfie's long, dark hair was pulled straight back, and he narrowed his eyes to mere slits so he could see better. The patchwork of sand and sea grass and surrounding forest below them and the wide ocean receded, grew smaller and smaller by the second.

"Look!" Alfie called out with delight. "I can see my house from here!"

Benny chuckled. Alfie always said that even though he had never invited Benny to his house, and all he could see for miles around was sand and sea and forest.

"Do you see the pirates?" Benny asked.

Alfie took a moment to look around, and then, raising his arm and pointing—even though everyone knows it is not polite to point—he cried out, "Over there!"

Benny turned in a wide, swooping circle and scanned the bay until he saw the ship. It was anchored close to shore on the lee side of the headlands, almost—but not quite—hidden from sight in the gathering gloom. The ship's brightly painted spars glowed like fire in the setting sun. On the deck, the pirates were swarming about in a flurry of activity. It didn't take Benny or Alfie long to figure out what they were doing. They were priming their cannons, getting them ready to shoot.

"Do you think they're going to shoot at us?" Alfie shouted.

The wind whistled past their ears, making it all but impossible for either of them to hear, but Benny caught the gist. He considered for a moment what to do, and then he nodded sagely.

"Why else would they get their guns ready?"

"Maybe they're going to attack the town," Alfie said. From this high up, they couldn't see the tiny town of South Port, but it was supposed to be just a short distance down the coast.

Alfie and Benny didn't have long to find out what the pirates intended. Far down below them, they heard one of the pirates shout a command as he pointed up at them with the hook that used to be his left hand. A black tricorner hat with a billowing white ostrich plume that draped down his back identified Skipper Black. Within seconds, several of the pirates rolled the cannon backward, angling it up . . . up . . . up into the sky. One man, a short, squat fellow wearing a red and white striped jersey and canvas pants torn off at the knees, touched the fuse with a torch. A second or two later, a puff of smoke issued from the mouth of the cannon. The cannonball hurled past them with an angry scream, close enough so both boy and dragon felt the wind as it passed. Then, as though from the bottom of a deep well, there came an echoing boom that was actually more frightening than almost getting hit by a flying cannonball.

"Let's get out of here! Quick!" Alfie shouted, but Benny ignored him. Swooping first to the left and then to the right, he gave his wings several mighty flaps until he was heading straight toward the pirate ship.

"Are you crazy?" Alfie shouted.

His knees dug into Benny's back, but Benny ignored him as he stalled in the air and then plummeted straight down, heading toward the pirate ship like an arrow in flight. The wind shrieked in their ears.

On board the ship, there was a flurry of action as the pirates scrambled for their weapons. Guns and swords and knives flashed like flames in the setting sun. The clatter of metal against metal rose into the sky. Alfie clung tightly to Benny's neck, positive that the pirates would get in a few good shots before they were within range of Benny's fiery breath.

"We could be hurt!" Alfie screamed. He didn't say the word "killed" because no one ever died when they fought the pirates . . . except pirates.

Below them, a few muskets smoked, and lead balls whistled past Benny on left and right. The pirates' upraised swords made the deck of the ship bristle like a silver porcupine. A mighty roar went up from the scurvy crew as Benny swooped down on them, gathering speed as he fell. Benny waited until he was less than fifty feet away from the bow of the ship before unleashing his fire. Flames belched from his nostrils and mouth, roaring like a tornado as they swept across the deck.

Moving as fast as he was and coming almost straight down, the heat of Benny's breath washed back over them, but both dragon and boy watched, laughing, as the pirates' shabby clothes caught fire, and they screamed as they dove overboard to extinguish the flames. The deck was set afire, and those few pirates who were still on board tried mightily to put them out, but Benny and Alfie both saw the small line of flame that ran across the wooden planking, heading toward the stack of gunpowder barrels.

"Oh-h-h . . . this is going to be fun," Benny said, loud enough for Alfie to hear him above the sounds of mayhem on the ship. They swooped to the right, swinging out over the water past the headlands. Benny was braking and just coming about when the first barrel of gunpowder exploded. A terribly bright flash of orange lit up the sheltered cove just before a thunderous roar shook the earth and sky. Alfie clung tightly to Benny's back, and they were both laughing as they watched one keg of gunpowder after another go off like a string of huge firecrackers.

Pirates howled and wailed, their burning clothes turning them into tiny comets as they flew through the air and then landed with loud sizzling hisses in the ocean. All the while, Skipper Black stood as though rooted to the deck, glaring up at them. He raised his good hand in a fist and shook it at them.

"Come down here!" he shouted. "Come down here 'n fight, if ye be a man!"

Both Alfie and Benny chuckled because, between them, there wasn't anything close to a man . . . They were just a boy and his dragon . . . or a dragon and his boy.

"Shall we oblige him?" Alfie asked in a voice that was too high pitched to sound really brave. But the expression on his face, in his eyes, was one of grim determination.

"Oblige," Benny echoed. "Such a fancy word for what you and I want to do to Skipper Black."

Benny sailed around in a wide arc over the burning pirate ship. A huge column of black smoke spiraled into the darkening sky, bending toward the shore with the breeze. Some men, their hair and clothes singed, their faces smudged with soot, splashed about in the water while others still on deck struggled to extinguish the last of the flames.

"Well, it doesn't seem very sporting just to blast them with fire and not give them a chance, now. Does it?" Alfie said.

"Do you have your sword?" Benny asked.

He knew Alfie always carried his sword strapped to his side, but truth to tell, it was a rather pitiful sword. It was made of two pieces of wood. The "blade" was a flat piece of wood that would better serve as part of a picket fence, while the crossguard was a small piece of a tree branch tied into place with several loops of yellowing string.

Without another word between them, Benny stalled in the air and then dropped lightly onto the heaving deck of the pirate ship. The crew made a collective *oohing* sound as they drew back. The weapons in their hands were all but forgotten as Benny and Alfie eyed Skipper Black.

"Well, so ye be not so cowardly as I thought," Skipper Black said as he approached them. His good hand dropped to the hilt of his sword. There was a loud rasp of metal as he drew it out. In the gathering gloom of evening, the blade appeared unnaturally bright. Benny and Alfie wondered if there might be some magic in the pirate captain's blade, but Alfie slid to the deck from Benny's shoulders and stood up straight, his feet braced widely apart. A faint smile twitched the corners of his mouth as he faced the captain. He was secure with Benny at his back.

"Are you sure you can beat him?" Benny asked, leaning his huge head close to Alfie's ear and whispering so as not to be heard. "I could shoot flames all across the deck and destroy the entire ship, and we could fly away."

"No," Alfie said. "It wouldn't be sporting. I want to fight him."

He gripped the hilt of his wooden sword so tightly his knuckles went white. The fire in his eyes was much brighter than the lingering glow of the setting sun in the west.

Without another word, the pirate captain and the boy closed the distance between them. There was a loud *clank* as their swords crossed, and then they set to it. Metal clanged against wood as man and boy fought without mercy. They slashed and parried, lunging and ducking slashing blows. Chips of wood flew from Alfie's blade at the same time his rapid strikes put deep dents into the metal blade of Skipper Black's sword. Alfie fought with a grim determination, his arm swinging tirelessly back and forth, his wooden blade whistling as it sliced through the air.

They pressed each other back and forth, moving gingerly across the charred wooden deck. The crew gave way, allowing them plenty of room to fight, but it was clear after a while that Skipper Black was tiring. He began to give ground.

"Go! Go! Finish him!" Benny called out, urging his friend on.

For a moment, Benny was afraid Skipper Black might have an evil trick up his sleeve. What if he was backing up only to lure Alfie into a trap? But the look in the pirate chief's eyes was gradually changing from angry determination to concern and then to gathering fear.

It was obvious he knew he was losing . . . and to a mere *boy!*

Their blades whooshed and sliced back and forth. The pirate crew was silent as they and Benny watched, captivated by the spectacle. Alfie kept moving forward slowly, steadily pressing his advantage. His bare feet inched across the deck, nimbly avoiding the charred remains of ropes, weapons, and barrel staves. Skipper Black's eyes widened as he fell back with a look of growing desperation.

"Ye think you can get the better of me, do yah?" Skipper Black said between black and broken teeth.

He may have sounded brave, but his sword arm was dropping lower by the second as fatigue took its toll. Alfie didn't let up. He kept coming at him, his arm swinging back and forth like a harvester, slashing . . . cutting . . .

"I don't *think* I can," Alfie said through clenched teeth. "I *know* I can."

With that, he suddenly lunged forward and swung at Skipper Black with all his might, sweeping the pirate's sword from his hand. It twisted end over end as it flew out over the water and then went *plunk* into the sea, disappearing below the surface with barely a ripple. Skipper Black stopped and looked at Alfie with amazement. Then, without a word, he dropped to the deck on both knees and raised his hands while lowering his head.

"I yield," he said in a low, broken voice. "Curs'd be ye."

A collective gasp went up from the pirate crew. In all their battles, in all their raids, they had never seen Skipper Black bested . . . and by a mere *boy!*

"Do with me what ye will."

Alfie didn't say a word as he approached his victim. Sweat beaded his forehead, glistening like dew. He was breathing fast, but his face looked as fresh as the morning sun compared to the abject defeat etched on Skipper Black's face.

"What I want is—"

"Yoohoo!"

Everyone looked around as the sound of someone's voice echoed in the stillness that had dropped like a curtain over the deck of the pirate's ship. Alfie and Benny froze where they stood. After a breath, they turned and looked each other straight in the eyes.

"Oh, no," Benny said.

"Don't tell me—Is it—?" Alfie's voice choked off.

"Hello . . . Where are you?"

The voice—a female voice—sliced through the gathering gloom. Skipper Black stood up and looked at Alfie, his face floating like a pale moon in the deepening darkness.

"What be this?" he asked, his upper lip curling into a sneer that raised his pencil-thin moustache.

"We—uhh, we have to go," Benny said as he took a cautious step backward. The shifting of his weight made the ship heave from side to side. Seawater sloshed into the scuppers.

Alfie looked at Benny with gathering surprise in his eyes.

"*Yoohoo . . . It's time to come home now!*" the voice called. "*Where are you, child?*"

Benny looked wistfully at Alfie, and then he turned his head, looking over his shoulder at the shore. Night had settled across the land like a heavy blanket.

"I . . . I'm over here," Benny called out, his voice laced with a low, mournful note.

"But the battle's not over," Alfie said. "I haven't taken my prize yet."

"I'm sorry. It's getting late," Benny said. "I have to go home now. My mom's calling."

"If he don't be acceptin' my surrender," Skipper Black said, "then he doesn't win, says I."

"I'm really sorry," Benny said, lowering his head and looking at both Alfie and Skipper Black with the most mournful look possible for a dragon. Then he turned and watched the huge, dark shape that had appeared over the nearest sand dune. The silhouette of a fully grown female dragon towered against the night sky, blocking out the stars.

"Ah-hah . . . there you are," said the hulking dragon as she walked down the slope toward Benny.

"Hi, Mom," Benny said, lowering his head until his scaly jaw almost touched the sand.

"Benedict. How many times have I told you that I do *not* want you playing down by the water alone . . . especially once it gets dark?"

"Sorry, Mom. I didn't—"

"Who were you talking to, by the way?" Benny's

mom asked, looking at him with a strange mixture of worry and anger lighting the golden disks of her eyes. "I thought I heard someone else talking."

Benny sighed and then jerked his head back when a tiny lick of flame shot out of his nostrils.

"No," he said. "No, it was just . . . me."

"Are you sure? If you've been playing with that Lambert boy again—you weren't, were you?" His mother shook her head with a stern look of disapproval.

"No, Mom."

"I don't want to be telling tales out of school, as it were, but I know that young boy is the one who put you up to lighting those fires in the woods last spring. We were lucky the entire forest wasn't destroyed."

"No, it was just me and . . . and Alfie."

"Alfie?" The expression in Benny's mother's eyes softened, and she moved close enough to him to lean down and nuzzle Benny with her neck. "Darling, how many times have I told you that Alfie is just a—"

"I know . . . I know." Humiliated, Ben was unable to meet her gaze.

"There *is* no Alfie . . . There's no such thing as 'people' . . . not any more. They're figments of your imagination. And I say it's time you grew up a little. I want you to promise me you'll forget all about Alfie from now on. All right?"

When Benny didn't answer her right away, she nuzzled him again until he couldn't help but smile.

"I have . . . I will," Benny said, and with that, they both turned and started toward home across the sand dunes.

At the crest of the hill overlooking Mockingbird Bay, Benny hesitated for just a moment. When he sighed, he blew out a plume of flame that lit up the deepening night as he looked back at the sea one last time. A piece of driftwood caught fire, blazing with a blue flame from the salt-saturated wood. Benny gazed into the dancing flame, as blue and hot as a midsummer sky. A single tear ran down his scaly green cheek when he considered that his friend might now be lost to him forever. He sighed as he stomped out the fire, and, just before he turned to follow his mother into the forest, he whispered, "Psst . . . Hey . . . Alfie . . . See you tomorrow."

STANDS A GOD WITHIN THE SHADOWS

Anne Bishop

1

Hesitant to leave the safety of my bedroom, where the windows were shuttered on the outside and let in nothing except a little light and the illusion of fresh air, I hovered in the doorway that opened onto the main chamber of my prison. It was a large, well-furnished room with comfortable chairs, a sofa, and tables of various shapes and sizes. The overlapping carpets were thick enough to challenge the cold that rose from the stone floor. The center of the room was clear of furniture and provided enough space to serve as a little dance floor or exercise area.

Not that I was diligent about exercise—or anything else for that matter. What difference did it make if I was sloppy fat and smelled or if I was trim and freshly bathed? *He* wasn't going to care.

As I crossed the room, I kept my eyes averted from the one large window that had shutters on the inside—the one window that looked out on the land beyond my prison. The shutters were safely closed, but I still kept my eyes focused on the chair . . . and the mirror on the wall that matched the window's size exactly.

I was forbidden to look at the world directly. My jailer wouldn't tell me what the penalty would be if I disobeyed. He simply insisted that I would be cursed, and the implied threat was that I would not survive the punishment.

Some days I wondered whether not surviving would be such a bad thing. Would that really be worse than a lifetime of solitary confinement?

No. My confinement was not quite solitary.

I sat in the chair and closed my eyes. A moment later, as some device registered my weight in the chair, I heard the shutters pull back from the window. I opened my eyes, focused on the mirror, and breathed a sigh of relief as I looked upon the world.

I couldn't figure out whether I was on the bottom floor of this gray tower or the top, but I suspected that, if viewed scientifically, the mirror shouldn't be able to reflect what I saw regardless of the room's position. Since I was a writer, a storyteller, and a dreamer, I ignored science and accepted the view.

A piece of the river, flowing clean and clear. Lilies growing near the bank, their buds swelling as they waited for their turn to bloom. A bright fuzz of green that indicated new grass. Then the section of dirt road framed by mirror and window. Beyond that, there was a scattering of trees and a lane that divided two fields, but they looked vague and out of focus.

"Fields of barley and rye?" I asked the mirror, thinking of the old poem.

"Is that what they should be?"

My pulse raced at the sound of his voice. Not because it was *him,* but because I was glad to hear *any-one's* voice.

Steeling myself for whatever would be lurking in the deep alcove that hid the entrance to this prison, I turned my head and looked at the male figure half hidden in the shadows.

The horned god today, bare chested and barefoot, but wearing jeans that had the softness of long wear.

Oddly enough, the incongruity of his looks and his choice of clothing made it less easy to deny that he was what he seemed—one of the old gods who, for whatever reason, had decided to keep me as a pet.

"Good morning, Eleanor," he said with the same quiet, courteous respect his voice always held when he spoke to me.

When I woke and found myself here and he asked me my name, I had told him I was Eleanor of Aqui-taine, a small act of defiance and a shot of courage on my part to claim to be an imprisoned queen who was centuries gone.

He had accepted the name without question, which was when I began wondering a few things about him.

My keeper. My jailer. My only companion. He never came into the room. I had never felt the touch of his hand. Sometimes I wished he would try to touch me, just so I'd know that he was real and not an illusion created by a broken mind.

"I'm not Eleanor," I said, fixing my eyes on the mirror and the world beyond the stone walls.

A silence that asked a question.

"I'm the lily maid."

A different kind of silence before he said, "Ah. The Lady of Shalott."

I struggled not to smile, pleased that he understood

the reference since he understood so few of them. Then I got down to the business of watching the world reflected in the mirror.

Blue sky and some white, puffy clouds. No sign of rain.

Maybe tonight, I thought. *That would make the spring flowers bloom.*

Birds flashed in and out of the mirror. A man on horseback trotted down the road, heading for the village. Then a young woman on a bicycle rode by.

After that moment of distraction, I saw Peggy coming down the lane. Plump and solid, her quick walk covered the distance and brought her to the spot where the lane met the road. She crossed the road, looked up, and positioned herself dead center in the mirror. Then she set down the satchel she was carrying in one hand and held up the bouquet filling her other hand.

She was smiling, but even at this distance I could see a weight of sadness in that smile. She knew I was imprisoned in this tower. That was why she came and stood there every morning on her way to the village's school. Maybe, unlike me, she even knew why I was imprisoned. But regardless of why I was there, Peggy would support a friend and do whatever she could to help—even if that meant standing on the edge of the road in all kinds of weather, waving to someone imprisoned in a tower that was set on an island in the middle of a river.

Peggy held up one flower at a time so that I could see them clearly. Daffodils, hyacinths, tulips. Crocus. Wild iris. But . . .

"They're all white," I murmured, trying to hold on to the pleasure of seeing flowers.

"Shouldn't they be?" came the question from the shadows.

I shook my head. "They're a celebration of spring. They should be yellow and orange and red and purple and pink. Even striped. And some," I conceded, "should be white. But not all."

I ignored his thoughtful silence and focused on the scene.

Robert rode up on his bicycle and stopped to chat with Peggy. He pointed to her satchel. She made a dismissive "it's no trouble" wave of her hand that was so typical of Peggy it made me smile.

Robert pointed again, insistent. After going back and forth a couple more times, Peggy put the satchel in the empty carry basket attached to the back of his bicycle. The satchel would be on her desk at the school when she arrived, but she'd have been spared the trouble of lugging . . . whatever she was lugging to the school that day to show her students.

Another minute went by. Then Peggy waved to me and headed down the road to the village.

I spent the morning watching the shadow world reflected in the mirror. Birds. The sparkle of sunlight on the river. Clouds. A few people on the road, but anyone who worked in the village had already reported to their jobs.

Finally tired of staring at fields of grain, I stood up. In the moment before I closed my eyes and the lack of weight on the chair triggered the device that closed the shutters, the mirror reflected something else, something dark.

Something terrible.

A bad angle, I told myself. Nothing more. The mirror was positioned to let me see out the window when I was sitting. Ordinary things wouldn't look the same when I was standing.

Despite what I told myself, I kept my eyes tightly closed until the shutters covered the window completely. Then I turned and walked to my bedroom.

"Will you come back to the mirror after your meal?" he asked.

I paused in the doorway but didn't turn around to look at him. "I don't know."

The bed had been made, and there were clean towels in the bathroom. A meal had been laid out on a small table, a cover over the dish keeping the food hot. The book I was currently reading was next to the dish.

I didn't know who tended these rooms. I never saw anyone but my jailer, but someone kept things tidy and filled the bookshelves with new offerings on a regular basis. And . . .

I lifted the cover on the dish and let out a *whuff* of pleased surprise. In the beginning of my imprisonment, all the food was gray and had a soft mealiness. It was nourishing enough but awful to look at. That was one of the reasons I began reading while I ate. Today's roast beef, red potatoes, and broccoli and carrots were identifiable. Even their tastes were more distinctive.

After the meal, I spent the rest of the day in my bedroom, reading, sleeping, and listening to the music *they* had scrounged from somewhere. I didn't go back to the mirror. Maybe I was mistaken, but when he had asked the question, I thought there had been a hint of yearning in his voice.

*   *   *

The next morning, when I looked in the mirror, Peggy held up a dazzling rainbow of spring flowers.

2

Weeks passed. In the evenings, I sometimes saw the moon reflected and marked the passage of days by its waxing and waning.

Were there others like me, imprisoned in the other towers? Even imprisoned here? Some nights I stamped on the floor, hoping to hear an answering thump that would confirm there was someone else trapped in this place. Some nights I stood near a window and screamed—and wondered if anyone could hear me.

Except him.

On those nights, I felt his presence in the alcove, but he still didn't enter the room. Didn't even speak to me.

Then one night . . .

I had finished dinner and the current book. My keepers had found some Celtic music, which was more to my taste, so I listened to music for a while. I put another disc in the player, then went over to the bookcase that held the "new" selection of books. I now had a bookcase of favorites that was never disturbed by whoever tended the rooms and a bookcase that rotated on a regular basis, offering me an eclectic mix of fiction and nonfiction.

A fat, leather-bound volume caught my attention. As I pulled it out, I noticed the cover was heavily stained and the pages had a rippled, swollen look. I opened the book and riffled through a few pages.

Dark stains, as if the book had fallen near a puddle of coffee or tea and no one had pulled it away before it had gotten a good soaking.

Not coffee or tea, I decided as I continued riffling the pages, not taking in the content. Then I hit a page . . .

Splashes. A spray of dark blotches on the paper. Not dark like coffee; dark like old . . .

Memories came back in flashing images, like seeing a fast slideshow of stills from a movie that had frightened you badly as a child.

I dropped the book and screamed.

"Not true," I panted as I rushed out of the bedroom, stopping when I reached the chair positioned before the mirror. "It's not true."

I took a step, intending to sit in the chair. Then I turned and looked at the window.

Rage filled me and with it, an insanity that eclipsed madness. I'd been told I would be cursed if I looked upon the world directly. So be it. The answer could not be found in the mirror.

Since the shutters had been opened mechanically each day, I had expected them to resist being opened by hand.

Not so. They flew open with almost no effort.

I looked. I saw. I screamed again, but this sound was full of denial and terror.

I slammed the shutters closed and . . .

"Eleanor? Eleanor!"

He stood at the alcove's threshold, scanning the room until he found me pressed into a corner, curled in a tight ball.

"Eleanor, I'm sorry. They didn't know, didn't understand they shouldn't bring you such things. The book is gone. Eleanor?"

"Go away."

The shock on his face was real, but even that wasn't enough to make him step into the room.

Or maybe he's unable to step into the room.

He studied the shutters over the window as if trying to decide whether they were in the exact same position as when he'd seen them earlier in the day. Then his body sagged. His head sank forward.

"Eleanor," he said as he took a step back.

It wasn't the sorrow in his voice that prodded me. It was the defeat that made me call out, "Wait!"

Still there, but I knew with a heart-deep certainty that if he took another step back into the shadows, he would be gone forever.

"Just for tonight," I told him. "I need to be alone tonight. Come back in the morning."

A hesitation followed by a sigh of relief. "In the morning," he said. Then he was gone.

I uncurled slowly. Holding on to my heart and my courage, I went back to the window and opened the shutters.

No fields, no trees, no grass or flowers. The river flowed sluggishly, choked with bloated, decaying bodies.

Even after all these weeks—maybe months by now—the river was still choked with bodies.

Had some fool finally pushed the button that began the end of the world? Had some storm been Earth's answer to global warming and toxic waste?

Something cataclysmic that caused a chain reaction. Unstoppable once it began. The end of the world I had known. Not even the damn cockroaches had survived.

I couldn't remember the how or why. Maybe that was a blessing. When you're the only survivor, those questions don't matter anymore.

I turned away from the window and walked over to the mirror. It showed me the same image, the same desolation.

Was that the curse? Had I torn away the veil of magic that had given me the illusion that a piece of the world had survived?

What *had* I been seeing in the mirror?

Now that I no longer blindly accepted what I'd been seeing, I remembered that Peggy had been killed in a car accident several years ago. And Robert? I saw him as I remembered him—a friend of my youth—when he should look middle-aged if I were seeing something besides a memory. As for the land . . .

Country village just down the road. I couldn't see it, but I knew it was there. Something more like the Avonlea in the Anne of Green Gables stories than Arthur's Camelot, but pieces of both those places could be found in the streets and houses and public buildings.

And what about *him*? He came to me most often as the Celtic horned god—the Green Man, the Lord of the Hunt. An earthy, primal male. But he came in other forms as well, and the only reason I knew it was him was because his voice didn't change along with his face or body shape.

What was he? Some old earth spirit that had returned to try to mend a broken world? An alien from another planet whose people were trying to keep the few surviving humans alive and sane for however many years they had left to live?

When I told him to go away, I'd frightened him. Truly frightened him. Why?

Because he needs something from me.

I closed the shutters and returned to the bedroom. The book was gone, as he'd said. But the thought of selecting another book from those shelves made me tremble, so I kicked off my shoes and lay down on the bed fully clothed.

Slowly I became aware of the music that was playing—had been playing in the background.

Hammered dulcimer and other string instruments playing the songs of Turlough O'Carolan, a blind Irish harper and bard who had lived centuries ago. I recognized the song "Mabel Kelly," which had been one of my favorites. I got up long enough to program the player to keep repeating that song. As I listened, the music lanced a wound that had been festering in my heart, and my quiet tears washed the wound clean.

The world I had known was gone, but another world existed—a shadow world I could only see reflected in the mirror. A world that, somehow, had been layered over the real one.

Real world? I was a writer and a dreamer. A storyteller. I had never been chained to the "real world." And since I couldn't touch either one, why should I let desolation be given the solidity of the word "real?"

As the music and the night flowed on, I made some choices, found some answers. Perhaps they were not factually accurate, but they were answers I could live with. That still left me with a question.

When he looked at me, what did he see? Who was I that he thought me so important to *his* people's survival?

3

The next morning he was waiting at the threshold, wearing a different form.

I walked to the center of the room and studied him, trying to determine if this was a message.

The Celtic horned god was primal, earthy. This male had a youthful maturity and a handsome face with the Black Irish coloring of blue eyes and black hair. The white, feathered wings brushed the sides of the alcove, and the white jumpsuit he was wearing . . .

"Angels are androgynous," I told him.

"Andro . . . " He frowned as he tried to find the tail end of the word.

"They have no gender."

"No . . . ?"

I circled my hand at a height that vaguely aligned with his groin. "No."

As I walked over to the chair, knowing I was about to change the rules, I heard him mutter, "I don't think I like this form."

Hope. If I'd had to guess at the reason he'd chosen this form from the myriad images or symbols humans had created over millennia, I would have said it was meant to symbolize hope. And hope must walk in the world.

"It's a good form," I said. "As necessary in the world as your other form." I hesitated, then added, "I'm not an expert on angels, so I suppose the ones who deal directly with people would need to look more like people and have . . . " Again I waved vaguely at his groin.

His sigh was gusty and heartfelt. Then he offered a hesitant smile and said, "Good morning, Eleanor."

I met his smile with a grim expression. "There is something I must show you."

I sat down in the chair and watched the shutters being drawn back from the window.

I glanced at him and noticed that his skin had turned sickly pale as he realized what the mirror revealed. He made some inarticulate sound of despair.

I focused on the image in the mirror. "This," I said in a clear, firm voice that would turn words into the stones of truth, "is the Land of Armageddon. It is a dark place. A terrible place born of death and destruction. What oozes out of its festering skin is dangerous, deadly. Know the names of the creatures who call this place home."

"I will learn them," he said, his voice stripped of everything, even hope. Especially hope.

I nodded to acknowledge that I'd heard him. "This is the Land of Armageddon. It is a dark place. A terrible place. It is also far away"—I turned and looked him straight in the eyes—"and it will never again be seen in the mirror."

His eyes widened as he realized what I'd just told him.

I stood up. The shutters closed.

"I must rest today."

He hesitated. "I should come back tomorrow?"

"Yes." I smiled. "Come back tomorrow." I headed back to my bedroom, truly in need of rest. But I paused at the doorway. "If *they* should come across books about gardening—books that have pictures of flowers and shrubs and trees, I would like to see them. And books on yoga."

"Yoga?" He tried out the word.

I spelled it for him, and he nodded.

He was gone before my bedroom door fully closed.

Gardening and yoga.

I wasn't sure why I had survived or what I was doing in this place, but if I was going to keep the Land of Armageddon far away, it was time to start setting a good example.

4

During the afternoons, I did yoga. At night I danced to O'Carolan's music and envisioned a gentler world than had ever existed. I pored over gardening books, fixing the look of flowers and trees in my mind's eye, focusing on how they would look in their own particular seasons.

I remembered the faces of friends and family, conjuring them out of memory until I could recall their voices, their particular ways of laughing, the way each of them moved.

And I saw each one of them walk down that little stretch of road that was framed by window and mirror, pausing to wave before they headed for the village and another kind of life.

It wasn't much different from world building for a story, I thought one afternoon while I was trying to figure out what fruits could be grown in this climate—and then wondered if that was even a consideration anymore. Then I thought, no, it was more like being a stage manager and director for an improv theater. I supplied a description and character sketches for the people and a stage and props that had as much detail as I could bring into focus. After that, it was up to the beings who took on the roles to interact with each other.

So I did yoga, I danced, I studied.

The sloppy fat burned away. The meals, once I concentrated on the gardening books that contained fruits and vegetables, became tastier and offered more variety.

Every day he was there within moments of my leaving the bedroom. He alternated between horned god and angel, on occasion trying on other forms to see what reaction I would have.

The minotaur form, after leaving a steaming pile in the alcove, was banished from the tower but was allowed to roam the countryside as a "natural disaster."

After all, even the most benign story had to have *some* conflict.

The night I saw a unicorn cantering up the lane between the fields brought tears to my eyes and took my breath away.

The seasons turned. The fields were nothing but stubble under snow. The river froze. Through the cold winter days, I talked to him about the feel of things, the smell of things, the taste of things.

And then, when the first cracks appeared in the river's ice, I tried to expand my horizon.

5

"Why can't it show the fields on the other side of the village?" I asked for the fourth time. My frustration rose in direct proportion to his strained patience.

"The mirror can only reflect what can be seen from this window," he replied.

But it doesn't reflect what is seen from the window,
I thought bitterly.

"I cannot change the nature of the mirror," he said
after several minutes of stony silence.

His tone came awfully close to a plea, and I felt the
jolt of his words. But I still wasn't ready to concede.
Except . . .

The nature of the *mirror*.

I had thought that because I was creating the stage
set, what I saw reflected in the mirror could be
changed simply by wanting it to change. But I had
forgotten a basic truth that every storyteller knows:
Whether it is science or magic that creates the won-
ders in a story, there are rules that must be followed—
and there are limits to what an object can do.

That's what he had been telling me—the mirror
could only do this much and no more.

"It doesn't matter," I said, already feeling the deep
ache of disappointment.

Hours passed. I kept my eyes on the mirror but
didn't see anything.

Finally he asked, "Why did you want to see another field?"

"I didn't. Not exactly." How to explain when I still
wasn't sure *what* I was talking to every day. "I just
thought there might be a field on the other side of
the village where the festivals were held and . . ." *And
I could see more of the people. I miss the people.*

Of course, I'd be looking at empty ground for much
of the year, so maybe seeing a handful of people go
up and down the road every day was a better choice
after all.

"Festivals?" he asked. "What is festivals?"

As an unspoken apology, because he really did try

to make my confinement as comfortable as possible, I told him about fairs and festivals. I told him about competitions that would be typical of a country fair. I told him about the game of horseshoes. I explained the concept of picnics. I tried to remember the various small celebrations humans had enjoyed, assigning one to every month. And feeling whimsical and impulsive, I told him about the famous rodeo tournaments that had been held in some villages.

His delight was a tangible thread between us, and his thirst for details melded with my flights of imagination.

For the first time, I saw him as something more than a jailer. I saw him as a friend.

When I finally stood up, stiff from so many hours in the chair, he stepped back into the shadows.

"Wait," I said, rushing to the alcove.

He stepped up to the threshold, his alarmed expression warning me even before I felt the invisible barrier that separated the alcove from my rooms.

Whatever supplied me with breathable air, food, and clean water did not extend beyond my rooms. Did not extend into the alcove.

Which meant that whatever he was didn't need those things the way I did. Or maybe it meant that the environment that sustained me would be poison to him.

That was one explanation for why he had never tried to enter the room. But there was another explanation, one I had feared from the very beginning of my imprisonment.

"Are you real?" I asked.

A long pause before he whispered, "I don't know."

Then he was gone. I heard no door close, saw nothing change in the alcove, but I knew he was gone.

*   *   *

Throughout a long, sleepless night, I thought about that moment, and just before I finally fell asleep, I realized something. Even though I was the one who had asked the question, he had been hoping I would also be the one who had the answer.

6

They didn't plant barley and rye that year. At least, not in those fields.

They made a Place of Festivals.

Of course, I couldn't see more than the strip of road and land that could be seen in the mirror. Not with my eyes anyway. But he came each morning with more information about what was being built and where it was in relation to the road, and as I put the pieces together, I could visualize the place.

They had a racetrack that served as a place for athletic foot races as well as horse races. They had dug a reflection pond in the center of the racetrack and would use it as a skating rink during the cold months.

They had other areas for games and competitions, but like the racetrack, those were things I couldn't see.

Closer to the road and on one side of the lane, they built an open-sided pavilion that served as both concert hall and dance floor.

They built a small stone building on the other side of the lane. There was a bench along the side of the building that faced my tower, giving me a clear view of whoever sat there.

I understood the purpose of every structure except the stone building, but no matter how I phrased the question, he refused to tell me what it was used for.

I stopped asking once I realized that structure had a deep significance for him or his people. It was enough that the building drew the villagers to my little piece of the world.

They seemed less uniform than when I'd first begun viewing the world through the mirror. Peggy still came every morning. Sometimes she sat alone on the bench outside the building, but, more often, someone else came along to chat for a few minutes. Friends who were no more than shadows and memories I held in my heart were alive again, looking exactly as I'd last seen them. But there were others as well, who had been conjured from some other well of memory. There were the angels, who varied in coloring but were all handsome, well-endowed young men. There were no female angels, but there were fairies, who were equally diverse in coloring and just as lovely as their angel counterparts. There were several who walked in the skin of the old Celtic god and seemed to be the groundskeepers for the Place of Festivals.

Was it their confusion or mine that had declared all these things equally real?

Did it matter?

7

Every month they held a Major Festival and a Minor Festival. They used some human celebrations, but most seemed to have no significance for them, despite the way most of them looked. So they didn't celebrate Valentine's Day, but there was a Crab Grass Festival in the summer. When I asked why, he said his people remembered crab grass causing a great deal of excitement in certain types of males, so it had to be important. Therefore, its existence was now formally celebrated.

The rodeo tournament was a dubious success. There was no calf roping or bronc riding, and those participating in the jousting tried to strike a target attached to bales of hay rather than strike each other.

When he told me about the barrel races, I agreed that, even though they were bulkier and not as fast on their feet, the centaurs did have an unfair advantage over the Quarter Horses because two heads were not always better than one and that next year there should be a separate event for each kind of participant.

They had a Festival of Trout, a Festival of Deer, and a Festival of Turnips.

I understood the trout and the deer. I didn't want to know about the turnips.

"Apples," I said, as I watched Michael and his ever-present toolbox enter the stone building. "Next year you must have an Apple Harvest."

"Apple?"

He had become braver, this god who stood in the shadows. More often than not, he stood closer to the barrier, and his expressions were easier to read.

I closed my eyes and remembered *apple*—the glossy red skin, the white flesh of the fruit, the sweet juice, and the satisfying crunch. Of course, there were green apples and tarter varieties, but the reds had been my favorites, and for a few moments I relived the experience of eating an apple.

That fall, people gathered at the small orchard that had appeared near the stone building. I spent the day watching them pick apples. Michael, Robert, and William organized the pickers and the distribution of ladders. Nadine and Pat organized the baskets that every family in the village had brought, fairly distributing the fruit, while Julie and Peggy bustled around the orchard with pitchers and glasses, offering water to the pickers. Lorna sat in the shade, playing her harp to entertain people as they came and went, and Merri and Annemarie entertained the children with games and stories.

I barely left the chair that day. And he never left the alcove.

I wasn't sure what he could see from that angle, but he seemed able to watch the reflection just as I did. That day, when I finally forced myself to look away from the mirror . . .

I had never seen him so happy.

That evening, when I reluctantly took a break, I found a bowl of ripe red apples on the table along with my dinner.

8

Seasons came and went, counting out the measured beat of years. The people in the mirror didn't change. Neither did my companion. But I was a canvas upon which time painted.

My health was failing. My body was failing. A walker that had been found somewhere allowed me to shuffle from bedroom to chair. The day was coming when I wouldn't be able to get out of bed. The day was coming . . .

"What happens when I'm no longer here?" I asked him after I had gotten comfortably settled in my chair.

"No longer here?"

"I'm old," I told him gently. "I'm dying. I won't be here much longer." My gnarled hand pointed at the mirror. "What happens to that when I'm gone?"

A long silence. Then, "Eleanor? Look out the window."

I shook my head.

"Please," he said. "Look out the window."

"Just got myself comfortable," I grumbled. But I hoisted myself out of the chair and shuffled over to the window.

The shutter mechanism was a little stiffer than I remembered. Or maybe I had simply gotten weaker. I got one side of the shutters opened and decided that was enough.

Then I looked out the window and struggled to open the other side.

The Place of Festivals.

Peggy sat on the bench, chatting with Pat and William while Merri crouched nearby, pointing out some wildflowers to her two daughters. Robert and Michael and one of the angels were exchanging news. Nadine was in the Pavilion with Julie and Lorna, organizing baskets of something.

"Must be a minor festival," I muttered. But I couldn't remember which one. Couldn't even remember the month.

Didn't matter. The people were all there.

"How?" I asked, not willing to look away. "How can I see them?"

"They're real now. At least, real in this other way."

I shuffled the walker a little so I could look at him but still easily watch the world.

"When Armageddon swallowed the world, some of the Makers survived. Not many, but some."

"Makers?"

"Beings like you."

Like me. "What are you?"

He took a deep breath and let it out in a sigh.

"Are you aliens from another planet?"

That surprised a laugh out of him. "No, Eleanor. We have been here since the world was young, a part of the world but always apart from the world. We did not have form, could not inhabit the space that was already filled. So we only had the shadows, the . . . reflections . . . of the world you knew. We existed, but we could not live. Not like you.

"After Armageddon, the world was empty. There were no reflections. We did not want to exist in a dead place, so when we found some of the Makers, we used what we are to create small places where they could survive."

Four gray walls and four gray towers. A confinement shaped to order by the fevered dreams of a mind trying to save itself from self-destruction.

"You used an image from my mind, didn't you?" I asked. "Something I had projected as a tolerable kind of prison."

"Yes," he said quietly.

"So not every place has the lily maid's mirror."

"No, but each place had something in which to see the world reflected."

"Why?"

"When the Makers looked upon the world directly, they could not see anything but the dead place."

The Land of Armageddon.

But here, now, the river flowed clean and clear. Lilies bloomed along the banks. The people I'd known . . .

"I provided you with shapes to inhabit?"

"That was all most of the Makers were able to do. But a few, like you . . . an . . . echo . . . filled your remembering, so there was more than shape. There was . . . feeling."

An echo of friends long gone but still remembered. A village still inhabited by these good people. That wasn't a bad legacy to give to the world.

"Since you're answering questions, will you tell me what that stone building is?" I asked.

Some strong emotion, there and gone, filled his face. "A . . . temple?" He paused, looking thoughtful. "A place to sit quietly and give thanks."

"To you?"

He jolted. *Me?*

"Aren't you the god who stands within the shadows?"

He looked shocked.

"No, Eleanor," he stammered. "*I* am not the god here."

My turn to feel shock.

"They call you the Lady of Shadows," he said quietly. "You are one of the Makers who dreams the world, and the reflection of that dreaming is the place in which we live."

I wasn't sure what to say. If I'd known I'd been assigned the role of deity, would I have done things differently?

Well, I wouldn't have mentioned something as stupid as the rodeo tournament, but that didn't last for more than a few years anyway.

As I mulled over my promotion from prisoner to god, I thought of something. "If I'm the Maker, what are you?"

"Companion?" He pondered for a minute, clearly trying to put his thoughts in order. "These places can only hold one Maker. It was all we could do. But we knew that Makers needed company, so some, like me, were chosen to remain with the Makers."

"Remain? Don't you go down to the village when you leave here?"

"No. I cannot leave this place. I am not like the Tenders who take care of your rooms. They can come and go. But I act as . . . go-between? . . . so I, too, am in between while I am companion. Once I leave here, I cannot come back."

"Then how did the people in the village know any of the things I've told you, described to you?"

"I was go-between. There were ways to communicate, much as you and I do."

I had thought he'd been free to come and go, but he had been as much a prisoner as I. Had been as isolated as I. All these years, he'd had no one for company but me.

"So I ask the question again: what happens when I'm gone?"

"I will go down to the village and live with the others," he replied. "Our place will stay as it was made."

We kept silent for a while and watched the world, already having said too much—and maybe not quite enough.

When my old legs got too tired to stand, I shuffled back to the chair where I could watch the world in comfort.

"There is something I would like to ask you," he said once I was settled. "We could make a starting place that could be seen as reflection. Besides what we wanted for ourselves, we had wanted to give some comfort, some hope that the world was not so dead. All the Makers were warned not to look out the window. All were warned that they would be cursed if they did. And yet all of them looked. Some resisted for a long time. Some didn't try to resist the temptation for a single turning of the sun. They looked—and nothing was the same. They stopped Making. Some broke and died. Some turned dark, and their Making was a terrible thing."

"What happened to your people?" I asked. "The ones who were caught in the dark Making?"

"They did not inhabit the shapes, and the Making had no substance and faded away. But you. You looked, and you were still able to see the reflection in the mirror. You still continued Making. How did you do this?"

How could I explain? It was more than being a storyteller, more than being accustomed to seeing worlds that didn't exist anywhere except inside my head.

An . . . echo . . . filled your remembering, so there was more than shape. There was . . . feeling.

That's what he had said. And that, I realized, was the answer.

"When I looked in the mirror," I told him, "I didn't see with my eyes. I saw with my heart."

A moment's silence. "Ah," he said, as if I had explained a great mystery.

We watched the world. I couldn't tell if there was supposed to be a specific festival. People came and

went, but the people I had loved remained, staying
around the pavilion or the stone building, or crossing
the road to stand on the river's bank and raise a hand
in greeting.

Or farewell?

"This place," I said. "It's an island in a river?"

"Yes."

"What do you call it?"

He smiled. "The Island of Shalott."

"And the village?"

The smile faded, and a touch of anxiety took its
place. "It was never named."

I hadn't understood my role. I'd thought of it as the
village, assuming it already had a name that I was not
aware of.

A legacy. A word that would hold shining hope
within its sound.

"Camelot," I said. "The village is called Camelot."

A hesitation. Then, timidly, he asked, "Do I have
a name?"

All these years he'd spent patiently waiting. Exiled
by choice in order to give as much as he could, not
just for my sake but for his own people. I thought of
the faces and forms he'd worn over the years.

"You are Lancelot Angel Greenman," I said.

His eyes widened. "So many names."

"You earned them."

Stunned pleasure.

Not much time left. But enough.

"I want you to do one last thing for me, Lancelot."

"Anything that I can."

"I want you to go down to the village. I want you
to leave now."

He jerked forward. Reached out. Almost touched the barrier. "No."

"Yes. I want to know you're safely in the village. I want to see you in the mirror, with the rest of my friends. Do this for me."

He lowered his arm but still hesitated. "What form should I wear?"

"You only get to have one form once you go down there?"

He nodded.

"Then you must choose for yourself who you want to be."

He took a step back into the shadows. Took another. "Thank you for our piece of the world," he said softly.

The silence and the solitude had a weight it had never had before. He was gone from the tower.

A few minutes later, a young man stepped onto the part of the road framed by the mirror. He had black hair and blue eyes. He had the face of an angel, but he'd given up the wings of that form in order to look more like the others. When he turned toward the tower and raised a hand in greeting, there was something in his smile and his stance that told me he had kept a bit of the old god too, at least in heart.

I watched him as the others came over to greet him. I saw his face when the simple act of being touched by the others confirmed that he no longer just existed in the shadows; now he truly lived in that world.

I saw his joy.

Then I breathed out a sigh—and saw no more.

NEITHER

Jean Rabe

The age-faded sign read: "Please don't give money to the vagrants. They are either professional beggars or addicts who use the money for drugs or booze."

Sig was neither.

He was a beggar, but certainly not a professional. A professional would be good at it and would have enough coins in his outstretched paper cup to buy something decent to eat. And he wasn't an addict, at least not anymore. Sig used to drink more than a little bit of whatever was strong and cheap or could be found in near-empty bottles discarded behind the Wild Horse Saloon, but he'd been sober for the better part of two years.

When he drank, his senses got so muddled he couldn't properly hear the music, and he could barely see the dog.

It was a good dog.

Sig sat on a clean piece of sidewalk along Broadway in downtown Nashville. His back against the red brick of the T-shirt shop, his head came up just far enough to obscure the lower corner of the front window that displayed the vagrancy sign. There were plenty of vagrancy notices in downtown Nashville, but most of the beggars avoided sitting directly beneath them. Sig sat here for several hours every day because the dog favored this spot. It was a convenient location from which to hear the music drifting out of the various bars.

The dog obviously didn't mind the fare that roiled off the juke boxes in the diners, but it seemed to like the live music the best, feeling the beat from trap sets and basses pulsing through the concrete and reverberating against its paws. Sig could feel the beat, too, when he set his fingertips against the sidewalk and concentrated, as he was doing now. It was the heartbeat of the city, and it brought out the people—the regulars who lived and worked in the area, the bums like himself who preferred the freedom and sounds of the colorful sidewalks to the blandness of the homeless shelters, and most importantly it brought out the tourists, who occasionally tossed scraps to the dog.

The city was said to have a black heart and that the beat masked it with lively tunes and sad songs, with electric guitars and expensive mandolins, with busty girls lip-syncing for videos that would be played on CMT—all of it distracting folks so they didn't look too closely. But Sig looked. And the city's dark heart showed itself to him from time to time on this very sidewalk in the forms of pickpockets and purse snatchers—several of which the dog had thwarted through the years at Sig's encouragement. Sig had also spotted drugs and money changing hands on a few corners after sunset; the dog had fouled a few of those sales, too.

A very good dog.

Sig liked bluegrass the best, even when the singers wailed too loudly in off-key feigned country voices, as someone was doing this very minute. The dog's preference? It didn't seem to matter: western swing, rockabilly, traditional, folk, honky-tonk, gospel, country rock, swamp opera, or boogie-woogie. Sig figured the dog liked just about everything—except for that damned accordion that started wheezing almost every afternoon from an apartment just above Ernest Tubb's Record Shop across the street. The dog howled like a coonhound when the accordion played.

The dog came to just above Sig's knees, the shade of an expensive Gibson mahogany guitar, with large, kind eyes and sharply pointed ears that were always tipped toward whatever joint was offering the best music at any given time. It looked as though one of the street artists had lovingly dry brushed white paint against the dog's otherwise dark muzzle and just above its eyes to give it brows. Just a hint of age to the dog. Distinguished looking.

Sig could not have imagined a more wonderful, beautiful dog.

He didn't know how old the dog was, only that he'd spotted it in an alley some six or seven years ago, or maybe it was eight, sniffing around a trash bin it couldn't quite reach. Sig had rummaged in the bin for it that night, coming up with some soggy French fries and a few partially eaten pork chops, which they shared. They'd been together ever since that night—except for when Sig had been drinking.

They slept in the morning when the music was dead, in the hazy time between three and nine when they would find a Dumpster in an alley to curl up behind so the light from the bare bulbs that hung above back doors didn't quite reach them. The air was always dead then, too, and was thick with sweat and filth and rotting lettuce and cabbage and whatever else had spoiled in restaurant kitchens and had subsequently been tossed out.

Promptly at nine, when the music started up again, they'd rise as if to an alarm clock. They'd stroll out to the sidewalk and sit in their spot. They'd wait for breakfast, which if Lee didn't stop by would consist of donut halves tossed in the trash can on the corner— of which they had a perfect view—or sometimes there'd be remnants of those sausage and egg sandwiches that the tourists bought at fast food shops and found too greasy to finish. Grease rarely bothered Sig and the dog.

It was such a good, good dog.

"Lee's late," Sig mused. She was special to him. She was one of the few people on Broadway who never looked the other way when she passed Sig and the dog. A bartender at Legends on the corner, she always stopped on her way to work each morning. Sometimes she gave them leftovers after her shift was over. Lee worked from nine to five, and so her comings and goings fit rather well with traditional mealtimes.

Sig always looked forward to seeing her. Lee's skin was the color of pale peaches, even-toned except for a hint of blush on her cheeks. And her hair was long and dark and always gleaming, her teeth as white and sparkling as new snow. Sig's own hair was always a tangled buggy mess, and so he kept it stuffed up under an old Tennessee Oilers cap so not to offend people.

Her smile . . . well it was beyond Sig's ability to describe. It melted him, made it difficult for him to think and to breathe, and it always set the dog's tail to wagging goofily.

She wouldn't always be a bartender, Sig knew. He'd heard her sing. Sometimes they'd shuffle down to Legends, and go around the corner to the side door, which was always open. They'd sit and listen to the young men playing acoustic guitars and hawking their CDs between sets. Every once in a while, on afternoons when business was slow, Lee would come out from behind the bar and sing a couple of songs she'd written.

"You're gonna be a star," Sig told her once. It was just a matter of time until she was discovered and swept away from this life. "You're gonna be at the Opry someday, Lee. Name in flashing lights."

"Me and everyone else on Broadway'll be there," she'd return with a dazzling snowy smile.

"She should've been here by now," Sig told the dog. "Not like Lee to be late." He craned his neck this way and that, thinking maybe she had to park somewhere else this morning and had gone in Legend's side door and thereby missed them. "Maybe she's sick. Not like her to be sick, though." He couldn't remember a time when Lee had been anything but perfect. "Not like her at all."

The dog tipped its ears toward Tootsie's, just a few doors down, where a man who sounded vaguely like Kris Kristofferson had begun a set. The dog pressed its front paws against the sidewalk, and Sig set his paper cup down and did the same with the palms of his hands, both of them feeling the steady beat rise through the concrete.

Shortly after the accordion started that afternoon,

Sig rose and gestured for the dog to follow; its howling was bothering the T-shirt shop customers. They ambled up the street, past Tootsies, where Sig paused to peer inside. Sig didn't care much for the place, and he was glad Lee hadn't been hired there. "World Famous" maybe, but it looked more ragged than his scruffy self. It was murky inside, always, the shadows helping to mask the cobwebs in the corners and the spilt beer on the floor. And it had a fusty pong that made even his nose wrinkle. The walls were interesting, though. They were papered with autographed photos of country music stars, all of them curled on the edges and yellowed from decades of cigarette smoke.

A bartender frowned and waved a towel at a horsefly. But Sig knew the gesture was aimed at him.

"Just looking," Sig said. He ducked back out and continued west, the dog dutifully following. He stopped at a plastic Elvis, little bigger than life-sized, arms outstretched waiting for a tourist to step into his embrace for a photograph. The dog hiked its leg and peed on the King's pantleg.

"Ain't you got no respect?" Sig asked the dog. But he smirked and winked. The dog always peed on the King.

They went around the corner and headed to Legend's side door. Sig looked in, sniffed, and scratched at his ear. At his feet, the dog did the same. Elvis's first five records were framed on one wall. Sig had heard they were worth thousands, the only five recorded on 78 RPMs on Sun Records. Kabuki-faced Kiss dolls were on a shelf near a large portrait of Johnny Cash and a guitar gaudily covered with shells

and buttons. A saxophone, trombone, and a sitar hung
near the ceiling. Album covers, some of them signed,
were everywhere.

A guy with a battered guitar was singing about the
"hits of the day" at a place called the Roadkill Café.
Cute music, Sig thought, scowling. "Get to the serious stuff."

When Sig stood at the side door sometimes Lee
would come out and bring him a soda or coffee, and
the dog a cup of water. Sometimes a sack of micro-
wave popcorn, still warm. But he couldn't see her inside, not behind the bar or at any of the tables, and
not around the stage with the Roadkill man. Maybe
she was in the kitchen or in the bathroom. Maybe she
was getting ready to sing a song or two, as the customers were few and didn't look to be demanding much
attention. Sig tuned out the Roadkill man and kept
glancing around.

Sheet music and photographs were displayed here
and there, none of them yellowed like at Tootsie's. A
notice, but not for vagrancy. It offered a reward of
$100 for anyone reporting pilfering of the memora-
bilia. A sequined shirt that would have been worthy
of Porter Wagoner caught his eye. Framed dollar bills,
Canadian and US, hung behind the bar. There were
lots of things to ogle in this place.

"That'd be nice, wouldn't it?" Sig mused, eyeing
the reward notice again. "Get me a night in a hotel,
a hot bath, get you a flea dip. A soft bed for us to
sleep on for once. Get me a new shirt, too. Maybe
like that sequined one. A pretty collar for you."

The dog's nose was pointed down the street, quiv-
ering in the direction of the Ryman Auditorium. A

gang of toughs in the back parking lot were admiring each other's tattoos.

"Maybe Lee's got a new job, dog. Maybe she went back to school."

She'd told them once that she was going to be a veterinarian . . . once upon a time . . . before she decided to move to Nashville and look for her big break, singing and songwriting. Sig remembered her saying that one of her songs was being considered by Tanya Tucker or Loretta Lynn or somebody else famous.

"Maybe some big record producer discovered her, dog. She would've told us, though, don't you think?"

The dog growled softly, and the hair rose in a ridge along its back. The toughs were parting ways, but two of them lagged behind, eyes fixed on the steps leading to the Ryman's backdoor.

Sig returned his attention to the barroom. "Dog, maybe I should call you Shep." He'd spotted a piece of sheet music called "Old Shep," by Red Foley, autographed and displayed behind a square of plastic in the hallway that led to Legends' bathrooms. "Elvis sang that." He looked down at the dog. "That leg you like to pee on? That's Elvis. He recorded 'Old Shep' some time ago. Sad, sad song. Not really country, though Elvis gave it a little twang. Do you want a name, dog?"

The dog continued to rumble at the two toughs until they eventually left, their eyes on the pavement as they passed by Sig, voices low in a conspiratorial whisper.

Sig settled down just outside the door, back against the brick, legs stretched out. The Roadkill man started singing about cigars and former presidents. "Get to the serious stuff," Sig repeated.

The dog nestled next to him, paws firmly against the sidewalk to better feel the beat, chin on Sig's knee.

"You're a good, good dog," Sig said.

They dozed until just before sunset, when a tour bus pulled up belching smoke and offloading a bevy of blue-haired women and balding men, the driver ushering them in the side door, all of them doing their best to ignore Sig and the dog. Not one dropped a coin in his paper cup. He listened to them shuffling across the hardwood floor, imagined them gaping at the memorabilia on the wall, prayed that one of them would take something—maybe one of those ugly Kiss dolls so the dog would thwart them and gain Sig a reward.

"That hundred bucks would buy us a fancy time," Sig told the dog.

The dog listened to the people, too, but also to the music. The Roadkill man had packed up his guitar some time ago, replaced now by a five-piece group with a well-known bluegrass man on keyboards. They'd been playing something soft until the tourists came in. Cranking up the volume now, a little thing with a big, high-pitched voice started singing country pop. Sig thought she was pretty good, her five-piece band that barely fit on the stage a bit better.

Not as good as Lee, though. Not close.

Two songs later the tourists shuffled back out, and a few of them dropped pieces of pizza crust on the sidewalk for the dog.

Shortly after sunset the rain started, making the street look like a slick black snake that wound its way past Legends and the back of the Ryman. The streetlights flickered on, and the neon beer signs sparked bright, sending rivulets of color streaming down the windows and across the sidewalk. The music got louder, still the little thing singing, sounding like Cyndi Lauper with a country twist. Hard to pick out all the words to her song, as a large crowd had gathered inside, and the quiet conversations, punctuated by calls for the bartender, mingled with the lyrics.

Sig knew there'd be a crowd at Tootsie's, too, and at all the other spots around the corner on Broadway. Music City's pulse quickened after dark, regardless of the weather. The beat brought more and more folks out the later the hour got.

Sig lolled his head back and closed his eyes, faintly heard the rain pattering on the sidewalk and felt its feeble attempt to clean the grime off his face. Soon he imagined that he'd be getting a good whiff of the dog. It always picked up a musty funk when it got wet. Sig certainly could pick out all the good things cooking inside: potato skins and roast beef sandwiches, minipizzas and popcorn. Sig had an amazing sense of smell.

"I'm hungry," Sig told the dog.

Glasses clinked, and a cheer went up. It was somebody's birthday.

"You don't mind the rain, the two of you?"

Sig's eyes flew open.

Lee stood in front of him with a hand on one hip, an umbrella held in the other. Black pants, white shirt, face shadowed except for her incredible smile.

"I'm on the late shift for a few days, filling in for Karen," she explained.

Sig smiled back. He was always at a loss for words in her presence. Maybe she thought him mute. The dog wagged its tail goofily and gave her a soft bark.

"I'll bring you out something on my break. Do you like roast beef?"

Sig nodded.

"Coffee?"

Another nod.

She looked at her watch and stepped into the doorway, taking down her umbrella and shaking it off before she disappeared into the crowd. Sig imagined he heard her high heels clicking against the hardwood.

He knew she wouldn't be singing tonight. Too many customers, all of them too demanding on the bartenders. He suspected that's why she liked the day shift, not as many people, meaning she had more opportunities to sing. He rested his head back against the wall, ignored the rain, and waited.

Sig didn't notice the dog pad away, down to the corner so it could raise its leg on the King again. And he didn't notice the beat of the city alter beneath his fingertips, heralding the reemergence of the two tattooed toughs that had walked by before. If Sig had been watching, he would have noticed that they'd changed clothes, or rather had added to what they'd been wearing earlier. Each had a black longcoat, a little too big with the shoulder seams drooping halfway down their arms. The toughs went in Legends' side door.

If Sig had been alert, he might have heard the first shout of surprise coming from the barroom, cutting above the music as the two men wrenched the big frame off the wall holding Elvis's five 78s. Instead, Sig was rudely jostled awake by the dog, returned from its pee break and now yapping.

"What?" Sig reached out to scratch the dog's ears, but then realized something was amiss inside. He got up, nearly slipping on the slick sidewalk, steadying himself against the wall as the two men forced their way out, the bulky frame held beneath the larger man's longcoat. They started to run.

Sig tried to take it all in, but everything came at him so quickly. The dog was still barking, people shouted, a whistle blew.

"Call the police!" someone inside hollered.

Suddenly Lee was out the door, a gun in her hand. She sidestepped Sig and dashed down the sidewalk, following the two men, who were fast losing themselves in the shadows that stretched out from the back of the old Ryman Auditorium. The dog barked a staccato rhythm that jolted Sig into action.

"A robbery," Sig stated. "Lee's after them." Then he and the dog gave chase.

Others came in their wake, but not as fast. They were curious patrons, mostly, wanting to see if the men were going to be caught and not wanting to get too wet. None of them ventured past the Ryman. The rain was coming harder now, rat-a-tat-tatting against the pavement and against the two thieves' longcoats, against Sig and Lee and the dog's back.

Car horns bleated from somewhere behind them on Broadway, and music poured out of the honky-tonks and dinner theaters and from open windows of apartments. The beat pulsed up through the sidewalk and into Sig's feet, and he set his legs to pump in time with it, his old shoes slap, slap, slapping against the wet sidewalk, the rain rat-a-tat-tatting, the music blaring, the beat coming louder and harder and not doing a good job right now to mask the city's black heart.

"He's got the Elvis records!" someone shouted from well behind them.

"The 78s!" another called.

The dog was just ahead of Sig, loping along at what looked like an easy pace, closing the distance to Lee, and then passing her.

A very, very good dog.

Their course took them farther from the downtown, the lights getting dimmer here, the music softer, the rain coming louder, and thunder booming and rattling windows. A siren keened.

"Get 'em, dog," Sig urged.

The thunder rattled the windows of an old apartment building they ran by.

Sig balled his hands into fists, swung his arms, and gulped in the wet air. He lost his Oilers cap and felt his hair fly free, whipping the back of his neck.

A taxi cruised by, slowed, and the driver rolled down the window. He shouted something that Sig couldn't hear, was shouting at the dog and the two men, then rolling up his window and driving away.

Around another corner the thieves dashed, this street better lit.

Lee dropped to a knee and fired. She was a good shot, and the bullet slammed into the concrete near the larger man's feet. The dog growled and the men stopped and spun. The smaller one pulled out his own gun.

The beat of the city changed again, pulsing now in a syncopated rhythm that felt uncomfortable against Sig's feet. He felt his heart rising into his throat, his chest grow tight. He tried to call out to the dog, which was heading straight toward the man with the gun.

Don't let it be like the song, Sig prayed. He remembered Elvis's recording of "Old Shep," the King singing about having to shoot the dog because it was old and the vet couldn't do anything for it.

The dog was pretty much everything to Sig.

Another shot rang out and Sig closed his eyes. He didn't see the pavement chip up at the dog's feet. He didn't see the dog vault off the sidewalk, pads losing contact with the pulsing beat of the city and ramming into the chest of the tough with the gun. He didn't see the dog tear at Nashville's black heart when it sunk its teeth into the tough's cheek.

But Sig heard the man scream and heard the clatter of a gun striking the pavement, and he heard the baying sound the dog made just like when the accordion started up. He heard the clack-clack-clack of Lee's high heels, and, finally, he heard a siren come louder.

Sig opened his eyes.

The larger man stood riveted, watching the dog maul his companion. He cursed when the police car pulled up, the red and blue lights playing against an old apartment building. The framed 78s slipped from beneath the thief's coat and landed to lean against his leg.

The dog took another bite out of the downed man, who moaned softly.

"Put your hands up!" A car door squeaked open as a burly policeman got out. "Do it now!"

The larger man complied, eyes still on the dog.

"Should I shoot the mongrel?" This came from the other cop.

"No," Sig croaked. "Please no."

"No," the first policeman answered. "It's just a stray. Seen it hanging around on Broadway a few times. I'd say it did us a favor."

The dog backed off and shook its head, blood flying from its muzzle. It trotted toward Sig and Lee, all of them standing in the driving rain.

"Good dog," one of the cops said. "Good, good dog."

The dog wagged its tail and retreated the way it had come, Lee following, heading back to Broadway. Sig waited a moment, watching the cops load the two men and the framed 78s into the car, listening as one of them got on the radio and reported their success.

"A hundred dollars," Sig said. "If we get that reward, I'll buy us something fancy." It took him a few minutes to catch up to Lee and the dog and to set his feet in time to the beat of the city again.

The dog continued to wag its tail, happy over the excitement of the past several minutes. Good thing Lee's "work schedule" had changed, the dog thought, otherwise this very real robbery might have been missed.

Sig should get a reward for his part in this, the dog decided, even though no real money would come the bum's way. Sig could "buy" a new shirt and a new pair of pants, a Tennessee Titans ball cap and get a proper haircut, maybe even think he'd passed the night in a hotel. And the dog would reward Lee, too, let her think she was getting her big break and that Tanya Tucker and Loretta Lynn were vying to record her song.

Lee and Sig were the best imaginary friends a good dog could have.

Neither of them real. Except in the dog's mind.

WALKING SHADOWS

Juliet E. McKenna

"LESHINA! Stop flirting with the troopers!"
The old woman's bark ripped through the
clamor like a knife through silk. Everyone froze; servants, delivery boys and all the horsemen making
ready to depart.

Leshina ducked her head as she hurried through the
yard, clutching the laundry basket to her generously
filled bodice. A trooper's low laugh prompted color in
her plump cheeks as a horse shook its head with a
rattle of harness.

"We've enough to do without your men distracting
my maids." Hands on hips in the entrance to the castle's lower halls, Sarese glared at the cavalry captain.
"When do we expect their majesties?"

He spared her the briefest of nods. "Tomorrow,
shortly after noon, all being well."

Sarese nodded curtly. "Safe journey, Captain."

As he led the troop out through the ancient arch,
everyone returned to their tasks. Leshina hurried

toward the servants' doorway, barely needing to feign
the embarrassment everyone would expect.

Sarese's wrinkled hand caught her above the elbow,
painfully tight. "A word, my lass."

Leshina meekly allowed herself to be steered
down a side corridor. Sarese followed so closely she
trod on the younger woman's embroidered hem.
Plainly gowned, keys and silver-mounted purse jin-
gling on chains at her waist, the old woman shut
the door.

"Wait a moment." Creases deepened in Sarese's
gaunt face as she closed her eyes. A low murmur ran
around the room.

Leshina half-smiled. "What will nosy ears hear
you saying?"

"Don't expect any sympathy when you're all tears
and swelling belly." Sarese wasn't amused. "Well?
What did you learn?"

"There were several keen to get a hand in my bodice." Leshina sat down on the low stool by the hearth
of the little chamber and retied the blue ribbon in
her long blonde hair. "Out to impress me with their
closeness to their highnesses."

"I know you don't like playing the tease." Sarese laid
a consolatory hand on the young woman's shoulder.
"But we'd be fools not to take advantage of the way
you look."

"Never mind." Apprehension clouded Leshina's
azure eyes. "Only Kemeti still concerns us."

Sarese wasn't pleased. "Jastro?"

"No." Leshina was certain.

Sarese frowned. "Jastro was pretending he had a
hound-whelp—"

"His majesty gave him a brindle from the spring

litters," Leshina said helplessly. "He has no need to imagine a puppy now."

Sarese clicked her tongue, exasperated. "And Kemeti?"

"She's still so young." Leshina knotted her hands in her lap. "Can't we wait? This time next year, the question might not even arise."

"This is her ninth summer. If she were going to outgrow imaginary companions, she'd already have done so. Jastro's barely out of his sixth winter." Sarese's faded eyes were hard as diamond. "And she's the paramount king's daughter. If she truly has the magic within her, think what it will mean? The rest of us can come out of the shadows and see our defense of this realm acknowledged." She laughed without humor. "Cavalry captains boast about their swift horses but we're the ones who really watch the distant borders out in the empty plains, making sure no one encroaches—"

"I may be new here, but I know that much." Leshina stared at her lap.

Sarese sniffed. "So the sooner we know if Kemeti has the magic within her, the better. The sooner she can be taught its strengths, warned to keep its secrets. Is her imagined friend still the same?"

"It's still the river boy." Leshina looked up. "Why is it so often a river child?"

"If you're six or seven summers old, at everybody's beck and call, realizing everyone else's wishes are consulted before your own?" There was some sympathy in Sarese's fleeting smile. "Wouldn't you want a friend who's seen realms upstream that minstrels have barely heard of? Who knows what's truly in the lands downstream that no two tales can agree on? Prince or peasant, children envy the river traders' freedoms."

"Maybe." Leshina was unconvinced.

"What's his name?" Sarese demanded. "What does he look like?"

"Like any river boy. Yellow hair, dark eyes." Leshina twisted her fingers together.

"Does he have a name?" snapped Sarese.

"She calls him Achel." Leshina closed her eyes. "And he has a dog."

"If that appears—" Sarese looked thoughtful, "—that'll mark the strength of Kemeti's imagination."

"But she's so small." A tear ran down Leshina's cheek.

"No matter." Not a pin shifted in the iron-gray twist of her upswept hair as Sarese shook her head "We'll only have tonight before the barons start paying court to their majesties."

Leshina shivered despite the spring sun warming the room. "What if she fails?"

"White Pastures is a big castle." Sarese folded her arms tight across her bony breast. "With servants used to caring for Rasun."

Tears welled in Leshina's cornflower eyes. "He was older than Meti when he faced his trial—"

"Don't you wonder whether if we'd intervened earlier, perhaps his magic could still have been safely shaped?" Sarese snapped. "Not testing Meti won't save her from herself if the magic within her is strong enough." She broke off to lay her hand gently on the girl's shoulder again. "It wasn't your fault though, what happened to Rasun. You must believe that."

Leshina managed to nod but couldn't speak.

"Get about your usual duties until their majesties arrive." Sympathetic, Sarese was still implacable.

"Then spend as much time as possible around Kemeti. Whenever you catch a glimpse of her friend, fix him in your mind's eye."

Leshina nodded, still silent. As she went out, she let her fearful tears fall. Since weeping would convince everyone she'd taken an undeserved tongue lashing from the old crone.

The rest of that day kept her too busy to fret. Housekeepers set every maid of all work to polishing the bedchambers and making up beds with fresh, scented linens. Every dust sheet was removed, the fine furnishings brushed regardless while the footmen fetched silver, glass, and statuary out of storage. Barechested yardmen beat the dust from carpets out beyond the gates while the girls swept hearths clean and polished fire irons and servant boys replenished log baskets against the evening chill still coming off the river. Dusk was falling by the time the white stone steps of the main entrance were finally scrubbed.

While the other girls slept, unheeding, exhausted, Leshina stared at the ceiling of their garret. What if Meti failed the test? What if she passed? What would she think when she learned what power she had within her. Would she realize what had happened to Rasun? Would she ever know that Leshina . . . ?

The slam of the door startled her awake. The uncurtained window was pale with dawn light, and the other girls were already pouring icy water from the ewers to wash away lingering sleepiness.

They breakfasted in the servants' hall watching the yardmen unloading barrels and sacks and provisions wrapped in muslin or oilcloth. Errand boys brought

baskets of more precious foodstuffs, wrapped and
sealed in the coarse yellow paper the river traders
brought from some downstream land.

Then the maids were set ornamenting every room
with fresh-cut flowers and wiping away any trace of
dust brought by night breezes. Leshina had barely returned to the lower hall for noon's bread and cheese
when the first outriders' arrival echoed around the
courtyard.

"Klyssa, Isette, Asteri, to go to the front of the
house and attend to the children's carriages." Sarese
clapped her hands. "And you, Leshina. And stop
yawning!"

Leshina hurried after the other girls, scarlet-faced.

"You weren't here this time last year, were you?"
Isette slid her a sympathetic look. "Don't worry.
We've done all the really hard work."

That's what you think, Leshina thought silently.

They ran up the stone stairs to the heavy door separating the lower halls from the castle's upper reaches.
Eyes demurely fixed on the black and white floor tiles,
they walked swiftly to the front entrance.

Leshina hoped anyone noticing her nervousness
would put it down to the searching scrutiny of the two
senior housekeepers already waiting there.

It seemed like an age before the first carriages
crunched around the broad gravel sweep to draw up
in front of the steps. An age, and yet, far too soon.

The housekeepers acknowledged the children's at-
tendants with cordial reserve before welcoming the
princes and princesses.

"Highness, what a beautiful gown."

"Prince Perisen, you'll soon be as tall as your
sister."

As elegant as her mother, Princess Giseri swept past with a rustle of lace-trimmed skirts, perfumed ribbons coiling amid her auburn ringlets. Tarifa followed, doing her best to mimic such poise. Perisen spared the gathering a good-natured, short-sighted smile before returning his attention to the book he carried.

"I have a hound pup." Tousle-headed, shirt rumpled and breeches creased, Jastro ran up the steps. "Mirich, I'm training him myself."

One of the other footmen nodded at the girls. "Go and help with the luggage."

Leshina looked hard at the empty air behind the youngest prince. Not even the slightest trace of his once-imagined dog lingered at his heels. Disappointment hollow in her stomach, she followed the other girls out into the spring sunshine.

A prudently aproned maid of honor was helping Kemeti out of the second carriage. Another was bundling muslin into an incongruously plain pail. The acrid smell of vomit momentarily rose above the spice-studded pomander thrown on top.

"Everyone keeps saying I'll grow out of it." A blush of embarrassment stained Kemeti's pallor. "I'd like to know when." The faintest echo of her father's famed temper colored her tight words.

Sarese knew how ill travel made the child, Leshina thought with silent anguish. How could they put her to the test?

Then she glimpsed the shadow behind Kemeti. A shadow strong enough to defy the sunlight. Looking around. For an instant, looking straight at Leshina. Then he vanished.

"Quickly," another maid of honor scolded, standing by the first carriage. "Before their majesties arrive."

Leshina hurried to take Jastro's toys and games, Giseri's jewel casket, Perisen's books and Tarifa's embroidery basket.

It was wholly dark when Kemeti woke. Where was she? Then the sourness at the back of her throat reminded her of the horrible journey.

Why couldn't they just live in one castle, she thought crossly. Why did she have to be jolted over endless leagues with the turn of every season? Because her father had to make his presence felt in every corner of his vast kingdom, yes, she'd been told that often enough. Because the great river was the kingdom's heart not its boundary. But why didn't Jastro ever get sick?

At least she felt better now she had slept. If she could just rinse away the foul taste in her mouth. As she sat up, she was puzzled to realize her bedroom was unusually dark. Who had laid the fire so badly it had left no glowing embers? As the feather-stuffed quilt slid down to leave her exposed to the night chill, Kemeti shivered.

"Feia?" Her words fell oddly in the dead air. "Feia, I want some cordial!"

There was no reply, and Kemeti realized no light from her night maid's candle was edging under the door. She scowled and swung her legs over the side of her soft, warm bed. Feia was supposed to stay awake in case she was needed.

As her bare feet found the rich wool carpet, she realized her bladder was uncomfortably full. She dropped to her knees, reaching beneath the carved bedstead for the chamber pot.

A hand fastened on her wrist. "Meti?"

She screamed and tried to pull away, but the grip on her wrist didn't yield. She screamed again and again, so hard she tasted bile, her heart pounding.

A spiteful chuckle in the darkness silenced her. "No one's coming."

It was true. All she could hear was her own rasping breath. No cries of alarm, no running feet, no guard throwing open her door.

"It's just you and me, Meti." The iron grip released her, and she fell backward.

Horrified to feel a hot thread of urine between her legs, she clamped her knees together. "Who—" Words stuck in her throat. She scrambled to her feet, stumbling on the hem of her long cotton nightgown.

Whoever had been hiding beneath the bed crawled out with another soft laugh. "It's me, Achel."

"What?" She stood uncomprehending in the darkness. Then she ran to the window to wrench open the shutters, and moonlight streamed in. Outside, the wide silver loop of the mighty river embraced the castle park's carefully nurtured copses. The city sprawled beyond the outer wall, beyond her mother's pleasure garden. Everything just as it should be outside. But something was very wrong in here.

Long fingers fastened on her shoulder and pulled her back around. "I was talking to you."

Kemeti shoved the hand away, clumsy with fear. "Who are you?"

He was taller than she, older, blond hair drawn back from his sallow, angular face. His dark eyes were hard beneath scowling sandy brows.

"I'm Achel, your friend." Irritated, he planted his hands on his hips, bare-armed in his long leather jerkin and coarse breeches, barefooted as every boatman standing proudly on his deck. "You don't seem pleased to see me."

"But—" If some curious boy from the river traders had managed to sneak past the gates and the guards, incredible as that might be, how did he know to call himself Achel?

"I'm dreaming," Kemeti realized aloud.

His sudden slap stung her face. "Are you?"

As she gaped at him, she couldn't deny a shock of recognition. How could that be? She searched her memories of all the times she'd watched the river boats, out in the gardens, from the towers of the other castles the seasons took her to. No, she hadn't ever seen him, not really.

But somehow she knew deep inside her that he was the boy she'd imagined so often by her side. But he wasn't the friend she had longed for.

"Go away!" She couldn't help glancing beyond him towards the closed door.

"No one's coming." He laughed, cruelly amused.

"You're not real," she protested. "You can't be."

"No?" He reached forward and pinched her upper arm, twisting the tender flesh through the cloth of her nightgown.

"Ow!" The unexpected pain redoubled the ache in her bladder.

"You wanted me here. You imagined me." He scowled.

"What do you want?" She was not going to wet herself. Pressing her thighs together, she blinked away furious tears. "What are you going to do?"

"Whatever I please." He looked idly around and picked up one of her books from a side table. "To pay you back." He started tearing out pages with slow malice.

"Stop that," she shouted, outraged.

"Afraid you'll you get into trouble?" he sneered. Dropping the book, he swept a fine china dish from the mantelshelf into the hearth. "You will, you know." Laughing, he smashed a crystal tree hung with necklaces beside it. "Because no one else can see me but you."

Kemeti rejected the futile hope of saving her treasures and ran for the door. She slammed it behind her, fumbling for the lock. As her fingers fastened on the key, Achel threw his shoulder against the other side. The jolt threw her backwards, the key lost in the darkness.

"You won't get rid of me that easily," he promised ominously as he pulled the door open.

Kemeti didn't waste breath replying, bolting from the antechamber into the corridor. But everything was wrong. There were no lanterns. Window shutters that should be safely closed stood wide, uncaring moonlight pooling on the narrow carpet.

She rounded a corner, then another, shivering with cold and fear. Was there anyone here? She threw open the door to Giseri's rooms but the antechamber was empty.

Kemeti pushed the door shut without actually latching it. She bit her lip as she hitched up her nightgown and used a shapely vase as a chamber pot. This had better be a dream, otherwise she'd have some explaining to do. She was just setting the vessel down when a deep-throated bark startled her. A dog?

"Seek, Scaff, seek." She could hear Achel encouraging it.

Dry-mouthed, she remembered imagining a dog at his heels, one of those rangy brindled curs that leaped from deck to deck. But she'd never imagined a name for his dog, she thought bemused.

Panting echoed louder as the dog turned into the corridor. She shoved the door all the way shut with a frantic whimper. The river cur barked triumphantly, and she heard its feet thud on the floorboards. Its claws scraped at the wood as it growled, low and menacing.

Memory paralyzed her. She couldn't breathe. That terrible night when Rasun had been taken ill, he'd shrieked about birds in the room, birds that no one else could see.

He'd screamed for his servants, for Giseri, for their mother and father. When they'd already been standing there. Only Rasun's empty gaze had slid straight over them, unseeing. He'd blundered about, weeping for fear of the darkness, when their father was summoning countless branches of candles.

She knew from servants' whispers that Rasun was still lost in his incomprehensible madness. Had she gone mad too—

Her panicked thoughts dissolved in utter confusion.

"Good boy, Scaff." Achel raised his voice on the far side of the door. "Kemeti, come out of there at once!"

A feeble flicker of indignation countered the wretchedness overwhelming her. He presumed to command her? Kemeti bit her lip and concentrated on holding the door closed. The river cur growled angrily, scrabbling harder, faster. As it snuffled at the base of the door, she could feel its breath hot and moist on her bare feet. She screwed her eyes shut, fighting the choking terror rising in her throat once again.

"Come out," Achel snapped. "Or you'll be punished all the more."

Outraged, Kemeti's eyes snapped open. Only her father and mother could order her punished. And she hadn't done anything wrong. He was the intruder here, him and his horrid cur.

One of her father's big hounds would defend her from this horrid river boy, she thought with desperate fury. She wasn't afraid of the robust hunting dogs, and they liked her. They wouldn't tolerate this cur in their castle. Introducing them to Jastro's new whelp had taken all the kennelmen's guile to save the pup from being torn to pieces.

A questioning whine made her yelp with fright. Spinning around, she pressed her back against the door. There was a shape in the room with her, a shadow beneath the window. Only it was made from moonlight rather than shade. How could that be?

She realized she could make out the outline of a sizable hunting hound. Long muzzled, its head cocked to one side, floppy ears pricked with curiosity. Its ruff of thick white fur was fluffed up, curled tail held high over its muscular rump.

Only it wasn't real. Kemeti could see right through it. But as it whined again, expectant, she realized she couldn't see the upright of the lamp stand through its flank any more. Somehow it was getting more real.

On the other side of the door, the river cur barked furiously. The hound's silent snarl drew its black lips back from perfect ivory fangs, but it didn't move, still looking keenly at Kemeti. Now she could see the darker gray inside its ears, under its belly, inside the curl of its wagging tail. It made as it to take a step forward but paced on the spot instead, as the best-trained hounds did until a command released them.

"Come here, boy." She bent to offer her hand. The hound thrust a solid wet nose into her palm, its warm tongue licking her icy fingers. She stroked it, feeling thick softness beneath the harsher upper coat. It hadn't been here a moment ago but it was undoubtedly real.

The river cur was barking hysterically now. The hound kept its eyes fixed on Kemeti's face as it growled low deep in its chest. She felt its hackles rising beneath her hand. It was real, and it was an ally. Wrenching the door open, she urged the hound on with hand and voice. "See him off, boy!"

The white hound sprang on the river cur. Taller but lighter-boned, the other dog was unable to resist the solid impact. Snarling, the hound crouched astride the cur as it whimpered, bowled over, pale belly exposed. Moonlight shone on the hound's gnashing teeth then they fastened in the river dog's throat. Gurgling, the cur drew up its hind legs to rake at the hound's belly but the heavier dog shook it like a rat, breaking its neck with an audible snap.

Kemeti stood, staring, mouth open, shivering with cold and fright. Achel swore an oath the stable boys used. She looked up, startled, to see him running away though the moonbeams and shadow dappling the corridor. Where was he going? Who else might he hurt? Jastro?

"Chase, boy!" She surprised herself by shouting to the white hound. "Bring him down!"

Obediently abandoning its kill, the dog pursued Achel, its eager barks echoing back from the stone walls.

Steeling herself, Kemeti edged past the slaughtered river cur. Her toes cringed at the thought of sticky blood on the carpet. But as she strained her eyes to try to see any stains in the gloom, all she could make out was the pattern of interlaced leaves.

Kemeti blinked, and there was no river cur. It was only an illusion wrought by the weaver's design meeting the moonshine's deceit. Like one of those pictures in Perisen's book, where a beautiful girl in a sumptuous gown became a hook-nosed old woman swathed in a wrap if you looked at her the right way. A cloud slid over the edge of the moon. When Kemeti looked again, she saw the hapless beast curled motionless in its death agony.

Tears stung her eyes. She hadn't meant to bring an innocent animal here to die in such pain, whatever that horrid Achel might say. If she had truly done something to cause this, she didn't know how, and she really hadn't meant to. She blinked, wiping her nose on her sleeve, struggling not to cry in earnest.

But this wasn't over. She could hear the white hound baying triumphantly and Achel shouting foul curses at it. It must have him trapped. There must be someone she could find, a guard who could throw him into a dungeon. If this really was all somehow her fault, she must try to put things right, mustn't she?

Trembling with apprehension, she screwed up her courage and opened her eyes. As she looked, she saw the dead cur fading away. Just as moonlight had shaped the white hound, now the river dog was dissolving into the shadows before her very eyes. She thrust a hesitant toe forward only to feel the soft dry wool of the carpet. The dog wasn't real. It had never been real.

You imagined me.

Achel's words echoed in her head.

She had. She had imagined him, and his dog. Because just about every trader's boat had a cur or two pacing its decks, splashing after the boys when they swam ashore, walking circumspectly behind the elders when a river clan anchored to pay formal visits to the city's merchants. But it hadn't been a real dog. Just the idea of a dog.

Kemeti groped for understanding but that was beyond her. She settled for concentrating on what was in front of her. Nothing. The dog had been nothing, not really. So Achel was nothing. Not real. And she'd tell him so. Not stopping to risk her new boldness foundering on some further inconvenient thought, she hurried towards the barking and shouting.

The white hound had Achel cornered. The river youth was pressed into a door recess where a side passage ended in a narrow window. He was cursing, vile as a trooper, and Kemeti saw him kick at the dog. The hound's gleaming teeth missed his tanned foot by a hair's breadth, and he hastily thought better of it.

As he saw Kemeti at the corner of the corridor, he yelled at her, enraged. "Call it off or I'll make you sorry!"

She could hear fear undercutting his wrath, but she wouldn't let satisfaction distract her. "You can't do anything to me," she said stoutly. "You're not real."

"I'm real enough to slap you senseless, you little bitch!" Achel tried to take a step forward, but the hound snapped at him.

"No, you're not." Kemeti couldn't help the tremor in her voice. She swallowed and pressed on. "You're just someone I made up when I was thinking about

river boys." She pictured all the youths she'd seen, on
walks with her maids, riding in the castle grounds.
There had been so many glimpses of different boats,
on journeys through the city or up and down the high-
road that followed the great river's winding course
across the vast plains of the kingdom. None of them
was Achel. They were all different from him.

"I am—" He gasped and fell back, the door re-
sounding with a hollow thud. "Hah," he spat. "Hear
that?" He hammered a clenched fist backwards to
bang the door again.

But Kemeti saw the weakness in his legs. His face
had blurred into uncertainty, a shiver of moonlight
running through his body. "You're not real," she insisted. "You're just—"

As she hesitated, Achel stood upright again,
stronger, bolder. "You know nothing," he said with
contempt.

"I just wanted a friend," she shouted with sudden
anger. "I was lonely. I wanted someone to share things
with, to play games, making up stories, like I used to
do with Rusan—" Anguish choked her as she recalled
all the times she'd been missing Rusan so badly, she'd
pretended she had someone there to replace him.
That's how all this had started. None of it was real.

Gritting her teeth, she forced herself to continue.
"You're not real. I made you up. You're not even
right. If you were a real river boy come ashore, you'd
have boots on." She was yelling at the top of her voice
now, infuriated. "They only have bare feet on board
their boats."

Images ran through her mind, of all the shirtless,
shoeless youths she'd ever seen. They were real. This
one was not. As she thought this, she realized she

could see the outline of the doorframe through Achel's shirt.

"And you'd have brought a cloak," she added scornfully. "It's a cold night, and you're dressed for high summer."

Insubstantial as smoke, Achel opened his mouth, but he could make no sound. Kemeti could see the moonlight through him now.

"Go away." Her conviction was firm, hard as iron. "And never come back."

Abrupt shafts of light pierced him, shining through the empty hollows of his eyes and mouth, and he vanished.

Sarese's vicelike hand restrained Leshina. The younger woman blinked away her own tears, her vision flickering back to the lantern-lit warmth of the real corridor. Somewhere overhead, she could hear a maid or a manservant's soft footsteps. The castle never entirely slept.

With an effort, she focused on the empty darkness again, where Kemeti stood alone with the white hound gazing obediently at her.

"I'm sorry." The little girl scrubbed at her tear-stained face with the cuffs of her nightgown. "I know you came to help me, but you're not real either. Please go away." Her voice broke on a sob. "I want to go back to bed and wake up and this all to be a dream."

Leshina held her breath, tense.

The white dog dutifully lay down, its nose on its forepaws, and dissolved into nothingness.

"Good girl," Sarese murmured with satisfaction. "Her magic's strong. She'll do well."

The two women stepped back as Kemeti came running toward them, unseeing, still lost in the deserted unreality of the castle confining her imagination. They followed her back to her room, where the maid Feia dozed in the antechamber, thanks to the powdered oblivion Sarese had dosed her supper with.

Entering the bedchamber, Leshina saw Kemeti scramble into bed, pulling the covers over her head to muffle her weeping.

Sarese was looking around, and Leshina knew she was seeing the real and the unreal side by side. "Don't break the necklace tree," the old woman decided. "But smash that dish in the hearth. She'll need something to convince her it was no dream."

Leshina nodded, not trusting herself to speak.

Sarese's thoughts were already moving on. "I'll let the others know in the morning, as much as is necessary. Make sure you're at hand to answer her questions." She chuckled. "You had better empty that vase she peed in. But ask her what she knows about it, if you think she needs a prompt. Right, let's get back to our own beds."

Satisfied, Sarese walked briskly from the room without a backward glance.

Kemeti's sobs were slowly subsiding beneath the quilt. Leshina slowly closed the window and the shutters, her heart wrung with pity and guilt. Then she closed the shutters on the unreal window too, and lit the thought of a candle besides, in case Kemeti woke in that terrifying darkness again.

She set the dish in the hearth and broke it with a savage stamp of her foot. Never mind Sarese's instructions. She'd wait out the night here in case Kemeti woke up before daybreak brought her securely back to reality. She could guide her home.

She was not going to see the little girl abandoned like Rusan. She owed him that. Since she owed her very existence to his fertile imagination, his adolescent longing shaping her seductive curves, her alluring blondeness. But she had been too bemused to help Rusan. Well, now she understood.

Now she could repay him by being Kemeti's friend.

SAY HELLO TO MY LITTLE FRIEND

Kristine Kathryn Rusch

HE was strange from the start, yet oddly compelling.

I can explain the strange. The compelling is harder.

He'd come into my bar about 3:30 Friday afternoons, thirty minutes before the official start of Happy Hour. He'd take a seat as far from the door as he could get. He'd order two drinks—one, a piña colada, the other light beer on tap.

Then he'd wait.

He was stunningly handsome. That's the thing you'd see first off. The square jaw, the black-black hair, the laughing blue eyes all accented his broad shoulders and perfect male model physique. Only he dressed like a regular guy: nice suit with a jacket he'd remove when he sat down, white shirt, and shoes that could use some attention. Before the drinks arrived, he'd loosen his tie and roll up his sleeves, revealing muscular arms.

And then he'd nurse the beer.

Any red-blooded woman would look at him, as well

as a handful of closeted males. So of course I looked at him. I'm as red-blooded as the next woman—even if it is my bar.

I'm red-blooded, but I'm not pretty. I'm perfectly cast in my role as bar owner. I'm muscular and broad shouldered too. My father used to say I looked like Bette Davis—and he didn't mean the young beauty of her early roles. He meant the battle-axe from *Whatever Happened to Baby Jane?* with the crumpled skin and the bugged out eyes and the voice that sounded as if she'd smoked a thousand cigarettes too many.

A few men like this look. They figure I'm easy (I'm not) because I'm lonely (I'm not that either), and they try to woo me with lies. The occasional guy who enjoys my friendship takes it a stage farther, but we usually agree to go back to platonic after a few months.

Men who look like this guy never give me a second glance. And if one of them had slept with me by accident (and none of them had), it would have been an invitation that came at last call, and the night would end with him chewing his arm off in the morning.

I know that. So when I started talking to Mr. Weird But Beautiful, I did it not because I wanted him (even though I did). I did it because he looked as though he needed some advice.

To understand why he needed some advice, you need to know what my bar looks like. It's not a fern bar or a sports bar. There are no big screens scattered around, all turned to ESPN. There are no giant booths with huge backs because I don't want couples making out in my place and getting us slapped with violating the decency laws.

There are round tables of various sizes scattered

across the floor, and they get pushed aside on Saturdays, when my favorite DJ comes in to spin the tunes—usually oldies, because I don't tolerate that hip-hop crap in my bar.

The rest of the time, it's the juke that's been here since I bought the place. A pool table against the back wall gives the regulars a reason to return besides my lovely presence.

The bar's the first thing you see when you come in the door. The back bar is large and mirrored, so it looks as though we have even more booze than we do. I put the expensive stuff back there because the business travelers who've just had a meeting in the big conglomerate across the street make it worth my while.

The bar is a classic U and made of expensive wood with a polyurethane top, so that I can wipe the thing off every night. Everyone vies for the twenty bar stools that surround the outside of the U, and during Friday Happy Hour, the line for those stools can be five deep.

Although it's not fair to call them stools. They're actually tall chairs with rounded backs that hug the backside of whoever's sitting there. I bought the things from a bar going out of business about five years ago, and they're the best purchase I ever made. They keep the hard drinkers—the guys who pass out with predictable regularity—in their chairs. These guys don't fall four feet to the floor, hitting their head on the bar rail on the way down and thinking lawsuit when they finally wake up.

Guys who drink like that—and every neighborhood bar has them—keep our local taxi service in business, especially weekend nights. I don't even have to call any more. At closing, half a dozen cabs show up here as if they'd been summoned. I confiscate keys, pour the hard drinkers into the cabs, and sign the tab. Then when the drinkers come back for their cars, I won't hand over the keys until I get reimbursed.

It works for all of us, and rarely does the hard drinker get mad.

I take care of my people. That's what I'm known for.

Which is why no one was surprised when I started talking to Mr. Weird But Beautiful.

He started coming in about February, with that uncomfortable look most first timers in a bar often have. He wore a shiny silk suit and a matching silver tie, and he looked good enough to eat.

When he sat at the bar, I was surprised. When he ordered his light beer and piña colada, I waited for the pretty business associate to show up for their meeting.

Only she never came. The beer got nursed and the piña colada disappeared, although I never saw him take a sip.

And as the bar filled up, a bottle blonde stopped beside the empty chair, leaned against the bar, and displayed her assets prettily for him. After she ordered, she turned to him, and he smiled one of those Tom Cruise mighty megawatt smiles, the kind that makes you hot just thinking about it.

She smiled back, and I could tell she was feeling like I was feeling—the right word and she was his.

He had one of those deep Barry White voices, which carried even though he probably didn't intend it to.

Her eyes danced and she leaned in, just a bit, as he said, "Please say hello to my little friend."

Then he looked down.

She flushed, grabbed her drink, and left the bar.

And he leaned back, looking very confused.

Now most guys, when they have a pick-up line that fails, try another one. And any guy who looks like him doesn't need a line at all.

It was a testament to his attractiveness that no woman ever dumped a drink on his lap or slapped him or called him names. Every woman he approached— and by April, he was approaching the desperate ones as well as the pretty ones—gave him that what-the-hell-did-you-just-say? look and fled.

But he never varied his line, he never altered his routine, and he never ever got anyone to say hello to his little friend.

Until, of course, me.

It was just after Easter when I finally had enough. When you have regulars in your place, you develop an emotional attachment to them. Sometimes that attachment is loathing, sometimes it's friendship, and sometimes it's pity.

With Mr. Weird But Beautiful, I found myself feeling oddly responsible. I wanted to sit next to him and say, "What? Your mother never taught you manners?"

But I knew that wasn't the way to approach him.

Instead, I pulled a bar stool over to his other side, the side away from the empty stool he hogged every Friday, and said, "Your little friend routine doesn't work."

He looked at me as though he didn't know I could speak English. Maybe he thought the only sentences in my repertoire were "Light on tap and piña colada, right?" and "That'll be six-sixty-five."

It seemed to take him a minute to process this new sentence, and then he said, "It's gotta work."

"Nonsense," I said. "You need a new line, that's all. Half the women in this place would go home with you if you asked them right."

"I don't want them to go home with me. I want them to go home with Marty."

That's when I sighed. I couldn't help it. "Look," I said, "to get them home with Marty, you need to charm them first."

"No," he said. "That's not fair. *Marty* needs to charm them."

"Marty can work his magic in the privacy of your own bedroom," I said. "You—"

But by that time, Mr. Weird But Beautiful was giving me the what-the-hell-did-you-just-say? look. He flushed and he was starting to get out of his chair when I grabbed his wrist.

His muscular oh-so-strong wrist.

"I'm trying to help you here," I said. "It's been nearly three months, and you can't get a girl to spend thirty seconds with you. You're going about it wrong."

He pulled his wrist from my grasp. "First, I don't want her to spend time with me. I'm trying to fix up Marty. Second, Marty and I do not share a bed or even a house. Third, what the hell even makes this your business?"

"Nothing, I guess," I started, but by the time I finished the third word, he was gone.

Without paying for his beer or his piña. And, as usual, the beer was barely touched, but the piña was gone.

It really bugged me that I never saw him drink it.

Especially this time. When I was sitting beside him from the moment I set the drinks down.

*   *   *

I figured that was the last I'd see of Mr. Weird But Beautiful, so I wrote off the drinks and went back to my routine. No one asked after him, even though a few of the regulars noticed he was missing.

These were the closeted guys, one of whom got very drunk on a Friday in March, sidled up to Mr. Weird But Beautiful, and said, "I'll say hello to your little friend," in a suggestive voice, and nearly got tossed across the room.

Mr. Weird But Beautiful left after that too, although that time he paid, hands shaking. He did come back, though, the following week, and when his closeted stalker came up to him a second time, Mr. Weird But Beautiful held up his hand.

"Look," he said in a polite voice, the same voice he used for his pick-up line. "I vote Democrat. I believe in equal rights. I know we should be flattered because you're probably a very nice man. But believe me when I say that my friend and I are not your type."

The closeted stalker nodded once, then went back to his chair, probably trying to maintain some dignity. He never approached Mr. Weird But Beautiful again, but he did watch from time to time, maybe hoping Mr. WBB might change his mind.

Although I could have told him that he wouldn't. A guy who doesn't change his pick-up line is not going to change his orientation, no matter how much the other party hopes he will.

Believe me, I know. Because most guys are oriented toward beautiful—or at least pretty—and no matter how friendly they are, no matter how much they talk to me or flirt with me, they're not going home with me, and they're certainly not going to invite me to spend time with their little friend.

At least, not when they're sober. And I've been a bartender long enough to know they're not worth a damn when they're drunk. After a while, you look for meaning, you know? Just a kind word, a phrase, a bit of understanding.

I try a little kindness once a night, just to keep my hand in the game, which was why I talked to Mr. Weird But Beautiful in the first place.

Sometimes kindness pans out. Sometimes it doesn't.

And sometimes it leads you places you never thought you'd go.

He came back the next afternoon. Mr. Weird But Beautiful, who never darkened my door on any day but Friday, had shown up on Saturday wearing a blue chambray shirt, faded jeans, shit-kickers with no added heel. If anything, he looked even more delectable. The blue shirt stretched just enough to show the muscles on his chest. The jeans hugged his ass the way . . . well, the way I wanted to.

He didn't sit at the bar. Instead, he took a table in the middle of the room.

And since none of the cocktail waitresses would go near him, I had to wait on him. From the bar, I said tiredly, "Beer and piña, right?"

He looked at me, those blue eyes flat, his expression reserved, his tone one you'd use with a six-year-old. "Just the beer."

So I brought him the light, still foaming over the stein, and onto the tray. Man, was I out of practice.

I set down the napkin, then the beer, and started to leave, when he said, "I've been thinking about our conversation."

"Good," I said, and returned the tray, wiping it down before I set it near the server's station.

"And I'd like to ask you a few questions," he said just a little louder.

Jodi, the cocktail waitress, raised a single eyebrow. It was her who-does-this-asshole-think-he-is? look.

But there was no one else in the place. So I told her to man the bar (she used to tend, but didn't make as much in tips; if I had assets like hers, I'd waitress too), and I walked back to him.

He kicked out the chair beside him. I sat. This wasn't going to be an easy conversation.

"So why doesn't it work?" he asked. "That line, as you call it."

My turn to give him the incredulous look, and I almost hauled out one of the sentences I'd been thinking since he first came in—"What? You were raised by wolves?"—but if I did, he'd bolt, and he'd spend the rest of his life trying this stupid gambit at bars all over town until he finally gave up and stayed home—alone—for the rest of his life.

I couldn't decide if that outcome was a crime against nature (his gorgeous nature) or just the way things should be.

For a minute, I toyed with answering the question delicately. But I'd tiptoed around delicately the day before, and it hadn't worked. This guy had spent *all night* wondering why "Say hello to my little friend" repelled women. He wasn't going to get delicate.

He might not even get blunt.

"Look," I said in my best I've-been-around-the-block voice, "we all know that most men name their penis, okay? We know you have a close relationship—

a friendship—with that part. We just don't need to know it from the moment—"

"You think Marty is my penis? Are you nuts?" He stood up, bumped the table, and knocked over the stein. I slid my chair back so I wouldn't get doused in light beer.

Jodi tossed me the bar rag, but she wasn't getting anywhere near good ole WBB.

"Who else would he be?" I asked as I set the rag on the table and went for some bar napkins.

"My friend," WBB said. "You know, the guy who comes in here with me. The guy who drinks the piña coladas."

"I hate to tell you this, pal," I said as I tossed half the napkins on the table and the other half on the stain spreading across the floor. "But you come in here alone."

I expected an argument. I expected him to tell me all about this Marty, who accompanied him. I expected to hear every detail about the delusion.

Instead, WBB said, "That fucking son of a bitch," handed me a twenty, and walked out of the bar.

He walked back in an hour later, dragging an ugly little man who had blood dripping from his nose. WBB picked up the little man—who couldn't have been more than three feet tall—and said,

"This. This is my little friend. Marty the fucking bastard. Say hello, Marty."

"Hello," the little man said in a nasal tone. He was dripping blood over the floors I had just cleaned the beer off of.

"Hello," I said. "Do you want to press charges? I can call the police."

The little man shook his head. Blood dripped everywhere.

"Show the nice lady what you can do, Marty," WBB said. "She's been kind to me. She deserves to know."

I flushed at the word "kind." No one had noticed before.

Marty closed his eyes. His nose was still dripping.

WBB shook him. "*Show* her."

And Marty disappeared. But the blood kept dripping on my floor. Ping, ping, ping.

Jodi and I exchanged glances. I'd seen a lot of strange things in my bar, but that was the first legitimate disappearing man.

"Now," WBB said. "Explain what was going on."

He shook his fists. Only Jodi and I knew that there was a little guy between them.

Either that or WBB was David Fucking Copperfield.

"*Tell* them," WBB said.

"We had a bet," the little guy said, and reappeared as he spoke. He was dangling between WBB's hands and looking as forlorn as a human being could. "We bet that no matter how good-looking he is, he couldn't get me a date."

"The rest of it," WBB said.

The little guy sighed.

WBB shook him again.

"We handicapped him," the little guy said, "by making him say, 'Say hello to my little friend.' You know, like in golf. Figuring the good player needed a level playing field with the ugly player. Me."

"Ugly." WBB said. "Damn straight."

I didn't say anything. I'd seen bar bets before. But judging from WBB's face the day he first came in—

all stunned at the way the bar looked and smelled—
he didn't. He had no idea that cheating was part of
the process.

"How much was the bet for?" I asked.

"The year-end bonus," WBB said. "Five grand."

"He doesn't need his," the little guy said. "People
give him stuff because he's so pretty."

I stared at WBB. His beautiful blue eyes flashed.
He was furious.

He shook the little guy one more time for good
measure. "Tell her the rest of it. I'd say, 'Say hello to
my little friend.' And then you *what*?"

The little guy cleared his throat. "I disappeared."

He vanished then quickly reappeared.

"To everyone except me," WBB said. "I could see
the little bastard."

"I hate to tell you this," I said, "but he disappeared
long before you came into the bar. If he really was
with you."

"He was," WBB said. "*Tell* her."

The little guy shrugged one imprisoned shoulder.
The movement looked like it hurt. "It's my only talent. It's all I can do. I trained it. Because people always looked at me with pity. I'm short and I'm ugly,
and you wouldn't believe the jokes."

"So you turned the table on your friend?" I asked.
"A man who was going to help you? You played a
trick on him?"

"He promised he wouldn't," WBB said. "He promised he'd stay visible."

"I did!" The little guy said.

"To me," WBB said. "And only me. The man who
believed in him. I figured once someone talked to him,

she'd want to go out with him. I used to think he was clever."

The little guy tried to wipe his nose but WBB held him fast.

"I *believed* in him," WBB said, and dropped him.

The little guy bounced in the pool of his own blood.

"Fucking bastard," WBB said, and left.

And, of course, I never saw him again.

His little friend, on the other hand, haunts my bar like an out-of-work Rumplestiltskin. I think he makes his living by winning bar bets.

Like, "Betcha I can't appear and reappear." Like, "I can make a piña colada vanish without even touching it." Like, "I bet a handsome man like you can't get a woman to give me a second glance."

I let him stay. He's a curiosity. Now that they're used to him, the regulars place bets right alongside his. The entire place is getting rich.

Except me.

Because there's a part of me that still wants the fairy tale. You know, you help the gorgeous guy, and even though you're a plain Cinder Ella, he sees through the grime and makes you his princess.

But WBB hasn't come back. I haven't even gotten enough courage to ask his little friend for WBB's real name.

I know real life is not a fairy tale.

But I also know that tiny men who look like Rumplestiltskin can't disappear at will.

And yet this one does.

Somehow that's not quite enough to overcome my belief in the way the world really works.

You see, I own a bar. I know that people never change their orientation. And WBB, for all his willingness to help his little friend, was oriented toward beautiful—or at least pretty.

And no matter how nice I was, and how much I was willing to help him, and how much his pride made him come back to talk to me, to explain he really wasn't crazy, I knew he wasn't going home with me.

I knew he was never going to invite me to spend time with his little friend.

JUSTINE AND THE MOUNTIE

Kristen Britain

JUSTINE staggered down the hallway, the floor reeling beneath her feet as though she were on a ship at sea—a rough, rolling sea—instead of at home in her calm, land-locked apartment.

"Dammit," she said, as she stumbled into a wall. She hoped to make it back to bed without needing to vomit again. She was not drunk—didn't even like to drink, except maybe for the occasional glass of wine. No, a problem with her inner ear was to blame. This was vertigo, and her doctor told her to hold tight, and it should pass.

Hold tight? Easy for him to say when he wasn't seasick without the sea.

Finally she reached the doorway to her bedroom and swept past the Mountie standing there.

Mountie?

She backed out the door and, fighting nausea, looked about. No Mountie. The vertigo must have really scrambled her brain. The only Mountie in sight was the little metal figure on her telephone table.

She'd picked it up on a whim at a gift shop during a business trip to Montreal. Everyone needed an iconic Mountie souvenir from Canada, right?

She named hers Ian because it sounded like a good Canadian name. Ian stood straight at attention with one hand raised in a salute. She thought him a very proper Mountie.

She left Ian behind and entered her bedroom, lunging at her bed as if the floor tilted her in its direction. Even after she was beneath the covers with her eyes closed and Oolong purring beside her, the world spun around and around.

She lay there thinking about the impending deadlines at work—*Nuts & Bolts Magazine,* the premier publication of the fastener and implements market of the hardware industry, was due to the printer by the end of the week. Not exactly glamorous, but it was a paycheck. She was the copyeditor and had learned more about screw esoterica than any thirty-something woman in her right mind ought to know. In any case, if the vertigo didn't lift in the next twenty-four hours as the doctor predicted, the magazine was, from a copyediting perspective, *screwed.*

The world finally stilled, Oolong lying close and warm. He was a big gray tabby Maine coon, and his rumbling purrs were enough to register as a minor earthquake. She started to drift off to sleep, thinking of her little toy Mountie trimmed out with his broad-brimmed hat and smart, scarlet coat. She'd never seen a *real* Mountie and thought maybe she should travel to Ottawa to watch the Musical Ride, in which Mounties rode their black horses in precise formations and cavalry drills choreographed to music.

As sleep deepened, her dreams were filled with

lance-bearing Mounties riding round and round in exquisite kaleidoscope patterns.

Until the phone rang, scattering all her Mounties and their horses into oblivion. She sat up too fast and the room whirled around her.

"Dammit." She tossed her sheets aside, burying the implacable Oolong, and stood unsteadily, gritting her teeth.

She ought to let the phone ring, but she so rarely received calls, it was difficult to resist answering it. For all she knew, though, it was just work. Someone was probably having a word emergency. *Do I use "that" or "which"? "Lay" or "lie"?*

Sometimes her colleagues treated her like a walking dictionary. There was the time Carl, a staff writer for *Nuts & Bolts*, burst into her office (really a space set aside in the supply closet) and declared, "I need a word!" Justine gave him a word, though not the one of many others she would have liked to, and it "galvanized" him to write his most spirited article ever: "Nails: A Lost Commodity in a Pre-Drilled World?"

She bumped her way into the hall again, rebounding off the wall, feeling very much like a pinball. A sick pinball. She grabbed the phone, knocking over a framed picture of Oolong and the Mountie figure. She tried to put the phone to her ear, but she missed and hit her nose with it.

"Dammit!"

"Justine? Hello, Justine?"

She closed her eyes, leaned against the wall to stay upright, and slid the phone to the appropriate orifices. "What?" she screamed into it.

"Justine? It's Liz. Hey, I heard you were sick. Anything I can bring over to you at lunchtime?"

A bucket, Justine almost said, relieved it was her friend and not one of the *Nuts & Bolts* crew.

"Justine?"

"I'm here. Yeah. Crackers—you know, saltines. And ginger ale." Those were always good for seasickness.

"You bet, honey. I'll be over at noon."

"Let yourself in," Justine mumbled.

"Will do."

Justine loved Liz, but her perky tone was tiring. She passed the phone to the Mountie to hang up. Carefully he replaced it on the receiver.

"Thanks," she said.

"You're welcome," the Mountie replied.

Justine stopped, heart pounding. She turned ever so slowly to minimize the vertigo, and there he stood, the Mountie, tall and broad shouldered, attired in hat and scarlet coat and shiny boots. With his square jaw and sandy, neatly trimmed hair, he looked as though he'd just walked off a movie set.

Justine screamed, and between the shock and vertigo, she fell to her backside.

"I don't see you, I don't see you," she said.

He bent over her, scrutinizing her. "May I help you?"

"I don't see you, I don't see you."

"You call me Ian," he said.

"I don't hear you either."

"You appear to be in some distress."

Justine laughed, and it held a hysterical edge to it. Here he was, her imaginary Mountie come to rescue the distressed damsel. He had to be imaginary, right? The vertigo not only unbalanced her balance but set reality akilter.

But then her imaginary Mountie helped her up and supported her to her bedside. Suddenly she was all too conscious of her old pink pajamas with the sheep on them and a hole beneath the armpit. She had vomit breath, too. Once she was in bed, she pulled the covers over herself, Oolong stretched out on his back beside her.

"How is it you are here?" she asked Ian.

"I have always been here."

Now that was a creepy thought. Had her little toy Mountie been watching her as she went about her daily routine all this time? Of course not. He was a figment of her imagination, at least this full-blown flesh and blood version of him was. The vertigo. It was the vertigo.

"You were distressed," Ian added uncertainly.

This was, Justine thought, a little like some books she'd read, a bit of a fantasy. She'd come to copy-editing out of a love for reading and writing. She'd never expected to be working at a magazine like *Nuts & Bolts,* but she'd stayed because it was a paycheck, and a habit. Occasionally she dreamed of moving to book publishing, but a real publishing house would probably look at her miniscule credentials and laugh.

She dreamed even more of finishing off her own long-languishing manuscript, but it always seemed like too much trouble to work on it. There was a time when she filled every spare moment with writing, when the ideas flowed, and she produced several pages a day. But in recent months? Not so much as a sentence. She'd hit the wall, had gone dry, lacked any fresh ideas. She'd pretty much given up on it, the whole dream. She wasn't cut out to be a writer, and so she stayed at the magazine. After all, someone had to keep Oolong in kibble and litter, and it wasn't gonna be Oolong.

Ian's appearance reminded her of why she loved those books she once read, and why she wrote. It was the magic of the story, how almost anything the imagination conjured could happen.

Justine yawned, and when she glanced about herself, she found only Oolong and no Ian. Well, unless you counted the toy figurine on her nightstand. It was the vertigo, she reminded herself, not "magic." Toys didn't just come to life and talk to you.

I am sick, I am sick, I am sick . . .

After a time, she drifted off.

She awoke to a presence hovering beside her bed. "Ian?" she murmured.

"Ian?"

The whole room went tilt-a-whirl as Justine sat bolt upright. After several moments of dry heaves, her friend Liz sat on the side of the bed. Oolong roused himself enough to come over and rub his face against Liz's elbow before flopping down again.

"I didn't mean to startle you, honey," she said, running her hand along Oolong's length. "My, but you're a sight."

Liz should talk. She was all shiny bangles, with multiple piercings in each ear and a stud through one eyebrow. Justine did not want to know if there were others elsewhere, though she heard a rumor that Liz had a literary tattoo—of Moby Dick—*somewhere.* Justine didn't want to know the truth of that, either.

"I got your ginger ale and crackers." She popped a can for Justine and produced the saltines stacked on a dish.

"Th-thanks," Justine said, easing herself against her

pillows. She accepted the fizzing can of soda and sipped.

"Who's Ian?" Liz asked.

"Ian?"

"Yes, Ian. Are you holding out on me? Is there someone new in your life?"

"Er, no," Justine said. "He must have been a dream."

"I thought you said you never dreamed anymore."

It was true. Justine used to dream vividly, with colors and details. As vivid as Liz's pink hair. Some were filled with mayhem and action, others proved more prosaic. One of her last dreams was of shopping in a store of Martha Stewart creations, with Christmas items on sale for half price. She'd been ecstatic, searching through hand towels and ornaments. When she related this dream to Liz, Liz had declared her a "sick puppy."

At some point, the dreams had simply stopped, evaporated, just like her writing.

"Is Ian some sort of screw?" Liz inquired.

"What?"

"You remember the Brads? How you kept carrying on about them? I thought you were dating several guys named Brad at once, only come to realize you were babbling about hardware. Honey, you have got to find another job."

Justine sighed, and glanced at her nightstand, where she last remembered seeing her Mountie, but he was gone.

"What about your novel?" Liz persisted. "It's as good as anything Evan Lord ever wrote. If he can be the world's bestselling author, I don't see why you can't get your book published."

"Because . . ." Justine simply let it hang there in the air. She'd been about to say, *Because I haven't had one stinking idea for months. Because I'm not Evan Lord with all his big concept novels.*

Evan Lord lived in the city, and she saw the signs of his success—not just the inclusion of his books on bestseller lists, but the sports cars he drove around, and his big mansion on the river. Many of his fans made pilgrimages to his neighborhood to gaze with longing and adoration through the security fence surrounding his property.

"Look," Liz said, "I know how good your stuff is, and I have access to all the latest and greatest."

It was true. Justine had met Liz three years ago at Bookwoods, a funky bookstore a couple blocks away where Liz was the assistant manager. Justine had ensconced herself in the store's café every Saturday, with her pen and pad to work on the novel. Liz noticed and struck up a conversation, and they soon became fast friends with their mutual love of books binding them together, to the point Justine trusted Liz enough to let her read the manuscript.

When it was clear Justine wasn't going to offer an explanation or excuses, Liz stood. "I've got to get back to the store. The rest of the soda is in the fridge. You give me a call if you need anything more, all right?"

"Okay. Thanks."

Liz started to walk from the room, but paused in the doorway. "Still not going to tell me who or what Ian is?"

Justine sighed. "An imaginary friend."

Liz smiled. "I hope he's good looking—mine is!" And with that, she was gone.

"Her hair is *pink!*"

Justine almost spilled her ginger ale all over her bed. Imaginary or not, Ian's appearances were startling.

"Er, yes, Liz's hair is very pink."

"I have never seen anything like it," Ian replied, "but there is much I've never seen."

"Right." Because Justine couldn't think of what else to say or do with an imaginary Mountie standing in her bedroom (well, maybe if she were feeling better, there was something else she could think of *doing* with the hunky fellow), she said, "Ian, why don't you tell me a little about yourself."

He brightened. "I am a member of the Royal Canadian Mounted Police."

"Um, I see that. Anything else? Any hobbies?"

"Law and order."

"Okay, I get that. You're dedicated. But beyond the job, anything about your past?"

"I was made in China," he replied. "Then shipped to the gift shop in Montreal where you found me. But I don't remember very much about it."

"And that's it?"

"I am your friend," Ian said with conviction. "I heard you say so."

Justine sipped her ginger ale, considering her Mountie. Why a Mountie? Why not a famous actor, or a superhero? Well, Ian was as good looking as any Hollywood star, and Mounties were known as heroic and brave . . . Perhaps more surprising, taking into account her job and her lack of creativity of late, was that she hadn't conjured up a carpenter or plumber. It pleased her she hadn't—she dealt with enough of those at *Nuts & Bolts*. Maybe it wasn't just the vertigo—maybe her creativity was coming back.

In any case, it was clear Ian needed some back story. He was a blank slate. "Ian," she said, "let's forget the whole made-in-China thing. Let's say you are on duty in the Yukon. Or the Rockies. I mean the Canadian Rockies, of course."

Ian frowned. "Then I cannot be here."

Justine scratched her head. "You are being too literal. I don't mean right now, but usually."

Ian nodded. "I am usually too literal."

Justine tried to detect if he was joking, but his expression was very serious, very earnest. This wasn't going to be easy if he didn't understand the nuances of basic conversation.

"Do you think you could relax a little?" she asked him. His ramrod-straight posture was tiring her. "You know, stand at ease?"

He widened his stance and clasped his hands behind his back, but it didn't look any more relaxed.

"This won't do," Justine said. "Come sit here." She patted the side of the bed.

"Are you sure?" Ian asked. "I'm certain it's not proper."

"You are *my* imaginary friend, and if I want you to sit there, you will sit there."

He obeyed, the mattress sinking beneath his weight. Justine thought her power of imagination was doing quite well to achieve such an effect.

"That's better," she said, though his posture remained rigid. "So normally you're on duty in the Yukon. Not that I know anything about the Yukon, but it's wilderness with bears and that kind of thing." It would have been less "romantic" to base him in Toronto working the streets from a patrol car. "In the Yukon you go after bad guys and . . ." And what? She remembered Mounties in the old silent flicks rescuing helpless females tied to railroad tracks. As amusing as those images were, if one thought further about what would happen to the victim if the train got there before the Mountie . . .

Yuck. She scrunched her face.

"I bring law and order to the Yukon," Ian said as if inspired. "I arrest bootleggers. I keep order in railroad camps. I ride down outlaws!"

"Hmmm." It didn't sound very contemporary, but that was all right. If it were a story she was writing, it would not have to be contemporary, and the emphasis would be on adventure—adventure and romance. Ian would make a good romantic hero. He just needed . . . hobbies.

And for good measure, she could throw in some space aliens.

Suddenly two bug-eyed, bulbous-headed creatures appeared at the foot of her bed. Ian jumped to his feet and reached for his sidearm. With a thought, Justine made the aliens vanish.

"What was that?" Ian asked, still gazing in suspicion at the spot where the aliens had stood.

"My imagination," Justine replied, very pleased with herself.

"I will protect you from it."

"Thanks, but that's all right. It's been a long time since it was functioning, and I'm glad it's back." Secretly, though, she thrilled at the idea of his protection.

Justine experimented with her imagination, planting giant saguaro cacti around her room, giving Ian a handlebar mustache with waxed, curling tips (and quickly removing it), filling her room with blinking fireflies, and having the three tenors serenade her with a disturbing version of "Muskrat Love."

She turned Oolong into a giant cat, which was not a good idea. The whole bed sagged, and his oversized, fluffy tail nearly suffocated her. Ian was pummeled by a huge back paw, and Oolong's already loud purrs turned into jet engines that shook the room. Knick-knacks and books tumbled from shelves. Justine quickly imagined him back to normal size, and there he lay unconcerned by the whole thing, still purring away as giant cat hairs drifted onto the bed.

"Now that's what I call a powerful imagination," Justine said.

"If you say so," Ian replied, straightening his hat.

"Yes. I think—I think I'm beginning to feel less dizzy." Then she thought, if that was the case, maybe she should call the office, find out how production on *Nuts & Bolts* was going. Maybe she could even drag herself into work . . .

But she did not move. She just couldn't bring herself to call in. She felt more inspired to—to write? She glanced about for pen and pad, thinking she could jot a few notes down for her novel, when she noticed Ian flipping through a book that had fallen from one of her shelves. It was *Queen of Tombs,* by Evan Lord, a door-stopper of a novel. She sighed.

Ian gazed at her quizzically. "What is wrong?"

She sighed again. "Evan Lord. Huge bestseller. I'll never get there. I'll probably never even get published."

"Why not?"

"It seems like every idea I ever had shows up in an Evan Lord novel before I even have a chance to write it down. And how can I write something so—so *big?*

You know, with the huge cast of characters and multi-layered themes?"

"I don't know," Ian said, "but you just proved how powerful your imagination is. Can't you out-imagine this Evan Lord?"

"You mean like a duel?"

"Dueling is illegal," Ian replied, all rigid again. "I mean, just write a better story."

"If only it were so easy. If only I could just write a *different* story. But all my ideas seem to pop up in his books."

Ian was flipping through the novel again. On the back cover was a black and white photo of Evan Lord with that smug expression of his, and with his slightly mussy sweep of hair and tweed jacket that looked just oh-so-bohemian. It was as if he were gazing right back at her and saying, "You're a loser. Look at me, the famous author!"

"You seem very sad," Ian said. "I am your friend. Do you want to talk about it?"

Justine almost barked out a sardonic laugh, but there was Ian, sitting beside her with that earnest expression of his, and she found herself pouring out her hopes and dreams, of how when she was little, she wanted to do something important and interesting when she grew up. She was one of those kids who always had her nose stuck in a book, so it was natural she aspired to be a writer.

She told Ian of how she wrote stories from an early age, how no one in her family understood her, of how other kids made fun of her for being quiet. And always, she took comfort in her favorite books and her own writing, escaping the difficulties of her life. Many of her best friends had been fictional characters:

Henry and Ribsy, the Black Stallion, Nancy Drew, Bilbo the Hobbit . . .

Now that she'd grown up, she found herself to be a disappointment without much to show for her life except a mediocre job. She cried as she explained how crushing it was that she could no longer seem to write. There were all those books in the stores and libraries, but none were destined to have her name on them. She was a failure.

By the time she finished, she was exhausted, and the light bleeding through her blinds had dimmed. Ian remained unmoving throughout, a thoughtful expression on his face.

"You *are* somebody," he said, "a real person. You weren't made in China, and you do not have to make up your past. And I am a witness to your creativity. Why not reimagine your future?"

Oolong yawned. Justine yawned. She was wrung out, and reimagining her future sounded tiring, like too much work, and yet there was wisdom in the suggestion.

Like the daylight, Justine began to fade; her last recollection before falling asleep was of Ian pulling the covers up to her shoulders.

As she slept, she felt as if she were in some eternal struggle, a tug-o-war to hold onto her dreams. The images tried to come her, to speak to her, to entertain her subconscious, but a huge, roiling vortex sucked them away, ripped them right out of her mind and into the black hole at its center. It slurped the forest of towering wedding cakes she'd been walking through; inhaled the parade of pink and green ponies, and the little bunnies hopping behind. She tried to cling to them, but they slipped inexorably, and totally, from her grasp, until nothing remained, not even a smear of frosting or a bunny trail.

Then she thought she heard someone calling her name.

"Justine!"

"Ian?" she mumbled, her mouth pasty and sour.

"Justine—help! Wake up!"

Her Mountie was calling for help? That couldn't be right. She opened her eyes, but the vertigo was back something fierce, and someone was standing over her. Her heart bumped in her chest—it wasn't Ian, and she knew it because this someone was wearing cologne and tweed. She wanted to scream, but the stench of the cologne and the vertigo combined made her sick and she vomited over the side of the bed.

"Shit," that someone said.

In the glow of her night light, it appeared she'd vomited on his expensive Italian shoes. "Who are you?" she gasped, fearing what the intruder intended and wishing desperately she had a phone at hand to call 911. She'd never make it to the hall phone. She should've told Liz to lock the door on her way out earlier.

She glimpsed her intruder just enough through cracked eyelids to identify him, before the swirling room forced her to close them.

"Evan Lord?" she croaked in incredulity.

"The one and only. Now, if you would hold still. I should be done in a moment."

"Done? Done with what?"

"Justine!"

It was Ian again, and his voice sounded faint. Justine opened her eyes once more to find him flickering and fading at the foot of her bed. "What the—?"

"He's stealing your dreams," Ian said. "You must hold onto them, or I'll disappear!"

Justine steeled herself and looked back at Evan Lord. He was his bohemian self, with a lock of hair hanging off his forehead just so, his collar open. He was waving something over her head. A wand? It glinted golden in the illumination of her night light. No, it looked more like a—like a fountain pen. She reached for it, but she missed and fell back into her pillows, the world spinning.

"You've gotten feisty," Evan Lord said. "Usually you just sleep through this."

Justine moaned. "This is not real. It can't be."

"Unlike your Mountie friend, I am very real, and so is the magic of the Golden Pen. You and the pen have made me a very rich man."

"I don't believe this."

"Justine!" Ian cried, his voice now distant. "Fight back!"

Ian. Her dreams. Her imagination . . . Evan Lord had been stealing from her all this time. No wonder she'd had to put her writing aside. No wonder she'd felt so desolate and stuck at a job she despised.

And how icky it was to think of him coming into her bedroom at night!

"Just relax," Evan Lord said in a cajoling voice. "I've a deadline looming for the current work-in-progress, so I've had to make extra visits. Sorry it's made you dizzy. This will be over soon, and you won't remember a thing."

As he waved the Golden Pen over her, she felt

lulled back toward sleep, toward giving away her dreams . . .

Ian. Her friend, Ian. She didn't want to lose him. If Evan Lord claimed him, he'd just go back to being a painted metal toy made in China. She would have no memory of him as her friend. She jammed her eyes shut and concentrated—concentrated on Ian and his scarlet coat, that hat of his, his square chin and blue eyes . . .

The vortex tried to claim the image, and it started to blur, scarlet and blue and brown running together. She focused on making it stop, tried to redefine the image.

"Now, now," Evan Lord said. "If you keep that up, I'll have to bring in Mister Dark, and you won't like what Mister Dark will do to the Mountie."

Mister Dark? Justine peeped one eye wide open. Evan Lord was glaring down at her, and Ian was no longer faded out.

"You can't have Ian," Justine said. "He's my friend."

"Tsk, tsk," Evan Lord replied. "I warned you."

A shadow congealed on the floor next to him and grew into the shape of a man, a man in a black fedora and trench coat. His face remained shadowed. This must be Mister Dark. He reminded Justine of a gangster, or possibly a Washington lobbyist. Ian reached for his sidearm, but the figure in shadow pulled out a weapon of his own from beneath his overcoat—a Tommy gun.

"Tell your Mountie to stand down," Evan Lord said, "or Mister Dark will fill him with lead."

"I am made of lead," Ian said.

"Hah! That will not stop figurative bullets."

"There will be no shooting in my bedroom!" Justine cried. "Figurative or not," she added.

Ian's hand still hovered over his holster.

"Then relax," Evan Lord said, "and let the Golden Pen do its work. I need more royalties, and a movie deal, too. I need to keep the missus happy, and there's a little silver Porsche I have my eye on."

"Never," Justine said, but he practically shoved the Pen in her face and the whirling of her room left her breathless. She tried to focus on Ian again, tried to make him solid in her mind so she wouldn't lose him, wouldn't give in to the thief, Evan Lord.

Mister Dark still aimed his Tommy gun at Ian. Ian flexed his fingers above the butt of his revolver. Was Mister Dark something from her mind, or a creation of Evan Lord's? Would she have created so bald a metaphor?

It took her only half a moment to realize that Evan Lord wasn't even capable of that much, that Mister Dark must have come from her basic store of archetypes, raw and unrefined. Evan Lord had taken him from her and used him as his own minion.

Ian grabbed his revolver and tugged it from his holster.

Mister Dark pulled the trigger on his Tommy gun.

"No bullets!" Justine cried.

Bubbles burped out of the muzzle of the Tommy gun instead.

Ian aimed and fired his revolver, but it had turned into a power drill.

Both of them looked at their weapons.

Then Mister Dark tossed his Tommy gun aside and pulled a hand grenade out of his trench coat pocket. Justine concentrated as hard as she could. Mister Dark threw the grenade, and as it sailed through the air toward Ian, it transformed into an egg. It hit Ian's chest with a *splotch!* Ian looked at the egg yolk dripping down his front.

"You can't do that!" Evan Lord cried, his face turning red with anger. "You can't tell Mister Dark what to do!"

"He's mine," Justine said, and before the shadow man could produce yet another weapon, she reimagined him into a new form. He grew still and solid. The pleasant scent of chocolate wafted from him. *Dark* chocolate.

"No! No! No!" Evan Lord cried. He raised the Golden Pen as if to stab her with it.

Oolong hissed beside her. She imagined him as a giant cat once again, and was immediately swamped by his tail. He knocked Evan Lord to the floor, and the Golden Pen went flying. Ian dove after it.

When Justine returned Oolong to his proper size, he sat on Evan Lord's chest hissing, and swiped his face with bared claws.

"OW!" Evan Lord cried, along with other words not suitable for print.

Oolong switched his tail back and forth and, using Evan Lord's belly as a springboard, leaped back onto the bed. His part done, he curled up among the blankets and licked his paw.

Justine wobbled out of bed and stood over Evan Lord. If she puked on him again, it was his own stupid fault. "You will leave *now,*" she commanded him with as much authority as she could muster. Her pink pajamas with the sheep and the armpit hole sort of ruined the effect.

"My pen," he said with a moan, "I need the Golden

Pen, or I'm ruined." He got onto his hands and knees and crawled around the floor searching for it. It was pathetic, really. Ian, who held the pen behind his back, winked at her. She removed the egg yolk from his scarlet coat with a thought.

"Get out or I'll call the police," Justine told Evan Lord. When he did not listen, she grabbed the tome of his Ian had been looking at earlier, *Queen of Tombs,* and *whapped* him on the head with it.

Evan Lord ran whimpering from her bedroom, with dust bunnies clinging to his knees, and out of her apartment. Justine staggered after him, through her apartment, and to the entry. She slammed the door shut and triple locked it.

Ian followed her out and held the Golden Pen before her. "This is yours now. What will you do with it?"

Justine smiled.

It had been a long time since Justine last sat in the café at Bookwoods with her pad of paper on the table before her. Liz—her hair a vibrant green today— brought over a mocha latte, set it before her, and took a seat.

"I'm glad you're feeling better," Liz said.

"Tons. The vertigo went away just like the doctor said it would."

"Hey, did you hear the latest about Evan Lord?"

Justine smiled and nodded as she sprinkled some cinnamon onto her latte. "Yeah. I read he quit fiction and is going on a speaking tour. Something about how to make millions on the dreams of others."

Liz chuckled. "I imagine he'll make even more money with the lectures than he did with his books."

It was true. Justine had seen him driving around

town in the newest addition to his fleet: a silver Porsche. She had considered turning him into the police for home invasion (she didn't think they'd believe her about the imagination stealing stuff), but she thought maybe without the Golden Pen he'd been rendered impotent, and the loss of his writing career was enough of a punishment. She hoped so, anyway.

"So how are things at *Nuts & Bolts?*" Liz asked.

Justine grinned. "You are looking at the new managing editor. The position comes with a raise. The magazine has been picked up by Giganta Media Corp, so there's a chance I might be transferred to their book publishing division." She reimagined her future, just as Ian suggested she should, and so had updated her resume and presented it to the editor-in-chief of Giganta Books. Didn't mean she'd get the job, but at least she was trying.

"Fantastic!" Liz cried. "Congrats. Consider this latte on me."

"Thanks," Justine replied.

Liz rose from her chair. "I've got to get back to work," she said, and she started to walk away, but paused and turned back to Justine. "How's Ian?"

"Ian?"

"Yeah, your imaginary friend."

"Oh, he's gone up north—back to Quebec. Decided to take up a hobby."

"Hockey?"

Justine shook her head.

"Curling?"

"Nope."

"Er, what else do they do up there?"

Justine sighed. "He said something about a sudoku tournament."

"Oh, you'll never see him again," Liz said.

"What makes you so sure?"

"I lent my guy, Sven, to a friend. He's a masseur, you know. I haven't seen him in months!"

"Your imaginary friend is a masseur?"

"Of course." With a toss of green hair, Liz wandered off between the tables, humming a tune as she headed into the bookstore section of Bookwoods.

"Huh," Justine said. She thought she should try conjuring up a masseur. That could be very useful.

For now, however, she was content to sit in the café, with its aroma of coffee and spices, and the murmuring voices of other patrons and soft jazz music in the background. Out the window pedestrians hurried by on the sidewalk and cars rumbled down the street, as though they existed on an entirely different plane than she in the café.

Her pad of paper sat before her empty of words, and she uncapped her ordinary black gel pen to begin anew on her manuscript. She could use the Golden Pen if she wished, but she would not do to others as Evan Lord did to her, so she locked it away in a safe deposit box and hoped to forget where she hid the key. Besides, she did not need the Pen and its magic, thanks to Ian helping her to restore her faith in her own imagination.

She had to admit the Golden Pen was an intriguing object, and maybe one day she'd try to learn more about its origins and properties. If magic was truly alive in her own mundane world in the form of so small an artifact, wasn't it reasonable to expect there were more such objects out there? Searching for them could be a whole new, grand adventure.

The mysteries of the Golden Pen, however, were

for another day. Right now she was more interested in rediscovering her own inner magic. Maybe she wouldn't earn the big bucks without the Pen's help, and maybe she wouldn't even get published, but now she had the confidence to try. If she could breathe so much life into an imaginary friend, it seemed her chances were tolerable.

With a smile, she applied the first words to paper in black flowing ink.

SUBURBAN LEGEND

Donald J. Bingle

MICHAEL knew that he shouldn't dwell on them, that he should let them go. He had better, more important, things to think about, to worry about, to resolve, like the fate of his eternal soul. But they rattled through his brain, interrupting everything he did, every bit of his concentration. When he brushed his teeth, his mind was otherwise unoccupied, and they screamed, whirling through his head, throbbing to the rhythm of the downward strokes, peppering him with doubt and self-loathing.

He focused hard, trying desperately to remember when his descent into this hellhole of confusion and madness had all begun. Three years, three long years ago, was the obvious answer, but he knew that was a lie. Others hadn't seen it, hadn't known, but it had begun months, almost a year earlier than that, and in the most innocent way.

Wow, Michael thought, Jennifer is really looking hot these days. Her smile is brighter, her curves are

116

curvier, and her latest haircut is really cute. He was pretty sure that dress was new, too, with a shorter hemline and a more daring neckline than what she usually wears. He should say something. He overheard her tell Barb once that he didn't compliment her enough. He should speak up.

"Gee, honey, uh . . . you've lost weight, haven't you?"

Jennifer stared at him with the same look of disgust tempered by enforced tolerance that one would give a small child who had just peed himself in front of company.

"What do you mean by that?"

Michael scrambled to find the right words, the words that would convey what his mind had intended, the words that would make this not become yet another of their more and more frequent and heated arguments.

"I . . . uh . . . mean you look good . . . uh . . . thinner. You had gotten a bit chunky there for awhile."

Those were not the words.   .

"You could stand to lose a few pounds, yourself, buster."

"Uh . . . sure . . . I mean, yeah, we've both porked up a bit since we got married. I was just trying to say that I like your new look, I mean you haven't shown so much cleavage or worn such a short skirt in . . . since we were dating."

Her eyes burned with the fierce, tiny intensity of the LEDs on the new flexible flashlight he'd gotten the week before at the Tool Shed.

"And just what are you implying, tubbo? That I'm some kind of tramp?" Her hip was thrust to one side and her newly manicured fingers were drumming at the edge where her brightly flowered sundress met the sexy tan of her surprisingly toned legs.

"Just . . . uh . . . just that it looks like that gym membership is paying off. You must be enjoying it." He tried desperately to change the subject from her appearance. "Met any exercise buddies, there?"

Her fingers stopped drumming, the pearlescent dawn rose of her nails providing a beautiful contrast to her dark, rich skin tone. "Don't do this, Michael. Don't let your imagination run wild. You always do this."

Earlier. He had to go earlier, obviously. What did he always do?

Jealousy? Was that what she meant?

He wasn't jealous. He was just protective of her, of his relationship with her. After all, she had dated a lot more than he had in college. A lot more. She was pretty and vivacious and attractive and, well, experienced. And he was portly and plain and . . . well . . . not so experienced.

She was chased and he was chaste.

A little voice inside his head had warned him, even then, that it couldn't last, that she would get bored with him, would leave him sooner or later (and most likely sooner) for someone smoother, better looking, better dressed, more exciting. Someone more virile, more worldly-wise, someone sexier than him.

Kip, his best friend, had told him so point blank once when he and Jen were on a double date with Kip and Barb and the women had trekked off to the powder room.

"You've got to snap her up, Mike," Kip said, as he

ogled the two women as they headed, their shapely asses swaying in unison, across the restaurant toward the restrooms. "There's just too much advertising going on for another buyer not to show up soon, real soon."

Michael had always been concerned about losing Jen, but what Kip said put him on edge. Michael and Jen had their first big blow-up only ten days later . . . ten nights later, to be more precise . . . when Jen had come back to the apartment they were sharing in the wee hours after an alleged girls night out with Barb.

The receipt had fallen out of the front pocket of her silk blouse, the one she always wore with her tight, hip hugger jeans on nights out with Barb, the one that always showed tiny strain wrinkles at the button hole two holes below where the blouse was buttoned up to when she came home in the middle of the night. The receipt was from some dance club in the city. Aside from evidencing a prodigious thirst for chocolate martinis and an overly generous approach to tipping, the receipt came with a message. "It was fantastic servicing you, Duane."

When he looked up from the receipt, she was posed, backlit, leaning against the doorjamb in the doorway to the bathroom, wearing nothing but her bra and panties. Gorgeous. Sexy. Alluring. Obviously trying to seduce him, to distract him, to fool him into forgetting where she had been and what she had been doing.

He refused to fall for it. "Who's Duane?" he said with a sneer that washed away any trace of romance from the moment, from the room, from their life together.

She stiffened immediately and clutched one arm to the opposite shoulder, covering her bosom as she reached to the nearby hamper for her cotton night-dress. "Who?"

"Duane." He lifted the receipt to face her and pointed to it in the pale glow of the nightlight. "The guy who has been servicing you."

"Jesus, Michael, you're imagining things." She plunked herself down on the bed, her back to him. "Go to sleep."

But he didn't go to sleep. He couldn't let it go. And they had fought for hours, until she had stormed off in her night clothes, grabbing her keys, her laptop, and her purse, to spend the weekend at Barb's. Or at least that's what she said.

The voice inside his head didn't believe her. It said that she was going to Duane's, to screw him again, and that if Michael didn't watch out, he would lose her forever.

The next day he called her and begged her forgiveness, groveling, blaming himself. It was just that she was so beautiful and sexy, he couldn't imagine why she was living with him. And she came back to him and they made love in the moonlight and all was good.

He proposed three weeks later near a small, unnamed waterfall, during a weekend getaway hiking trip in their favorite nature preserve downstate. They were married the next summer, just six weeks after their best friends, Kip and Barb. All their friends and family were there. Joe and Bonnie and Ted from the dorm, Kela and Brittany from the women's field hockey team, Uncle Fred and Aunt Mary on his side of the family, Jen's numerous relatives, and all the rest, all toasting them and kissing them and shaking hands in congratulations.

They bought a house in a sleepy suburb near where

Kip and Barb had settled and started their own version of the American dream. And for awhile, they were happy.

But it didn't last. Soon the voice in his head began asking questions and Michael didn't like the answers.

There was nothing he could pin down at first, just that she was more sullen and moody than a new bride should be. She also spent a lot of time with Barb, or so she said. And then, shortly after their first anniversary, he began to notice other things.

She seemed to get less done around the house during the day, while he was at work in the city running actuarial spreadsheets.

The number of local calls per month on the phone bill crept higher and higher—not really a financial issue, given their billing plan—but, still he noticed.

She joined a gym and started to pay particular attention to her appearance, dropping all the way to her wedding weight after a year of adding on the pounds. That one had led to the fight he had just been thinking about.

There were occasional hang-ups when he would answer the phone and conversations that seemed cut short when he arrived home.

She played the "credit card game" whenever she went to lunch with her girlfriends, paying for the group with her credit card and collecting cash from the others so "she wouldn't have to go to the bank so often," or so she said. He had noticed the charges, but, of course, had no idea where she actually spent the cash, the untraceable cash, afterwards.

He also noticed one evening that during the day she had used the shredder he had in his home office. They

only used it for annoying preapproved credit card
come-ons and for Michael's business documents, so
that he could destroy spreadsheets from the company
when he was working from home. She said that he
must have left it on from the night before, but he
was too environmentally conscious to ever have done
something like that. It was a waste of power.

Things were strained. They grew apart. And everyone noticed. They rarely went out with Kip and Barb
anymore. Jen's old friends from the field hockey team
never chit-chatted with him anymore before they
asked him to hand the phone over to Jen. The last
time Michael had tried to organize a poker night with
the gang from the dorm, there weren't enough takers
to pull it off.

It all hit the fan when he came home early one
Friday afternoon because of the flu and found her on
the computer in his home office, wearing not very
much and looking flushed.

"What the hell is going on?" he demanded as she
flipped off the unit.

"Jesus, you startled me, Mike." She stood up from
the desk and turned to him before continuing. "I left
my laptop at Barb's and realized during my shower
after my Pilates class that I hadn't reserved a location
for the field hockey team's booster club award lun-
cheon, like I promised Kela. I figured I would do it
before I forgot." Her tone had started out ragged, but
firmed up as she progressed in her tale. "What are
you doing home? You look awful." She started to
move toward him, but he backed away.

"You were online with him, weren't you?" Michael
was feverish and not just from the flu.

"Who?"

"Duane. You were having online sex with your lover, Duane, weren't you?"

Her eyes narrowed. "You're delirious, Mike. Duane is a figment of your deranged, and, quite frankly, filthy imagination. He doesn't exist. I was searching for banquet facilities."

"Then why did you shut off the computer when I came in?"

"I know you don't like it when I use your work computer. You're always fussing about viruses and worms and Trojan horses, whatever those are. But I couldn't use my laptop because I forgot it at Barb's."

"Bull," he said, advancing on her. "You are nothing but . . ." She slapped him, hard, with all the force that a former field hockey forward could muster, one long fingernail slicing into his cheek. He stopped cold, reaching up to feel the hot blood on his clammy face. He never could stand the sight of blood.

"I think I'm going to be sick," he mumbled as he lurched to the bathroom to vomit.

She wasn't there when he came back out.

He gave a primal scream of frustration and pounded the door to the garage, his blood pressure spiking and causing the scratch on his face to flow freely. Flecks of crimson spattered the white door and wall. He cursed both Jen's behavior and his response, then leaned against the cool door, the pressure against his cheek stemming the flow of blood, and simply wailed. Then he pulled himself together, held down his bile, and fetched some bleach, cleaning the blood off the flat white of the door and wall. Afterwards, woozy from the fumes and the flu, he collapsed down on the couch with the remote. He was asleep before Oprah introduced her second guest. The next thing he knew, he was waking up as the late news was signing off.

Jen wasn't home yet and he didn't know if she was coming home.

He was still surprisingly tired—physically weary as if he had been working out. Emotions could do that, he guessed. He trundled into the bedroom and cried himself back to sleep.

Michael did his best to remain calm the next morning when Jen still hadn't returned or called, but by midmorning he had lost his composure, pacing frantically, then pawing through credit card receipts for some clue as to where she might be. When he found nothing, he started to search for the receipt she had brought back that time from the club, the one with the note from Duane. Maybe he could call the club or there was a code on it that he could ask the manager about which would identify who "serviced" her. And then he could find where Duane lived. Three hours later, the house was a mess, his flu fever had spiked to a hundred and two, and his hatred of Duane was still climbing.

But no Jen. And no clues.

On Sunday morning, he called the gym, thinking that Jen might still work out, no matter where she was staying. The idiot staff member who answered refused at first to check to see if Jen was there, but when Michael became more belligerent, the guy finally put down the phone and made the rounds. Or at least that's what he claimed when he picked the phone back up, reporting in bored tones that nobody responded when he said there was a call for someone named

Jen. Michael didn't believe him and threw a tantrum, berating the clerk's nonchalance, demanding to know the address of every club member named Duane, and asking in increasingly frantic tones how often Jen came to the gym, who she exercised with, and whether she ever left with anybody. The clerk refused to answer him and finally hung up on him when Michael started to curse.

Michael didn't flinch at demanding information about his wife from strangers, but it galled him to have to ask their friends about her. But, eventually, he could not think of anything else to do. Finally, on Sunday evening, more than two days after Jen left, Michael called Barb, admitting he and Jen had been fighting and asking if she'd seen Jen, perhaps when she had come over to retrieve her laptop. But Barb claimed not to have seen Jen and not to have her laptop. He hung up without thanking Barb and re-treated back to the bed, where he slept fitfully.

Finally, on the third day, he rose again from the dead sleep of the emotionally drained and shuffled back to the phone. He notified work that he was tak-ing a sick day. Only then did he call the police to report his wife missing.

Two detectives came over straightaway. Michael im-plored them to search for his wife, but they seemed more interested in the scratch on his face, on the de-tails of his and Jen's last encounter, and on the reasons he had delayed for so long in calling the authorities. He told them everything he knew, or that he thought he knew, about her lover, Duane, but they kept ex-plaining that if she had simply run off with another man, that wasn't a police matter. But even as they said that, he saw them glancing around at the disarray of the house, sniffing the faint chlorine odor than still hung near the door to the garage, and making notes in small, spiral-bound pads.

It probably didn't help when he started raving at them, insisting that Duane had kidnapped Jen, had stolen her, and had to be stopped, had to be found. They called into the station and arranged a trace on Jen's credit cards and cell phone usage. Then, they left to talk to Barb and others of Jen's friends. When they returned later that day, they said no one they talked to had ever heard of Duane. Still, they were worried that Jen had fallen victim to foul play. There was no activity on Jen's credit cards or phone since Friday midday, which troubled them. So they agreed to begin a search, starting with the nearby forest preserve and lake.

Michael's and Jen's friends and families, their entire neighborhood, two Boy Scout troops, and most of the congregation of the church they had been married in, but rarely attended, showed up for the search. It was a big story on the local television news that night and front page the next day in both the paper in their suburb and in the big city daily.

Michael made a plea for Jen's safe return at the news conference kicking off the search, holding up a 5" X 7"' wedding photo, but as a "person of interest" he wasn't allowed to help look with the others, lest he contaminate the crime scene or lead the searchers astray. He also wasn't allowed back into their home, as police had begun carting away bags full of alleged evidence. So, Michael alternated between the police station and a local motel. He had asked Kip if he could stay with him and Barb, but Kip had said no. He had tried to talk to his old friend, to explain what had happened, but Kip had begged off the call. Michael thought he had heard Barb in the background yelling for Kip to hang up.

Michael was a man alone. Kela and Brittany and Bonnie and Joe and Ted all joined the search, but they didn't return Michael's calls. His aunt and uncle were too overwhelmed with concern to even talk with him, and Jen's family obviously blamed him for her disappearance. No one from their church volunteered any casseroles for him, although they brought sandwiches and lemonade for the search teams. Beverly, from the HR department at work, called to say that Michael could use up his accumulated vacation and sick days and that they didn't expect to see him at work for "the duration."

There was nothing he could do to help. He had been warned not to leave the county. The two guys wearing suits inside the gray Ford Taurus that constantly seemed to be hanging around his motel probably would have stopped him if he tried, so he couldn't go into the city to the bars and dance clubs that Jen and Barb used to frequent to search for Duane. Besides, his car was being dismantled by the local town's CSI wannabes. His computer had been bagged and taken and Jen's laptop was still missing, so he couldn't do anything through the internet to find her—he didn't relish using a library or cafe computer to try to track Jen and Duane, not with Channel 6 looking over his shoulder. And, of course, he was still forbidden to join the volunteer groups, which had widened their search area and increased their number as word of "the missing suburban newlywed" was trumpeted by the media and their minions.

He called Jen's gym again from the hotel, to see if

he could pry any information out of a different clerk. But he got the same guy, who freaked out when he made the connection with what was now a constant story on the cable networks favored by the clientele working up a sweat on the myriad treadmills and stair-climbers at the gym. The guy hung up, then blabbed, first to the media and then to the cops, about how Michael had called over the weekend, stressed out and angry, stalking Jen or maybe trying to create some kind of half-assed alibi. And that's when Michael realized that the situation had spun out of control, that the damned media would say what they wanted, and that he wasn't going to crack the case for the police. He wasn't Columbo or Magnum or even Veronica Mars.

All he knew was that he was innocent, and he would have to have faith in the system.

He tried to relax by using the overheated and over-chlorinated hot tub at the motel. The two women already there when he arrived left hurriedly almost as soon as he got in, though, and the jets were too weak to ease the tension across his shoulder blades. The only result of the effort to ease his aching back was that he was greeted with pictures two days later in a national newsweekly with the caption "Hubby parties with unidentified women while search for missing wife continues." The article, which referred to him repeatedly as "the chief suspect" in his wife's sinister disappearance, contained anonymous quotes about his life and his relationship with Jen that he knew had to have come from Kip and a few, even more devastating ones, that he knew had come from Barb. "Irrational and psychotic loser" was one of the nicer ones.

The news media camped out at the motel where he

was staying. At first he thought the management would demand that he leave, but apparently the paparazzi were booking so many rooms, especially near his, that he was considered a plus from a business perspective. He found two "journalists" picking through his trash in the maid's cart one day, so he stopped letting her in to clean.

He became deeply depressed, lying in the sweat-stained sheets of the motel bed, watching news coverage about the case. As the search dragged on, the media spent less time interviewing Boy Scouts who had combed the nearby corn fields and more and more time dissecting Michael's life. He had not dated much before marriage and was considered an "odd pick" for a husband by Jen's friends. He was a loner, a loser, a possessive and jealous tyrant. He had a temper.

He paced the room much of the day, switching between the various news channels by hand (instead of using the remote) and keeping the volume low because he was convinced the paparazzi next door were trying to monitor his viewing habits. He stopped shaving and barely ate, especially after first his favorite pizza place and then even the local catsup-on-cardboard thirty-minute-or-less franchise cut him off because they didn't want their delivery guys filmed bringing him food.

His anger at Jen dissipated as his anger at Duane grew. Jen had been weak, yes. She had betrayed him. But Duane was the seducer, the home wrecker, the kidnapper, the villain. This was all, all Duane's fault and Duane would be made to pay.

Michael learned that Jen was dead at the same time and in the same way as the rest of the nation, on

Susan Vick's show, "Crime and Punishment," on CNN, almost three weeks after Jen's disappearance. He could have lived without knowing that her "badly decomposed, naked body" had been dumped, half in the water, below a small waterfall in a downstate nature preserve—their nature preserve. But, apparently the rest of America could not live without such information or without knowing that the body had been discovered by two birding enthusiasts who were horrified by what they had seen.

The "reporters" covering the story now seemed to spend almost as much of their time with his and Jen's friends and family as they did camped out on his doorstep, so it wasn't long before the location of Jen's body was linked to him, to them, and sensationalized as just one more sick, depraved aspect of the horrific crime.

An hour later, Michael was put on "unpaid, indefinite leave" from his job.

Two hours later, "unauthorized" photos of the "crime scene" and Jen's grisly body were on the news. The television shows used black bars to cover the intimate parts, but did nothing to censor the bruising or blood or bloating—the horrific parts—of her body. He was sure the postings on the internet weren't censoring anything at all.

Three hours later, Michael was arrested for Jen's murder. The light from the television setups outside his motel room was as bright as his future with Jen had once seemed, when the police entered the room with the maid's key and carted him off to a waiting squad car in his boxers and a white T-shirt, his eyes angry and red from crying and his chin sporting a ragged and splotchy, stubbled beard. Before the cops even got him into the vehicle, pushing his head to make sure it did not hit the door jamb as they firmly assisted him inside, he heard one energetic live-on-location journalist breathlessly telling his audience that Michael had apparently been growing the beard in an attempt to disguise himself before a planned run for freedom.

Reporters and photographers rushed the car as the police attempted to begin his transport. Michael couldn't make out their individual inquiries in the tumult and din of the assault, so he just shouted over and over as the car began to pick up speed. "I didn't do it. It was Duane." And then they were free of the mob, and the cop riding shotgun told him to shut up unless he wanted to make a confession. After that, he just sobbed hysterically until an hour after they put him in an interrogation room at the station house.

It was in the wee hours of the morning that the interrogation began. He knew from watching the cop shows on television that he should call a lawyer, and, of course, the detectives said so each of the three separate times they read him his rights. But he also knew that he was innocent, that Duane had done this horrible thing to his Jen, his dear, sweet Jen, and that asking for an attorney would make him look guilty, would distract them from their efforts to find Duane, to find the real killer. God, he thought, now I'm quoting O.J., but that's how he phrased it every time they asked him.

So he didn't ask for a lawyer. And no one, not his friends, not his fellow workers, not his family, and certainly not Jen's family, sent one on his behalf. He was on his own. But he knew he would be all right, just as soon as the authorities captured Duane. There would be dirt in his vehicle or blood—Jen's blood, oh, God—on his clothing, and footprints and fibers and all that forensics crap, and his nightmare would not be over, but it would be less. They simply had to find Duane.

The cops, however, did not seem to be too interested in Duane. They had no evidence that Duane existed, so they said. Although they had not yet recovered Jen's cell phone (they were searching the nature preserve downstate thoroughly, though), there were no calls to or from it during its active history except from home or from identified friends or businesses that were not suspicious. No one had seen this mysterious Duane. Jen had not confided to her best friend, Barb, that she had taken a lover.

"But, the computer!" shouted Michael, bone weary from grief and from lack of sleep. "She was having online sex with him, I know it." And the police, they promised that their technical guys were checking out the computer, but then the conversation would turn to other things for hour after hour. Let's talk a bit more about your love life, your temper, what crime shows you watch on TV, why you left work early that Friday, why no one saw you that weekend, and why there were bleached-out blood stains on the door and wall near the garage. Let's go over just one more time your trips to the nature preserve—it was highlighted on a map in your car—and the fight the two of you had that Friday afternoon and the scratch on your cheek, the one you are trying to cover up with that pathetic beard.

During the rest of the day, things got progressively worse for Michael, if that could be imagined. The police were testing DNA found under Jen's fingernails to see if it matched his, on the presumption that she had attempted to fend off her attacker. After all, the mess in the house clearly suggested that there had been some kind of struggle. And the stench of bleach suggested he had tried to cover up his crime.

He had just a few moments of elation when the police finally admitted to him that they had recovered sexually explicit instant messages on his home computer between sexybride186 and badboy4452. But then the detectives said the forensic techs had traced the source of badboy's raunchy chat to Jen's (although they kept calling it *his*) laptop computer and demanded that Michael tell them where he had disposed of it.

It made no sense. Jen wasn't talking dirty to him. It was Duane. He knew it was Duane. But he merely mumbled his insistence that the laptop was Jen's and he didn't know where it was.

It was late the next evening, with no respite for sleep for Michael, aside from fitful dozing in the straight-backed chair he was handcuffed to in the chilly interrogation room, when Michael first learned that Jen was seven weeks pregnant when she was killed. Susan Vick had told the rest of the world four hours earlier, just ten seconds before the first time she referred to Michael as a "depraved baby killer" instead of her usual reference to him as "the violent-tempered estranged husband" of the angelic Jen. But, of course, Michael didn't know that until later. Instead of receiving what would, at one time just weeks ago, have been the happiest news of his entire life from his loving wife, or a doctor, or even a social worker at the police station, Michael found out that Jen was pregnant when the detective that had been hounding him in shifts for almost thirty hours announced that a second count of murder was being added to his indictment.

And by that time, Michael was so weary, so beaten down, so anguished and afraid that he prayed, he prayed to the God of the church where he had been married, that the baby carried in his wife's womb wasn't his, that it was Duane's. He prayed that his dead wife was having her lover's baby, because he needed the police—the friendly, neighborhood, suburban cops that had been so helpful to him in getting a stop sign installed at the end of their block in their homey little suburban subdivision—to test the DNA and find that the child wasn't his.

It was Duane's. It had to be Duane's.

Michael tried to think back on the timing, on the last times he and Jen had made love, but he was too tired and it was too painful to remember.

He finally stopped answering questions and asked for a lawyer, not because he had wised up about his legal predicament, but because he just wanted the endless interrogation to stop and it seemed the only way he could make that happen. He got a nebbishy public defender who treated him with distaste and told him to say nothing and wait for the evidence to come in, then they would talk about strategy. So Michael sat in his cell, where no visitors came to call, and watched his wife's funeral on television and listened to all of their friends say wonderful things about her and say nothing about him in their eulogies.

And, then, a week later, the DNA analyses came in, and it was Michael's skin under Jen's fingernails and Michael's son in her womb, and Michael cried for his unborn son and for his family and for the life they could have had. And while the questions still raged through his mind about how and why Duane had ruined his life, he no longer raged out loud. Instead, he merely sat mute as the questions, the images, whirled through his mind. It didn't really matter anymore. Nothing mattered anymore. If he couldn't find Duane, couldn't kill Duane, there was no point to his existence.

The police and the prosecutor, of course, kept pressing for a confession. "We'll take the needle off the table," they said, as if confessing to Duane's crime in order to secure the living hell of a life in a cell without friends or family, his every thought preoccupied with the man who killed his wife and child being at large in the world, hurting others, was a desirable thing. So, he never confessed and there was a trial.

At first, the press was excited about the prospect of a trial, but when it became apparent that the public defender was just going through the motions, that Michael was just going to sit there, stony faced and silent, as the forensic evidence was presented, they raced on to the next circus, a missing Hispanic girl in Pensacola.

The public defender wasn't a hack—or at least he didn't want to look like a hack—so he brought up the issue of the mysterious Duane and the fact that there were no witnesses to the actual crime. But the prosecutor just smiled and kept referring to Duane as the "phantom lover" and "imaginary killer" and insinuating that it was all in Michael's mind, that Michael was Duane and that he had killed his beautiful Jen.

At times the prosecutor was so convincing that Michael had doubts, himself. Why was Michael so weary when he had woken up on the couch during the news, after sleeping for hours? Could he have possibly killed

Jen and forgotten, blocking out the violent rage of a hideous, jealous alter ego? Had some twisted part of him done such a thing to his dear, sweet Jen? Was it really all his fault?

But, no, he was the victim.

The guilty verdict on both counts was no surprise. Neither was the sentence: death by lethal injection. After all, Michael had not even presented a single character witness at sentencing. None of his friends— Jen's friends—would agree to testify. Even Uncle Fred begged off, because of his heart, he said. Michael didn't know the details, but apparently it was broken somehow.

Michael waived his appeals, but even without that tedious nonsense, the process of the criminal justice system was such that more than three years passed between the crime and the scheduled execution date. And now Michael became frantic. It wasn't that he was afraid of dying—that would be a pleasant release when it came. It was that he wanted to know. He wanted to know who killed Jen. He wanted someone to believe him. He wanted someone to keep looking for Duane, and he knew that once the plunger had been pushed on the needle, Duane would be lost forever. No one would ever open the case again.

And so the questions whirled through his mind, giving him no rest until the final rest.

Michael Gaylon Caufield was pronounced dead by lethal injection at 5:13 p.m. on March 1. There were ten witnesses, as prescribed by law. No one attended the execution on the convicted's behalf.

Susan Vick did a retrospective of the crime and the trial on her show that evening.

*   *   *

Darren Kraykowski watched Susan Vick's retrospective on the television in his motel room in Lubbock, Texas, while he played solitaire on a beat-up old laptop. The stupid cow of a reporter thought she knew all about killers and criminals, but Darren knew from real life and death personal experience that the key, the real key to being a serial killer wasn't just moving from place to place and avoiding falling into discernible patterns and, of course, working hard—working damn hard—to avoid leaving evidence behind. Simple things like being discreet, using a fake name, avoiding her friends, and wearing a rubber. And more clever things, like getting the lonely wife to lend you her cell phone and her laptop for your clandestine sex talk. No, the real key was setting up some poor sap to take the fall. Then no one would ever really come looking for you.

Of course, you couldn't really blame the cops— especially the safety patrol suburban types. Eight or nine times out of ten when you found a sweet young dead bitch naked in the woods, it was the husband or the live-in boyfriend that did it. The safety patrol played the odds.

Still, it was risky business for Darren. Of course, that was part of the thrill—not just the seduction, not just the sex, not just the glorious pleasure of the killing itself, and not just getting a twofer because the tramp was preggers or a threefer because her numb-nuts hubby took the fall, it was the chance of getting caught.

Even this loser schmuck, Michael, he might have stood a chance if he had called the cops sooner, or gotten a decent lawyer right away, or if his friends had stuck up for him in the interviews with the cops or even at the trial, itself.

This guy, this stupid, clueless, shit of a guy, he was alone even before his wife ran off to get slaughtered by a ruggedly handsome and surprisingly charming psycho serial killer drifter.

Michael never knew it until it was late, too late, but he only had imaginary friends.

BEST FRIENDS FOREVER

Tim Waggoner

"DADDY, is that a stuffed dog on the side of the road?"

Upon hearing his daughter's words, a cold pit opened up in the middle of Ron Garber's stomach. He gripped the steering wheel tightly and concentrated on keeping his gaze fixed straight ahead. If he could keep from looking, just for a few more moments, they'd drive past, and he wouldn't have to see whatever Lily was pointing at. If he didn't see it, it couldn't be real, and if wasn't real, he could forget about it.

"Daddy! Over there! Look!"

Lily was only seven, still young enough to be relegated to the back and be forced to endure the humiliation of a booster seat. But despite her age, she had a mind sharp as a scalpel. She'd know something weird was going on if he refused to look, and she could be tenacious as a pack of pitbulls when she wanted to. She wouldn't stop asking him why he didn't look until she got a satisfactory answer. He had no choice. He had to look.

It's probably nothing, he told himself. Just a toy some kid had been playing with and left outside, temporarily forgotten.

He turned to look in the direction Lily had pointed. On the opposite side of the road, sitting on the gravel shoulder, was a three-foot high stuffed St. Bernard. Brown and white fur, floppy ears, red-felt tongue hanging out, black plastic eyes. Eyes that did more than not reflect light but which seemed to absorb it, feed on it, drink it in and swallow it down.

Ron hadn't seen the toy dog in . . . in . . . *a while,* he decided. But he recognized it instantly. His nostrils filled with its musty odor—the result of the animal having been left out in the rain overnight once when Ron was only slightly younger than Lily. Though he continued to hold tightly to the steering wheel, his fingers felt the dog's artificial fur, and he whispered a single word.

"Biff . . ."

"Let's stop and get the doggy!" Lily said. "He looks lonely!"

Ron's foot pressed down on the accelerator, and their Toyota Sierra minivan flashed past the toy.

"Daddy, we can't just *leave* him there! Someone might steal him! Or he might get hit by a car!" Lily had always been a sensitive, highly empathetic child, and she sounded honestly worried.

Ron reached up and tilted the rearview mirror so he couldn't look back and see Biff.

"No need to worry, honey. Whoever the dog belongs to will come back and get it soon." He tried to keep his voice as normal sounding as he could, but his words came out edged with tension. He glanced over his shoulder at Lily to gauge her reaction, but his daughter wasn't looking at him. She was looking at the repositioned rearview mirror and frowning.

"Besides, there's a lot of traffic, Lily. I'm not sure I'd be able to turn around." Only partially a lie. Ash Creek was hardly the largest town in Ohio, but it was almost the lunch hour, and a lot of people had left work to pick up something to eat. There were a number of fast-food joints in this part of town, so there were a lot of cars on the road. Not so many that he *couldn't* turn their minivan around if he really wanted to, but even as smart as Lily was, he hoped she wouldn't realize that. She *was* only seven, after all. Still, before she could say anything, he added, "I have to get to my appointment on time. It's an important opportunity, and I can't afford to miss it."

This *wasn't* a lie. True, he'd made sure they'd left early enough to give him a comfortable cushion of extra time to get to Coleman Publishing, but he didn't want to squander that time by making any unnecessary stops. He glanced at the black portfolio case propped against the passenger seat next to him. *Important opportunity* was an understatement. It was the break he'd worked so long and hard for.

He'd been at his home office earlier that morning, sitting at his drawing board laying out ads for a newspaper insert for a local grocery, when he'd gotten the call. Kevin Armstrong, art director for Coleman Publishing, had finally gotten around to reviewing the samples Ron had sent several weeks ago. Armstrong had liked what he saw and told Ron that Coleman had been approached by a local church to print a line of Christian-themed children's books to use in Sunday school. Armstrong thought Ron might be the perfect choice to illustrate them. The gig wouldn't pay much, and Ron wasn't religious by any means, but if he landed the job, he'd get his first professional credit illustrating kids' books. A credit he could use as a calling card when approaching national publishers.

Because Ron was a freelance commercial artist who worked out of his home, it fell to him to care for Lily while her mother was at work. Normally, it wasn't much of a problem. Sure, his productivity had suffered to a degree, but he loved spending time alone with his daughter. Doing design work for ads, pamphlets, and brochures might've paid the bills, but for years he'd dreamed of illustrating children's books. And now that it looked like that dream might be coming true at last, he'd had no choice but to bring Lily with him. They had no friends who were home during the day who could watch her, and Lily was too young to stay home by herself, even if only for an hour or two. Ron had tried calling Growing Minds Discovery Garden (evidently *daycare* was too déclassé a term for them), where they sometimes left Lily. But Lily had a slight cold and was running a low fever, so they wouldn't take her. Ron had told the director of Growing Minds about his meeting with Armstrong and that other than a bit of a runny nose, Lily was acting perfectly fine. The woman had said that while she sympathized with Ron's situation, rules were rules, and there was nothing she could do about it.

Frustrated, he'd called Julia at work and asked her to tell her bosses that she was sick so she could come home and watch Lily for him. *That* had been a mistake. They'd nearly gotten into a fight over the phone. Julie had only recently returned to work as a paralegal, and she didn't want to do anything that might jeopardize her job. She worked for Sloan and Sloan, husband and wife lawyers who shared a practice. While Mr. Sloan was easygoing enough, his wife was a real hard-ass. No way did Julia want to risk the woman's wrath by lying to her so she could skip out of work. Couldn't he call the publisher and reschedule?

No, he couldn't, he told her. That would be unprofessional.

He could almost hear her shrug over the phone. "Then you'll just have to take her along, I guess."

He expected Lily to protest his excuses for not stopping to pick up the stuffed dog, but she said nothing. He thought maybe she was pouting, so—judging they were far enough away from the spot where Lily had spotted the stuffed St. Bernard—he readjusted his rearview mirror so he could see her. But when he saw her reflection, he experienced a shock that was equal parts surprise and stunned recognition. The image in the mirror was Lily, all right, but not the seven-year-old girl with bright eyes, round face, button nose, and curly strawberry-blonde hair. It was Lily as a baby, not quite a year old. Strapped snugly into her carseat, wearing a one-piece outfit that left her chubby pink arms and legs bare, fine curly wisps of hair on her head, nothing like the thick, rich locks she was destined to have. Lily's pudgy face was red, eyes squeezed close, mouth open wide. She looked as if she was crying, but Ron heard no sound.

He blinked, and Lily was suddenly seven again, sitting on her booster seat and looking at him expectantly.

"Didn't you hear what I said, Daddy? I said maybe we could pick up the doggie on the way back."

Feeling disoriented and a trifle dizzy, Ron said, "We'll see."

He was nervous about meeting with Mr. Armstrong, that was all. Coupled with his artistic imagination, his anxiety had caused him to momentarily "see" a memory. Weird, maybe, but nothing to be worried about.

He faced forward again and concentrated on his driving, but somewhere in the back of his mind, he heard a baby crying.

Ron was too young when he got Biff to remember the first time he saw the toy that, in many ways, was to become the best friend he'd ever had. But his mother had told the story to him often enough over the years that he felt he could recall every detail.

It had been his first birthday, and his parents had done all the usual things. They'd put him in his high chair, turned off the kitchen light, and brought out a cake with a single thick candle shaped like a numeral one on top. The candle was lit, and Ronnie's eyes widened as his mother set the cake down on the table in front of him—but not *too* close. Wouldn't want Baby getting burned. His parents sang "Happy Birthday" to him, and he smiled at the tune, though he couldn't quite understand the words. Then both his Mommy and Daddy blew out the candle flame. Ronnie liked looking at the flickering warm glow, and he was sad to see it go bye-bye.

Mommy cut the cake while Daddy took pictures. Mommy put Ronnie's slice on a tiny paper plate and set it on his highchair tray. He squooshed the cake with his tiny fingers, getting more of it on his bib, face, and in his hair than in his mouth. Mommy spooned a bit of ice cream into his mouth, and he dutifully swallowed it, only to make a horrified face at the unfamiliar sensation of cold in his mouth, followed instantly by tears. Mommy washed his hands, then Daddy took him out of the high chair and carried him into the living room. A half dozen objects were stacked on the coffee table, all wrapped in brightly colored paper. But Ronnie barely glanced at them. His gaze was drawn to the large brown-and-white thing sitting on the floor next to the coffee table.

Daddy put him down on the floor, and Ronnie took several unsteady steps toward the big fuzzy thing before giving up and falling to his hands and knees so he could make better speed. He swiftly crawled over to the fascinating object, reached out, and grabbed a handful of brown-and-white fur. It was so soft . . . he buried his face in its fur and grabbed hold of it, squeezing as hard as he could. It was soft like Mommy, big like Daddy, and warm, too. But it didn't pull away when he squeezed it, didn't say, "Ouch, that's too hard, sweetie!" Ronnie instinctively understood that whatever this furry thing was, it was his, and it would accept whatever he did without question, complaint, or reprimand.

From that moment on, Ronnie cried whenever anyone tried to separate him from his new friend. It was an "Oggy" he eventually learned, and he wanted his Oggy to go wherever he went, wanted it in the crib with him when he slept, despite how much room it took up, to protect him from the things that moved sinuous and silent in the dark. Wanted it sitting on one of the kitchen chairs when he ate, sitting by his side as they watched cartoons, looking on with its black plastic eyes while he got a bath. If he went outside, Oggy had to go outside. When Ronnie had to come back in, so did Oggy. This meant a lot of extra work for his parents, as Ronnie was too small to carry

Oggy around by himself. But eventually Ronnie grew, and he was able to drag Oggy along with him, giving his Mommy and Daddy a bit of badly needed relief. But Ronnie didn't notice or care about his parents' reaction. All he cared about was spending time with Oggy.

Ron glanced at the digital clock on the van's dashboard and gritted his teeth. 11:47. There'd been a wreck on Everson Road, not much more than a fender bender, really—but he'd had to wait in a mini traffic jam until a state trooper and a tow truck had cleared the vehicles involved from the street. He judged he could still make his appointment with Mr. Armstrong, but his margin for error was decidedly thinner than it had been.

"Daddy? I don't feel so good."

Those were the last words Ron wanted to hear. He felt like groaning, but he didn't want to hurt his daughter's feelings, so he worked on keeping his voice calm as he asked, "What's wrong, honey?"

"My tummy feels all shivery."

Ron bit back a curse. Lily had a tendency to get carsick, but usually only on long trips. He'd taken precautions, though. It was hot out today, but he had the minivan's air conditioning on, and though he'd been hurrying to make up the time lost to the accident delay, he'd tried to avoid accelerating or braking too rapidly and cutting corners too sharply when he turned. Still, it looked as if his precautions had failed.

Of course they did, he thought. That's how the universe works, right? The more you needed to avoid something, the more likely it was to happen.

He checked the time again. 11:50. He couldn't afford to stop, but how could he keep going, knowing Lily was in discomfort? And—to be cold-bloodedly practical about it—how could he continue on to his meeting with Armstrong if Lily threw up all over herself? He'd have to take her home for sure then.

He looked in the rearview mirror and saw Lily's pale, frightened face looking back at him.

And even if he was cruel enough to make her sit in her own sick while he kept his appointment, the vomit-stench would attach itself to him. He could just imagine introducing himself to Armstrong and trying to explain why he stank of his daughter's puke.

"Don't worry, honey. I'll find somewhere to pull over."

He saw a Hamburger Haven coming up on his right. He signaled, eased up on the gas, then gently pressed down on the brake. He turned into the restaurant's parking lot so slowly that the person behind him blasted his horn. Ron was tempted to give the sonofabitch the finger, but Lily was with him, and he didn't want to be a poor role model, so he resisted. There was a parking space near the entrance, and Ron eased the minivan into it and cut the engine. Trying not to think about the time, he got out of the van and hurried around to the side and slid open the side door. He hoped the absence of motion combined with exposure to fresh air would settle Lily's stomach, but it was so damned hot out, he wondered if he should've left the door closed and the AC running. He'd only been outside for a few seconds, and already beads of sweat were forming on his skin. He was wearing a nice shirt, tie, slacks, and dress shoes for his interview with Armstrong, and he worried about getting sweat stains on his clothes. Not much he could do about it, he supposed.

"How are you doing, honey?"

Lily was still pale and her breathing was coming in ragged pants. She kept swallowing, too, fighting to keep her stomach from emptying its contents.

"I . . . I'll be okay, Daddy." She attempted a smile, but it came out as a grimace.

Ron was overwhelmed by a sudden swell of both pride and guilt. His little girl was doing her best to be brave because she knew how important his meeting with Armstrong was for her daddy. He was proud of her for trying to act so grown-up, but he felt guilty that he'd been more concerned about wasting time stopping than about his little girl's physical condition.

He unbuckled her seatbelt. "C'mon, let's go inside where it's cool."

Lily was beginning to sweat now too, and she gave him a weak but grateful smile as she climbed out of the van. He took her elbow to steady her, slid the door closed, then locked the van using his keychain remote. Then together they entered the restaurant.

A blast of cold air hit them as soon as they walked in. Too cold, Ron thought. His own stomach lurched at the sudden extreme shift in temperature, and he doubted the transition made Lily feel any better. Worse yet was the smell inside the restaurant—hot grease, smoke, and frying meat. Lily's face went chalk white. Without saying anything, she turned and fled toward the women's restroom. Ron felt equal amounts of concern and frustration, the latter making him feel even more guilty than he had before.

This Hamburger Haven was set up like all the others Ron had even been in. A front counter where apathetic teenagers and bored retirees took and filled orders, tables and chairs where customers could sit while they gobbled down the muck the place passed off as food, and a play area outside with more seats and a configuration of plastic tunnels for small children to crawl around inside like hamsters. Ron disliked fast food in general—it always upset his stomach—but he had fond memories of bringing Lily here when she was little, of taking her to the play area and letting her explore the tubes. Not too far in, though, for she wasn't even a year yet and just starting to learn to walk.

"Can I help you, sir?"

He turned toward the voice, startled out of his memories. A stout matronly women in her fifties wearing a blue Hamburger Haven uniform stood before him. Her nametag said *Gloria* and beneath that *Manager*.

Ron was puzzled by the woman coming up to speak to him. Since when did Hamburger Haven get so proactive about customer service? Gloria stared at him as if there was something wrong with the way he looked. Her nose wrinkled, and she turned her head slightly aside, as if he had offensive body odor. But he was wearing clean clothes, and he'd showered this morning and put on deodorant. Sure, he'd started sweating outside, but not *that* much.

"I'm just waiting for my daughter," he said. "She's in the restroom."

The woman's eyes narrowed with suspicion, and Ron understood why she had come out from behind

the counter to check on him. The way Lily had run
from him must've looked as if she were trying to escape a captor.

He gave Gloria what he hoped was a reassuring
smile. "She gets a little carsick sometimes."

She frowned. "I didn't see you come in with anyone."

"Maybe you weren't looking. There's a lot of people
lined up at the counter." Which was true. It was the
lunch rush, after all.

Gloria's frowned deepened into a scowl. "Unless
you're going to buy something, I'll have to ask you
to leave."

Ron was starting to get angry. This woman was acting like he was some kind of dangerous nut instead
of a father doing his best to take care of his child.

"As soon as my daughter's okay, we'll get out of
here. All right?"

The woman looked as if she were going to say
something further, but then she glanced at all the customers waiting to place orders, and she turned away
and headed back to the counter.

Ron was glad to see her go, and he'd be even more
glad to get the hell out of here, after—

The women's restroom door opened and Lily came
out. She was still pale, though not nearly as white as
when she'd gone in. Her face was wet, and at first he
thought she was dripping with sweat, but then he realized she'd splashed water on her face.

"How are you feeling, sweetie?"

"Better." Her voice was shaky, but not as weak as
it had been. "I think I'm okay to go now."

He felt a surge of hope, and he immediately
squashed it. Lily was infinitely more important than
any illustrating gig he might get.

"Why don't we sit down for a little bit until you feel all the way better? I can get you something to drink, maybe some Sprite to settle your stomach."

"Really, Daddy, I'm okay. Let's—"

"I asked you to leave." It was Gloria again, only this time she wasn't alone. She'd brought a tall, beefy teenaged boy with her.

Ron's anger rose, and it was all he could do to keep from shouting at the woman. "I'm not sure my daughter is feeling well enough yet."

The teenaged boy—whom Gloria had doubtless brought along for whatever muscle he could provide— gave his manager a confused, questioning look.

Gloria didn't glance back at the boy. She kept her gaze focused on Ron. "I don't want any trouble. Just go. *Now*." She didn't sound mad. She sounded scared, and Ron couldn't figure out why.

Lily tugged at his arm. "Let's go, Daddy? Please?"

Now Lily sounded scared, and though Ron wanted to tear into the manager and give her hell for treating him this way, he didn't want to subject his daughter to any more of the woman's weirdness.

He gave Gloria a parting glare. "Fine. Whatever. But see if we ever come back here again."

As Ron and Lily headed for the door, he heard the teenager say, "We?" but he didn't turn back. They exited into a thick, syrupy heat that made Ron feel queasy. He looked to Lily to check how she was handling the abrupt temperature shift and was surprised to see a big grin on her face.

"Look, Daddy!" She pointed toward the van.

Sitting on the sidewalk in front of the vehicle, facing toward them, was Biff.

*   *   *

Ronnie was nine. He sat in his driveway, legs crossed, hands resting limply in his lap, ever-faithful St. Bernard sitting next to him. His Oggy was somewhat worse for the wear after eight years of accompanying Ronnie on his adventures. His colors had faded, and there were bare patches in his fur. A number of his seams had split over the years and had been sewn back up by Ronnie's mother, leaving bits of thread here and there. The plastic eyes had been scratched from too much hard play, giving them a somewhat milky cast, like an old person's cataracts.

He sat there, doing nothing, thinking nothing. Eventually Jerry Klauser came riding by on his new ten-speed. Jerry lived down the block, the youngest of seven kids, though he was a year older than Ronnie. For reasons that Ronnie had never been able to fathom, Jerry thought he was real hot stuff and teased Ronnie whenever he got the chance.

Ronnie hoped Jerry would ride on past, but he knew he wouldn't.

Jerry rolled up to the end of Ronnie's driveway and put his feet down to stop.

"Hey, it's Ronnie and his Oggy-Woggy!"

Ronnie didn't feel like talking to anyone right now, especially Jerry Klauser, but he knew the taunts would only continue and get worse if he didn't respond.

"His name's Biff."

As Ronnie had gotten older, he'd come to realize what a babyish name Oggy was. He'd tried out other names: Champ, Killer, and—least imaginatively of all—Bernard. But one day his parents had left him with a babysitter while they went out to the movies. He watched TV while she did homework, and he noticed she'd used an eraser to remove parts of the

cover, creating white lines like writing. The lines said
SUZE AND BROOKE: BFF.

"What's *Biff* mean?" he'd asked.

Suze had been puzzled for a moment, but when she
figured out what he meant, she laughed. "It's B-F-F.
It stands for Best Friends Forever."

Ronnie thought that was a great way to describe
him and his St. Bernard and so that day Oggy became Biff.

"Biff is a stiff!" Jerry said in a singsong voice. "I'd
like to throw him off a cliff!"

Ronnie's jaw tightened and his hands clenched into
fists. "Shut up and leave me alone, Jerry."

"What's wrong? The baby can't take a joke? Are
you gonna start to cry? Maybe Oggy will give you a
kiss and make it all better."

Ronnie rose to his feet. "I told you his name is
Biff." He could feel the pressure of tears behind his
eyes, and he fought to hold them in. He didn't want
to give Jerry the satisfaction of seeing him cry.

Jerry's eyes hardened. "You wanna make something
of it, Baby?" His words seemed false somehow, as if
he were repeating something he'd heard on TV. Jerry
had never tried to pick a fight before, but he sounded
serious. Ronnie had never been in a fight, but the way
he felt now, he'd almost welcome it. He took a step
toward Jerry but then thought better of it.

"Just go away. My grandma died this morning."

Though all Ronnie had done was talk, Jerry reacted
as if he'd punched him in the stomach. His eyes went
wide and his mouth fell open.

"No shit?"

Ronnie had never used a swear word before, but it
seemed only appropriate now.

"No shit."

"Aw, geez. I'm . . . sorry."

Jerry looked at him a moment longer, as if he were trying to think of something else to say but couldn't. Finally he put his feet back on his bike pedals and rode off down the sidewalk.

Ronnie's mom was inside the house, lying on her bed, crying. She'd been there all day, ever since Aunt Karen had called with the news of Grandma's death. Dad was still at work, and though he'd told Mom he'd try to come home early, he didn't know if his boss would let him. So Ronnie had been left alone with his grief all morning.

No, not alone. Never. Not so long as he had Biff. Ronnie sat back down next to his friend—the only *real* friend he'd ever had. He grabbed Biff and held him tight as the tears he could no longer hold back flooded forth.

"It *was* the same dog, Daddy! He followed us!"

Ron drove five miles over the speed limit. It was 11:57, three minutes before he was scheduled to meet with Mr. Armstrong, and he still had several miles to go to reach Coleman Publishing. He was going to be late, there was no helping that now, but maybe he wouldn't be *too* late.

"It *couldn't* be the same one, and it sure as hell couldn't have followed us. It's *stuffed* for Christ's sake!" He instantly regretted using such harsh language when speaking to his daughter, but he was so goddamned pissed off. Over Lily's protests, he'd taken the St. Bernard—which was *not* Biff, he kept telling himself—into the Hamburger Haven to tell the manager that someone had abandoned the toy outside her restaurant. The woman had vehemently refused to take the dog from him and had shouted for him to get the fuck out before she called the cops. Everyone in the restaurant—employees and customers alike—had looked at him as if he were insane, and so he'd plopped the stuffed dog that was *not* Biff down on the counter and left.

"I tell you what, honey. If you really want a stuffed dog, I'll take you to the toy store after my meeting and you can pick out whichever one you want, no matter how big. How does that sound?"

"But I don't want any old dog," she whined. "I want *that* one!"

Ron gritted his teeth and held his tongue. At least her carsickness had passed, he told himself. He thought he heard the sound of a baby crying softly then, but it seemed so faint and far away that it had to be his imagination. The sound soon faded away, as if the child had tired itself out and fallen asleep. He glanced in the rearview mirror. Lily sat looking out her window, lower lip pushed out in a little girl pout. If she'd heard the baby crying, she didn't show it. At least *she* wasn't crying. That was something to be thankful for. It had been a hard morning for her as well. He understood that and vowed to do his best to make it up to her—after his meeting.

They drove on in silence for the next few minutes, and Ron tried to remain calm as the digital clock moved from 11:57 to 58, 59, and then to noon. He was now officially late.

But there, coming up on the right, was the entrance to Coleman Publishing. He remembered the blue sign standing up in the grass out front, remembered the white letters that spelled out the company's name, including—in smaller letters below—est. 1967. The colors were a bit faded now, but—

He frowned. What was he thinking? He'd never been here before, had mailed his art samples to Mr. Armstrong. He'd probably driven past on occasion, but he'd never really noticed the place, certainly not to the point where he'd recognize changes in the sign's colors. He was probably remembering a different sign, a different company, getting the memories mixed up. Yeah, that was it. Had to be.

He slowed, signaled, and turned into the entrance.

"Looks like we made it, kiddo!" He felt suddenly light, cheerful, all anxiety drained away. The clock said 12:02. Late, but only a little. Mr. Armstrong probably wouldn't even notice. He glanced up at the rearview mirror to see how Lily was doing. She stared straight ahead, eyes widening with horror.

"Daddy, look out!"

He lowered his gaze, and through the windshield he saw a large brown-and-white shape dash across the driveway right in front of their van. Felt the heavy *thump* more than he heard it. He slammed on the brakes, squealing tires blending with Lily's screams.

Ron stood in his bedroom, looking at the two suitcases and bulging duffle bag sitting on his bed. For the dozenth time he took a mental inventory of everything he'd packed, and for the dozenth time he decided he hadn't forgotten anything. He knew he was stalling and that his mom and dad knew it too, but neither of them had come in to tell him it was getting late and they should get on the road. He appreciated that.

He was excited about leaving for college, was looking forward to moving into the dorm, starting his art classes, getting a chance to see what it was like to live on his own. Finally starting his adult life. He knew he wasn't leaving home for good, not really. He'd be back for holidays and summers. But this was the last time this would he *his* room, the place where he lived. From now on he'd only be visiting.

He hadn't thought it would be so hard to say goodbye to a place, to let go of all the memories that filled the room like light and air. But it was. And there was one memory that was hardest of all to let go of.

Biff sat on the floor next to his dresser, a fine coating of dust on his fur. The stuffed dog leaned sideways, head flopped over at an angle, its stuffing having clumped up and settled in odd places over the years. Biff had been sitting in this position since Ron started junior high, and he hadn't touched it since. He'd outgrown the need for make-believe friends. But then again, he hadn't stuck Biff in the closet with all the other toys he never played with anymore. And whenever his mom made noises about giving Biff to Goodwill or worse, just throwing him out, Ron wouldn't hear of it. Maybe Ron hadn't needed Biff the same way as when he'd been little, but that didn't mean he didn't need him at *all*.

Ron went over to the dresser and crouched down in front of Biff, just as though he were a real dog. Feeling only a little foolish, but still glad no one was here to see him, he reached out and scratched the top of Biff's head.

"I guess this is it, old buddy. I won't see you again until Thanksgiving. I . . . want to thank you. You've been a good friend to me." He smiled. "Tell you what. I ever have a kid, I'll give you to him or her, and you can be their friend. What do you think of that?"

Biff didn't respond. He never had. After all, he was just a stuffed animal. But if Biff had been alive, Ron liked to think his old friend would've been pleased.

Ron stood in front of the van, telling himself that he wasn't seeing what he thought he was seeing. Lily knelt on the ground, holding the crimson-splattered body of Biff to her chest, tears streaming from her eyes, her small body wracked by sobs. The animal that had run in front of the van had been a living dog, a *real* dog, Ron was certain of that. But the tattered wet thing his daughter held was the stuffed St. Bernard from his childhood. The impact had split open the seam that ran from Biff's neck, down his chest, and across his belly. Wads of gray stuffing that looked too much like internal organs protruded from the wound, along with thick red fluid that looked like blood but couldn't possibly be.

"You killed him!" Lily wailed.

Ron struggled to find words to comfort his daughter, but his thoughts were sluggish, and he felt a throbbing pain at the base of his skull. Still, he had to say something.

"He can't be dead, honey. He was never alive. You can't kill something that never lived . . ."

Lily kept on sobbing, and Ron doubted she'd heard him. His entire head was pounding now, and a wave of vertigo washed over him, causing his gut to twist with nausea. Something was seriously wrong here, and he instinctively understood that he had to get Lily away from this place before—

"Mr. Garber!"

Ron turned to see a bald man with a salt-and-pepper goatee hurrying toward them down the driveway, coming from the direction of the Coleman Publishing building. The man was tall, thin, and wore wire-framed glasses. He had on a gray suit and a tie that—even from this distance—Ron could see sported a design of tiny interlocking paint palettes. Ron had never seen the man before . . . had he? But he recognized the voice. It belonged to Mr. Armstrong.

Ron felt a surge of panic. He couldn't let Mr. Armstrong see him like this! How could he ever explain? *Sorry, sir, but I seem to have run over and killed a stuffed animal from my childhood. Most embarrassing.*

He put his hand on Lily's shoulder and gently squeezed.

"C'mon, honey. We have to go. We can't—"

"Mr. Garber!" Armstrong called again. He was much closer now, and Ron's panic gave way to fatalism. It was too late . . . in so many ways. He gave Lily a last squeeze before turning to meet Armstrong.

As the man reached them, sweat running down the sides of his face, breath coming hard from half-running the whole way, Ron said, "I know this looks bad, Mr. Armstrong, but I can—"

"Mr. Garber, when you called this morning, I *told* you not to come. You know I have nothing but the utmost sympathy for your situation, but you *cannot* keep doing this. I don't want to call the police again, but I will if I have to."

The man sounded at once sympathetic and exasperated, and Ron had no idea what he was talking about.

"What happened was a terrible thing, Mr. Garber, but it was six years ago. I'm not going to be insensitive and tell you to get over it. I can't begin to imagine the pain you've experienced. But you've got to come to grips with what happened. Can't you see that?"

Ron felt pressure building inside his head, so intense that he feared it might explode any moment. "I . . . I don't . . ."

And then the pressure, the pain, the confusion vanished, and Ron remembered.

Remembered driving to his appointment with Mr. Armstrong six years ago, on a day even hotter than this one. Lily in the back, not quite a year old, sitting in her car seat, Biff next to her. His childhood friend, now his daughter's companion, confidant, and guardian. Lily with her fever and without a babysitter, crying all the way to Coleman Publishing, falling asleep at last as he pulled into the parking lot. Ron trying to decide what to do: bring Lily inside and risk her waking up and squalling in the middle of his interview with Armstrong? He told himself she needed the sleep, that he wouldn't be long, that he'd leave the windows cracked, that she would be all right. After all, Biff was there to watch over her, wasn't he?

The meeting went well, and Ron got the job. But when he returned to the van, Lily wasn't all right. She was never going to be all right again.

Armstrong found him screaming his grief as he tore Biff apart with his bare hands. After all these years, his whole fucking *life*, his best friend had let him down when he'd needed him most. It was Biff's fault, not his. Never his.

Ron realized he couldn't hear Lily crying anymore. He turned to look at her and saw exactly what he feared he would. Nothing. No Lily, no Biff. No stuffing, no blood. Just empty, clear asphalt in front of the van's tires. The van, which looked older, scratched, dented, and badly in need of a wash. Ron looked down at his clothes and saw they were filthy as well, wrinkled and stained. He examined his hands. His nails were long, cracked, discolored. He reached up to his face, felt his unkempt beard, his long scraggly hair. He inhaled and smelled his own foulness. Now he knew why the people in the Hamburger Haven had reacted to him the way they had. He'd gone in alone, looking like this, talking to a daughter who had died long ago.

He ran his fingers over his sweat-slick face. "I'm sorry, Mr. Armstrong."

The profound pity in the other man's gaze was far worse than anger or revulsion. Ron shuffled back toward the van's open driver's door, climbed in, and shut it behind him. Mr. Armstrong stood and watched as Ron put the vehicle in reverse and began to back up.

Ron sat at a picnic table in the park, art portfolio on the seat next to him, sketch paper open on the table. As he drew, he thought. In a way, Biff *had* tried to protect him by preventing him from keeping his appointment with Mr. Armstrong—and from having to remember. Sure, Biff had been a hallucination, just like seven-year-old Lily, the age she would've been if she'd lived. But maybe Biff was the part of his mind that wanted to get better, to break the cycle he was trapped in. Maybe he was ready to go back to therapy, maybe he'd even call his ex-wife. He and Julia had barely spoken since Lily's death. Maybe it was time they did.

His thoughts were interrupted by the deep, sonorous bark of a large dog.

"Daddy, look! I taught Biff a new trick!"

Ron looked up. Lily pointed her index finger at the St. Bernard and said, "Bang!"

Biff fell onto his side and rolled over, tongue lolling from the side of his mouth. Lily giggled in delight and ran over and gave her friend a hug. Biff's tail thumped happily on the grass.

Ron smiled and looked back down at the picture he'd been sketching: a little girl playing with a St. Bernard in the park on a bright summer day. It was just a sketch now, but he thought it was good enough to finish. It might even turn out to be good enough to put in his portfolio. He hoped so. It would be nice to have something new to show Mr. Armstrong at their next meeting.

GREG AND ELI

Paul Genesse

"**D**AD, the light's red!" Greg's fingers dug into the armrest, and he ducked below the dashboard as his father stomped on the gas pedal. Their van streaked across the dark intersection, while the headlights glaring through the passenger window made shadow monsters on the dusty upholstery. His father would normally have cursed at the honking cars, but he remained silent as he guided the car faster than Greg could ever remember. Dad hadn't said a word since Vegas Valley Hospital had called. Greg had answered the phone, and when the doctor started talking, he thought the day had finally come; but his excitement about the birth of his little brother, Joe, had been replaced by teeth-clenching fear.

Dad pulled a hard left turn. Greg lurched against the door as their van bounced into a parking lot. They stopped with a screech in front of a tall white building with mostly dark windows. Greg ran after his father, and they passed a creepy old man in a wheelchair smoking a cigarette.

The desk lady in the emergency room said Mom was now in the "I See You" on the sixth floor. The sign at the elevator said: Labor & Delivery, Fourth Floor. "Dad, isn't Mom there? We took the tour there. Remember?"

The muscles in his father's jaw stood out as he poked the sixth floor button as if he were playing a video game and shooting space aliens rapid fire. When the elevator ride was over, Greg had to jog to keep up. The air in the "I See You" smelled wrong, as if someone had forgotten to clean up dog pee, then tried to hide it with orange-scented air freshener.

Dad talked to a man in a white coat while Greg took in all the strange beeps and bongs, trying to figure out where they were coming from.

"Hi, honey, I'm Megan." A freckled woman with short red hair wearing blue pajama pants smiled at him. "You sure are cute with those puppy dog eyes. How old are you, sweetie?"

"I'm six." Greg just wanted to find Mom and see his new brother. "Where's the glass wall to see the babies? This is the 'I See You,' right?"

She stifled a smile, and two more ladies in pajamas joined her. Dad went into a room with the tall man in the white coat, and Megan tried to distract him. "What grade are you in?"

"First." He shifted uncomfortably as they stared at him. "Where's my mom?"

Megan tried to keep her smile, but her eyes flashed with worry. She peeked into the room where Dad had gone, then slipped past the curtain. A moment later, Megan came out and knelt down, her brown eyes at his level. "Sweetie, your dad wants me to bring you to your mom's room. She was in a car accident to-night. She's hurt, but she's going to be okay."

"No," he shook his head in disbelief, "she's here to have a baby, my little brother." Greg felt his face squinching together. Megan was nice, and her freckles were cool, but she had to be wrong. Still, he let her take his hand and lead him past the curtain. Dad sat in a chair beside a tall bed with plastic railings all around it. Bags of water and what had to be blood hung from the ceiling. TVs with weird wavy-lined channels and flashing numbers were everywhere. He couldn't believe how many buttons and wires there were.

The pale-faced person in the bed didn't look like Mom at first; then Greg noticed her straight black hair, slightly matted and messy in the back. Her face was bruised, and her left cheek had swollen to the size of a baseball.

"Mom?" Greg's voice came out so high pitched he wondered if she would recognize it.

His father waved him forward, and Greg touched Mom's hand, which clutched her gold crucifix neck-lace. Her eyes opened, and she smiled at him.

"Hi, Greggy." Mom sounded tired, and on the verge of tears.

Greg's whole body started to shake. "Mommy, are you okay?"

"Yes, honey. Don't worry. Mommy's fine." Her smile looked weird because of her swollen face. He could tell she was just pretending. He could always tell.

"She'll be here for a few days, then she's going home." The man in the white coat gave him a reassur-ing look.

"Doctor Reed." Megan stepped behind Greg, her gentle hands resting on his shoulders. "There's a Doctor McNeil with OB on the phone for you, and Mrs. Lloyd's hematocrit is back; it's twenty-two."

"Okay," Doctor Reed said, "give her another two units and recheck the crit. Then page me."

"Are you giving her medicine?" Greg asked.

"Yes, and she needs some blood," Doctor Reed said.

"I can give her some," Greg held up his arm. "We're both O positive, Mom told me. Or I can give some to Joe. Does he need any?"

Mom's face froze in shock, and the doctor looked at the numbers on a TV that suddenly went from seventy to over a hundred and started flashing red. "Take some deep breaths, Mrs. Lloyd." Doctor Reed made eye contact with Mom until the numbers turned green again.

"Can you leave us alone for a minute, Doctor?" Dad glanced at Greg.

"Of course. I'll be at the desk."

When they were alone, Greg felt like he needed to either run or pee.

"Greg," his father's voice was quavering, "the baby . . . got hurt in the accident."

"Is he going to be . . . ?" Greg felt all numb and tingly. He leaned against the bed, trying not to shake. He remembered his brother high-fiving him through Mom's belly whenever he touched her. Greg reached out and put a hand on Mom's stomach. The flatness made him pull his hand back as though he'd touched a hot stove. "Where's Joe?"

"Honey," Mom started to cry, "your brother . . . Joseph . . . is . . . " She couldn't go on.

Dad said, "Joe's in Heaven now."

"He can't be." Greg shook his head. "He's going to be my best friend. We're going to ride bikes together."

"I'm sorry, honey." Mom's body shook as she cried.

Little tremors went through Greg's whole body. This wasn't fair. His brother hadn't done anything wrong.

Greg collapsed against the bed, but the tears wouldn't come. His mother stroked his hair and whispered, "Greggy, everything's going to be okay."

She was pretending again. Things weren't going to be okay.

Two months later, Greg added his house to the list of things he'd lost since Joe died. Mom said she couldn't live there anymore or anywhere in the city for that matter. She couldn't go near the baby room, and everything about kids made her cry. She could barely look at Greg anymore and didn't care that he got awards for spelling and multiplication three weeks in a row, or that he ate all his lima beans, or anything else for that matter. Dad didn't care either. He'd been working extra hours at the school where he taught drafting, engines, and other stuff. When he was home, Greg's father spent all his waking hours in the garage doing something with power tools or his welding torch. Greg had been banned from being nearby when the loud tools were out, so he almost never spent any time with him anymore.

Both his parents had made it clear. They didn't want him around.

The "Sold" sign wavered in the hot desert wind when they drove away. Mom kept up her blank stare out the front window of their green and white van,

not even acknowledging the waves from the small
group of his friends and their parents who had come
to wish them goodbye. He felt a lump in his throat,
and his eyes misted over as he waved to Jeff, Mike,
and Justin. Greg and his friends had ridden their bikes
and played in the vast desert lot near their subdivision
since kindergarten. He wondered if he would ever see
them again and stared out the back window of the
van trying to memorize how they looked. He hoped
he would never forget them, especially Jeff, who had
always been a great friend—never once had he teased
Greg about his height, even when the other kids were
piling it on.

Dad drove north on the bleak highway into the Nevada desert. Hot, dry air blew into the van and fresh
asphalt scented the breeze. Everything the moving
truck didn't carry was packed into their van. Greg
wandered between the couch in back to the seat behind Mom, staring out and rarely looking at his silent
parents who seemed more like statues.

The desert of sagebrush and scraggly creosote
bushes went on endlessly. The black rocky hills and
purple mountains in the distance looked lonely, and
the landscape was barren. They passed two tiny towns,
and one didn't even have a gas station. Greg kept an
eye out for animals, but all he saw was a dead jackrab-
bit and a few little birds. There weren't any buzzards.
Greg thought there should be buzzards. They were in
all the Western movies on channel five.

An hour on the empty highway felt like two days
to Greg. He didn't even have any toys to play with.
Mom had packed them all. The only thing he had was
a few markers and some thin brown paper that always
bled through to the other side. He drew buzzards, cir-

cling over a coyote, and a dragon guarding a gold mine that a Hobbit was trying to sneak into. When the paper ran out another hour later, Greg was sick of buzzards but not dragons. Who could ever get sick of dragons? He figured Joe would have loved dragons.

Finally, they reached their new home: Beatty, Nevada, population: 1,206—now 1,209. The old mining town was ringed by multicolored mountains of white, red, and black rocks. Beatty sat in the middle of nowhere along the banks of a trickle of water called the Amargosa River, which was lined with a few cottonwood trees. As they passed over a bridge, Greg thought the little green ribbon of water looked more like a small stream.

The rocky hills around the town were dotted with black mine tunnels that were probably filled with vampire bats and ghosts. Greg shuddered when he thought about how dark they must be inside.

The vibration when they drove over a cattle guard seemed to wake Mom up. She stared into the ramshackle town of scattered mobile homes and deteriorating shacks. After a long sigh, she said, "What a shit-hole. I told you to apply in Fallon."

Dad scowled. "Don't start with me, Doris. You didn't want to get off the couch and see it when I interviewed, remember? Just be glad I got something in the middle of the school year."

"I asked for quiet, not dead." She folded her arms as she took in the view of the small desert town.

The van slowed to a crawl as they passed an abandoned gas station, a small single level casino with a smiling burro on its sign, a tiny general store, and a dingy-looking motel with faded yellow paint. A larger casino and a bar sat at the intersection of the town's only stoplight. The red light blinked in four directions, but no other cars were there. Dad turned, passing an old sign that read, *Welcome to Beatty, the Gateway to Death Valley*.

Greg suspected there were buzzards in Death Valley. There had to be.

After taking a side street with more potholes than pavement, they stopped in front of an old brown house with a peaked green roof. A chicken-wire fence with a hexagonal wire pattern enclosed the squat looking home. A dead tree with sawed off branches sat in the front yard, but a few living trees grew around the property. Two big lots choked with dead tumbleweeds surrounded the house on both sides.

"*This* is where we're going to live?" Mom looked furious.

"You said you didn't want to live in a mobile home, *dear*, and this was all I could get. It's a good house. Mr. Parker built it himself back in the forties."

"This was not what I—"

"Look, you wanted out of Vegas. I got us out and this was all I could get. It's this or a trailer. Take your pick." Dad pointed to the white singlewide mobile home across the street sitting on cinder blocks. It looked like a dented beer can with rust stains running down the sides.

"Don't push me, or you'll be living here alone." Mom got out, slammed the door and struggled to open the swinging metal gate covered with desiccated vines. She went into the enclosed porch that sagged off the side of the house.

"May as well be already," Dad muttered, and he started to unload the van. The tension was so thick Greg had trouble breathing. He got out of the van and spotted a playground just down the street. He needed to get away and let his parents calm down. The green stagecoach, big teeter-totter, and tall swing set beckoned, promising refuge. "Dad, can I go to that playground?"

"That's the school. All the grades, 1 to 12 are there, and we both start tomorrow."

An oppressive sense of dread made Greg even more anxious. Going to school the next day would be terrible. He wouldn't know anyone, and his teacher would probably be mean. No teacher could ever be as nice as Mrs. Merritt.

"All right, go play for a few minutes." Dad carried some bags to the house and Greg started to reconsider. What if he ran into mean kids? But then he heard his parents yelling at each other inside the house. He sighed and marched toward the school.

He didn't know where to walk, on the empty street or in the weeds? There wasn't a sidewalk. He ended up on the side of the crumbling street, staying away from the potholes and cracked pavement. The weed-choked dirt was filled with pointy stickers that embedded themselves into the soles of his shoes. They clicked when he stepped back onto the asphalt. Greg used a flat pebble to pry out the three-pronged stickers, then found the gate into the schoolyard. He sat down on a black rubber seat on the swing set. The back of his thigh burned, and he realized he'd have to wear jeans next time, not shorts.

The wooden bench inside the metal stagecoach was better. He found a good spot and watched his dad unloading their van. A big moving truck appeared moments later and blocked off his view. Greg sat inside the coach for a while reading the bad words on the walls and wishing Jeff or Mike were there with him. They could all be cowboys fighting off outlaws who were trying to rob the stagecoach. He figured he'd probably never have friends like them ever again. There was a pain in his chest, and he sniffled a little.

All alone, he held his head in his hands. Beatty was so different from Vegas. The old neighborhood was always loud with kids playing or the music from the ice cream truck. All he heard here was the wind blowing some leaves. The town really did seem dead, just like Mom said.

Five kids on bikes streaked down the road and skidded to a halt in front of Greg's new home. They watched the two mover guys unloading boxes and furniture and shouted questions at them. He wondered who the kids were, but he was afraid to meet them. Being short tended to make him a target, and being a teacher's kid had never been a good thing. He felt even more alone and sank down so they wouldn't see him. Greg kept an eye on them, hoping they would go, but they stayed put for a long time. He knew he should go back and help move in. He could hold the door open or something. Greg started to get up.

"Where you going?"

Greg turned, and a boy a year or so younger than him stood outside the coach. He wore a red shirt with a bulldog on it and jeans with a hole in one knee.

"Duck down," the boy whispered, "or those kids will see us."

Greg and the brown-haired boy hunkered down together, peeking out as they spied on the five kids on bikes.

"What's your name?" Greg asked.

"Elijah." The boy smiled, showing he had a missing tooth in the front.

"I never heard that name before." Greg raised his eyebrows and thought the bullies probably made up some bad names for Elijah.

"It's one of them bible names. You can call me Eli."

"Okay." Greg smiled, silently vowing he would never make fun of Eli or his name.

"Hide here with me until those kids go," Eli said. "You don't want to meet them. Not today."

"My dad will get mad if I don't go back and help."

Eli shrugged his little shoulders. "Better if you stay here. I can't hold off the bad guys by myself." He aimed his hand and shot a pretend gun, closing one eye. *"Bang, bang!* Hey, Sheriff Greg, you got any more bullets? *Bang, bang!"*

Greg wanted to pull his own six-shooter—which almost never missed—but he glanced back to the moving van. Fighting outlaws would take a while. More than a few minutes. "Sorry, I'll see you later."

"Not if the outlaws get me." Eli kept shooting, *"Bang, bang. Click, click.* Uh-oh, I'm out of bullets."

Greg wanted to stay, but Dad needed him. "I gotta go now."

"Be careful." Eli reached for his spare gun. "Go 'round the back of your house, in the alley. They won't see you there. Trust me."

Greg slipped out of the schoolyard and tried to figure out how to get to the alley and avoid the boys on the bikes. Those kids couldn't be that bad. Could they? While he pondered how to sneak across the street, he was spotted by a skinny kid with a spiky flat-top haircut that was long in the back, way past his neckline. The boy said something, and all of their heads swiveled toward Greg. They all had a variation of the same type of haircut, which his dad had called millets, or something like that. Their eyes locked on him as though they saw easy prey. He couldn't avoid them now, so he stepped forward, keeping his eyes focused on the street and trying not to be too afraid. They were almost all older than him by a year or two.

"Hey kid, what's your name?" A boy with buck-teeth who looked like a fourth grader asked.

"Greg." He turned away from their leering faces.

"Greg? That's a stupid name." Bucktooth grinned. "You a chicken, Greg?"

"He looks like a little chicken boy," Flat-top said.

"Scrambled Egg Greg, a little rotten egg," Buck-tooth laughed as did the others. "Hey, Rotten Egg Greg, you got a bike?"

Greg walked past them, toward the moving van hoping they would shut their big fat mouths.

"Hey, Bobby," Flat-top said to the bucktoothed kid, "his bike probably has training wheels because he's too short to reach the pedals." The others laughed loudly.

Greg kept his mouth shut and looked away from them. He tried not to scowl, but his expression slipped. The short jokes always bugged him, and he was much shorter than the pack of town kids. Why did he always have to be the shortest one?

"Shut up," Bucktooth said to Flat-top, "or you'll make Chicken Boy cry."

Greg passed through the gate into his new yard, suppressing the urge to call them all buttholes. He went into his yard and still heard the kids making fun of him. Greg's face burned, and he wished he had listened to Eli and stayed in the stagecoach. At least he had one friend in this stupid town.

The next day his dad walked him to school and got him registered. Then the principal, Mrs. Melker, an old lady with broad shoulders, short hair and a deep voice, took Greg to his classroom.

"It's good to have such a promising student here." She smiled and Greg wondered if she had dentures.

Mrs. Melker opened the door to a classroom with nearly thirty students, all sitting in an array of mismatched desks with scarred tops and cracked plastic chairs. She explained that the first, second, and third grades were in the same room and that there were only twelve pupils in first grade.

"Hello, Greg." A lady teacher nearly as old as Mrs. Melker smiled. "I've been expecting you. I'm Mrs. Tolman."

The kids stared as though he were an alien from Mars. Bobby, the bucktoothed kid, was there. He appeared to be the tallest and oldest of all the students in the classroom. He'd probably flunked and had to be held back. Bobby laughed and whispered something to his friends. All the kids around him chuckled, and Greg felt his face burning again. In the very back of the room sat Eli, who waved, then tucked away his hand before anyone saw.

The principal left, and Mrs. Tolman introduced Greg, then sat him in a desk much too near Bobby and his pack of friends. He was far away from Eli and had to turn all the way around to see him. He did a couple of times, but a girl with blonde hair gave him a cold look and asked, "You got a staring problem, Chicken Boy?"

Greg wondered if everyone knew about the dumb nickname. He cursed Bucktoothed-Butthole-Bobby. He turned forward and listened to Mrs. Tolman teach the class about grammar, going over stuff he had already learned in his advanced reader class in Vegas. No one was answering her questions, and it was driving Greg crazy. Back in his school in Vegas over a dozen hands went up every time the teacher asked a question. Here, nothing. Greg finally raised his hand out of sheer boredom.

"Yes, Greg."

"Lavender is an adjective." Greg felt everyone glaring at him.

Mrs. Tolman smiled. "That's correct. Thank you, Greg."

It got even quieter in the room, and a moment later a spitball hit Greg in the ear. He turned around, and the girl scowled at him. She said, "Brownnoser."

Bobby and his friends had evil smirks on their faces, but he couldn't tell who shot the spitball.

Recess was called soon after, and Greg watched a vicious game of dodgeball where all the older kids abused the younger ones. He kept to himself and stayed near the door to the school building.

A ball smacked Greg in the face and knocked him over. His eyes watered as he sat up. A leather football bounced away, and a pack of kids were laughing at him.

"Told you he couldn't catch," Bobby said, then picked up the football.

"I would've caught it if I saw it coming." Greg stood up, rising to his full height of three feet.

"You probably can't see past your big brown nose." Bobby threatened to throw the ball at him again.

"Lavender is an ad'jec'tib," Bobby mocked him. "So what?"

Greg thought about what to say to the bully and his gang. Eli stood off to the side, shaking his head, telling Greg to walk away. But Greg didn't take his friend's advice. "I guess adjective is too big a word for you, you bucktoothed retard. Stick to nouns like idiot and dummy."

Bobby looked at him with a mix of anger and confusion. He cocked his arm to throw the football at point blank range. Greg flinched when he faked a throw. "Shut up, you little faggot, or I'll kick your ass into next week." He threw the football, and it hit Greg in the gut. He slid down the wall holding his stomach.

The bell rang and Bobby started to go inside with a big smirk on his face.

"Butthole!" Greg shouted.

"We do not use that kind of language here, young man." Principal Melker lifted Greg off the ground and marched him to her office. His stomach hurt, his pride hurt, and he had to fight to hold in his tears. Mrs. Melker gave him a stern warning in her office, which smelled like a smoky casino. She then showed him the large wooden paddle they used on children who didn't behave. It had a flat wooden head with holes in it to improve the speed of the paddling.

When he returned to class a while later, he kept thinking about how much the paddle would hurt. The rest of the day went slowly, and Greg didn't answer any questions—even when the teacher asked him directly. School finally got out, and Bobby blocked his way at the door, then let him pass. The older boy stuck out a foot and said, "Enjoy your trip," as he pushed Greg from behind. "See you next fall."

Greg fell, but then sprang off the floor and scurried away. Eli ran with him and said, "I told you to keep your mouth shut." Chastised by his friend and feeling quite embarrassed, Greg ran home and managed to avoid the bullies who were still unchaining their bikes from the rack. He locked the front door of his house. The brown house was old, but it was close to the school.

Mom was lying on the couch in the dark living room. Greg hated the dark. "Hi, Mom."

She turned her head a little but didn't turn to face him. "How was school?"

"Fine." He tried to sound convincing but failed miserably. He wondered how long it would be before Principal Melker talked to Dad and he told Mom.

"What happened?" Mom rolled over.

Greg held in the tears. "Nothing."

She sighed and turned away from him, just as she had for most of the past two months. Greg went to the back porch, wanting to get away from Mom. He rolled his bike off the back porch and went into the backyard. As soon as it was ready, he would get out of there and ride around the town, though he was afraid of who he might meet. He sprayed the chain with lubricant, holding down the red button of the blue and yellow can and coating the moving parts.

He heard Dad come home a few minutes later and talk to Mom. Her voice carried out the window, and he heard her upset tone. His father walked into the backyard soon after that. "Greg, Mrs. Melker talked to me."

"It wasn't my fault." Greg pleaded with his eyes.

"I know, but could you please not embarrass me? It was my first day on the job." Dad shook his head.

"I'm sure this Bobby kid had it coming, but you yelled a bad word in front of the principal. My boss."

The shame felt like cold needles against Greg's skin. "Sorry, Dad."

"Just don't do it again." His father stomped away and shut the back door harder than he needed to.

Greg went to the back gate and shook it as hard as he could. It wasn't fair that they had moved there, and it wasn't fair that all his friends were gone. It wasn't fair that he was short or that he got sent to the principal's office when it was Bobby who was bad. He went into the old garage that smelled of motor oil, dust, and cats. He found a stained cardboard box by Dad's camping supplies and smashed it with a three-foot long wooden rod he found laying around. Then he went outside to hit something else.

Eli stood outside the gate in the alley. "Greg, you want to go monster scouting?"

"Where?" Greg lifted his wooden sword, his rage starting to lessen. Monster scouting sounded fun.

"There." Eli pointed to the field next to the house and beyond the white propane tank that smelled a little like rotten eggs.

"Okay, let's go." Greg climbed over the back fence and followed Eli into the field. They searched through tumbleweeds, piles of dirt and rocks that had been dumped there, pretending they were hunters after big game.

"Giant scorpion!" Eli yelled and attacked a dead tumbleweed.

"We're surrounded!" Greg hacked at the bushes. Pieces of dry tumbleweed flew in the air as his sword chopped them up, one after another. Eli and Greg made a pile of the dead monsters, but there were too many of them. One stung Greg on the hand. He pulled the stinger out of his finger and sucked out the poison.

"Run! We have to tell the king about the monsters!" Eli led the way back toward the safety of the alley, and Greg—being the stronger warrior—covered their retreat. Both boys climbed over the fence into the yard. They hid by the garage, under an awning, squatting in the soft sand.

"Look at that anthill." Eli pointed to a mound where huge red ants crawled around, disappearing inside the ground by the big propane tank in the weed-choked yard.

"Greg, come in for supper." Dad called out from the back porch.

"Do you want to stay for dinner?" Greg asked.

"I better not." Eli climbed over the fence. "See you tomorrow."

Later that night after supper, Greg's dad tucked him into bed. "Did you say your prayers?"

"Yep." Greg glanced at the picture of Jesus and the wooden crucifix on his wall.

"Who were you playing with in the back yard today?"

"My friend, Elijah. He's in my class."

His father gave him a questioning glance and stood up to leave.

"Dad, will you leave that light on?"

"But you've got your night-lights." He gestured to the two dragon-shaped night-lights along the walls of the room.

Greg frowned. The house was way too dark and scary to turn out the big lamp.

"Okay, good night." Dad left the light on and shut the door. Greg put his stuffed brown and white dog,

Measels, by his pillow and tried to go to sleep. He couldn't. He got up and turned on the bright overhead light, gathered a few more stuffed animals onto his bed and went to sleep.

The next day at school, after lunch and before class started, Greg overheard Bobby talking to some of the younger students. "There was a huge anthill in the desert by my house."

"Yuck, I hate bugs." A girl named Stacy made a disgusted face.

"The ants ain't there now." Bobby stood by Stacy's desk, her full attention focused on him. "I got some oil spray and matches and burned a whole big nest of them. I made a flamethrower. It was awesome. I killed every last one of them, even the queen ant."

"Cool." Stacy grinned.

Bobby pretended he was pushing the button on a spray can while holding up a match. He made flame-thrower noises—aiming the flame right at Greg's head.

After school, Greg knelt in front of the anthill in his backyard by the propane tank. He had a book of matches and the can of oil spray. If Bobby could do it, so could he.

Eli knelt with him, worry on his face.

"I know, I know," Greg said, "but these ants might get into the house. It's better if I get rid of them now. Mom hates ants."

"This isn't a good idea," Eli frowned, "you know it's not."

"Let's just see if this'll work." Greg lit the first match, and the wind blew it out. He held the second one up and then pushed the button on the spray can. The liquid streamed out the little red tube stuck into

the push-button and instantly caught fire. A burst of
flame engulfed the ants, turning them into shriveled
little balls.

Greg rocked back, amazed at what he'd just done
and lit another match. The ants had been moving
slowly, but now they sped over the dirt and dozens
poured out of their hole to defend their colony. Greg
roasted them with a long blast of fire. Ants crawled
out and he kept burning them. The grass at the base
of the propane tank started to burn.

Eli pleaded, "You have to stop, please. This is
dangerous."

"Just one more time." Greg burned the winged ants
that had come out and backed away. He heard the
backdoor open and turned to see his scowling father
marching toward him. Dad stomped out the fire and
kicked dirt over the burned areas.

"What the hell are you doing?!" Dad snatched the
can out of Greg's hand and banged on the huge metal
capsule. "The tank could have exploded if there was
a leak. You know that."

Greg could only look at his feet, totally embarrassed
and feeling stupid for playing with the matches. What
was wrong with him?

"Who taught you to do that?" Dad asked. "And
don't say your friend Elijah."

"No, Eli told me not to—"

"Greg, stop it." Dad wagged finger at him. "There's
no Elijah in your class. I checked. There's no Eli in
the whole school and don't be mentioning that name
in front of your mother. She's got enough problems
right now."

What was Dad talking about? Eli was so in his class.
He was his only friend. Without, Eli, he had no one.

Mom came out the back door. "What's going on?" Dad explained what he'd caught Greg doing.

Mom put her hands on her hips, and Greg withered under her double-laser-beam glare. "Go to your room. Now!" She pointed to the house.

Greg went and listened to his parents arguing on the back porch. He was in big trouble this time. It wasn't as if he'd accidentally broken a lamp. He had intentionally played with matches. Near the propane tank. How stupid was that? Why hadn't he listened to Eli?

Mom and Dad's angry voices became louder and louder, though he couldn't make out all of their words. The words he did hear scared him to death. He heard "divorce" many times, and they mentioned a lawyer in Vegas and who would get custody. They kept arguing, and Greg guessed it was only a matter of time before they told him they were separating. Mom was leaving Beatty, and Greg would have to stay with Dad. The whole town probably heard them shouting.

As the arguing continued, Greg's heart beat faster. He paced around his small room, glancing at the window and wanting to climb out of it. With every passing moment he became more and more worried. This could be it. What if neither of them wanted him? What if they sent him away? He knew they didn't want him around.

Greg's parents stopped talking. He froze, afraid they had made a decision. They were coming to tell him they were divorcing. It was all his fault. If he'd been a better kid, it would have been okay. But if he wasn't there to be told, then maybe they would stay together. There was only one thing to do. He had to run away. Hide somewhere. Greg darted toward the open window, removed the screen, and scrambled over the sill. He dropped into the small space between the wall and the fence, then crept into the backyard, making sure his parents had left the back porch. Greg grabbed his bike and walked it out of the yard, then jumped on it and sped down the alley.

"Greg!" His father shouted after him.

He raced downhill, toward the river, crossing the highway and speeding through a neighborhood of decrepit old houses interspersed with mobile homes. He kept trying to think of a way to make his parents love him again. He had to think of a way to keep them together. If he was smart, he could do it. There had to be a way.

A big black dog ran out into the street and barked ferociously at him. Greg pedaled hard and fast, the slavering dog on his heels. It chased him past an intersection before finally leaving him alone. He kept going fast until he ran out of breath, then coasted down a dirt road that led across the knee-deep Amargosa River. It flowed down the center of a gravel-strewn ravine. The water was barely five or six feet wide, though the banks of the riverbed were ten times that far apart. He stopped and stared into the shallow water. Tadpoles swam around, and slimy green algae floated on the surface.

Greg wasn't sure what to do and glanced up at the tall mountain and rocky hills looming before him. He didn't want to go back into town, which was not far from the riverbank, and he couldn't go home. He sat by the stream, watching it flow by and wondering what made it smell funny. Dad would know. He wished Dad were there and remembered when they'd gone fishing in the Ruby Mountains. Trout tasted like mud, but it was fun catching them. He wondered if they would ever go fishing together again.

A flash of movement toward town made him stand up. Boys on bicycles rolled down the road toward him. It was Bobby and his friends. Greg jumped on his bike and pedaled across a dirt and rock bridge built over two culvert pipes. He went up the hill on the other side and glanced back. The town boys were coming after him. Greg pedaled hard and went up the road that snaked into the hills. His legs burned with exertion as the road kept winding uphill.

"We're coming, Chicken Boy!" Bobby taunted and stood tall on his pedals.

Greg took a fork in the road, hoping to lose his pursuers. It led him up a very steep hill, and he had to walk his bike after the incline became impossible. The road wound around the hill, then leveled out at the mouth of a boarded up mineshaft that went straight back into the rock. The ground in front of the shaft was a huge pile of rocks mixed with white clay from the mountain. It was very steep on all sides, and Greg didn't see a way to go except for straight down. He thought about hiding in the mine entrance, but his bike wouldn't fit past the boards. Plus, it was dark in there. Really dark. The longer he looked into the blackness the more he felt a primal fear take over.

Bobby and his four friends came around the bend huffing and puffing as they walked their bikes up the road. Greg was trapped. There was nowhere to go.

"What're you running from, Rotten Egg Boy?" Bobby asked. "You still a little chicken?"

Greg shook his head.

"Come on, you're chicken." Bobby pulled his bike up onto its back wheel, menacing Greg with his spinning front wheel.

"Am not." Greg thrust out his chin.

Eli walked up behind the other boys, following them like a lost dog. Seeing his friend there made Greg feel better, despite what Dad had said. Eli was in his class. Wasn't he? Doubt crept into Greg's mind as Bobby and the others didn't seem to notice when Eli came up beside them.

"What should we do with him?" Bobby asked.

"Toss him off the mountain?" Flat-top suggested.

Greg glanced over the edge. It was a long way down to the river. Bobby wheeled his bike forward, pressing Greg toward the drop. The tall third grader pushed his bike into Greg's, forcing him to back up. A rock skittered down and clattered below. Greg couldn't go back another step. The other boys blocked the road with their bikes. He had nowhere to go but off the cliff.

"Let's give him a chance to prove he's not a chicken," Bobby said, glancing at the tunnel. "We've all touched the back wall in there." Bobby pointed into the mine. "If he can do that, he ain't no chicken."

The thought of going into the mine without light made Greg forget how to breathe or speak. His hands trembled. He could see only a few paces inside, then the utter blackness took over.

Bobby and another kid grabbed him and hustled him toward the entrance.

"Now get in there. I dare you." Bobby pushed him against the graffiti stained boards.

"How far back . . . is the wall?" Greg's heart beat a hundred miles an hour.

"That's what you have to tell us, runt," Bobby said. "Walk back in the dark and touch the wall. Tell us how many steps it took you, and we'll know you went back there."

Eli shook his head vigorously.

"What are looking at?" Bobby pushed Greg against the boarded-up mine shaft, not paying any attention to Eli.

Fear contorted Greg's face as he stared into the tunnel.

"Egg Boy is chicken. Egg Boy is chicken," Bobby starting singing. "What's wrong, Chicken Boy, are you afraid of the dark like some little girl?"

"I am not." Greg scowled and Eli nodded in support.

"He won't go in there, Bobby," Flat-top said, "he's a chicken."

"Egg Boy is chicken. Egg Boy is chicken," they all started singing. Bobby picked up a pebble and threw it. Greg turned and the rock hit him in the lower back.

"Stop it!" Greg shouted as a painful welt formed. Bobby picked up another stone. Eli stepped beside Greg, but the kids didn't turn their hateful stares away from Greg.

"Then go in there." Bobby cocked his arm, holding the sharp rock like a baseball pitcher.

Chest heaving, Greg breathed in and out of nose, turning the fear to anger. He slipped past the boards, scraping his leg on some jagged wood. The town boys seemed shocked that he went inside.

"No," Eli said, "don't go back there. It's too dangerous."

Greg heard his friend's warning, but this was his chance. Maybe they would leave him alone after this.

He looked at the gang of kids. "I'll go back there, but then you all better leave me alone."

They laughed and Bobby threw the rock. It bounced off the old wood. "Sure, we'll leave you alone," Bobby said, "but you won't go back there. You're too chicken."

"Yeah, watch me." Greg flipped them off and turned to face the darkness. The first four steps were easy, as the late afternoon sun came through and illuminated the floor of the rocky tunnel.

The fifth step would be horrible. A wall of pitch black stood in front of Greg.

"He's going in!" One of the younger kids said.

"He'll chicken out," Bobby said, "just wait."

Eli came behind him. "Don't go. It's not safe. You don't have to prove anything to them. They haven't been in here. They don't know how far back this goes."

"It doesn't matter," Greg said fighting the fear that made his whole body seem heavy. "Go away, Eli. You're not real anyway."

There, he said it. Dad was right. He didn't have any friends in this hick town. He was alone. No one liked him, and they wouldn't—unless he showed them he wasn't afraid.

Greg took the next step into the darkness. He didn't care if he got eaten by bats or killed by some miner's ghost. His parents would rather have him lost forever in some hole in the ground anyway.

Greg's foot found the rocky floor. He took another—six steps total.

"You know this is stupid," Eli said from behind.

"Leave me alone."

"Just stop this and go home," Eli pleaded.

"They won't let me leave," Greg whispered and took another step. "Mom and Dad don't want me at home anyway. I don't have anywhere else to go."

"Will you listen to me for once?"

"Why?" Greg turned after his eighth step, but even if Eli was real, he couldn't see him in the darkness.

"Because you know you should."

Nine steps, and the darkness was so thick he couldn't see his hand in front of his face as he groped for the back wall. He found nothing as he reached forward. Greg tried not to stumble on some debris on the floor.

Ten steps. His heart was pounding in his ears, and he was totally enshrouded by the gloom.

Greg reached forward, hands extended. Eleven steps. Twelve. Thirteen. Still nothing. On his fourteenth step the ground fell out from under him. Greg screamed, flailing his arms as he fell into the hidden pit. His arm struck first. Then his body and head banged into jagged rocks. Greg heard a snap, and shooting pain went up his right arm. He fell unconscious on the cold stone as the darkness swallowed him whole.

Fear overwhelmed Greg when he finally opened his eyes. There were no night-lights, no lamps, no light at all. Nothing but impenetrable darkness surrounded him. Sharp rocks under him were definitely not his bed. This was no nightmare. He whimpered, remembering what had happened and wished that he had never gone into the mine. He had no idea which way was out and lay there on the ground, paralyzed with fear.

Why had he been so stupid? He tried not to cry

and cradled his injured arm. His head and knees ached
from the impact, but his arm hurt the worst, and his
stomach knotted with hunger. He tried to move, and
the pain in his arm pulsed through his entire body.
He touched the scabby wounds on his knees. His
touch made them sting,· and he withdrew his hand.
Greg managed to·roll onto his back and heard a high-
pitched rattling sound.

A rattlesnake. It was very close by, cloaked by the
darkness.

The echo of the rattle was all around. He couldn't
tell where it came from. He lay there in shock, trapped
with the agitated snake that couldn't be more than a
few feet away. He imagined the needlelike fangs sinking into his flesh and injecting him with a poison that
would kill him dead. A man might survive a bite, but
the TV show he saw said a little boy would die for
sure.

"Greg? Are you okay?" Eli's friendly voice gave
him a glimmer of hope, and at that moment, he had
to believe. His friend was real and hadn't abandoned
him.

The snake rattled louder, sharper, faster.

A whimper escaped Greg's lips. "Eli, my . . .
arm . . . hurts."

"Just move slow," Eli said, "so the snake won't get
more angry."

"Go get my dad, *please*." Greg cradled his broken
limb as he took in a shuddering breath, wondering if
the snake had come closer. The fear made him want
to pee so bad, but he held it in.

"I can't, Greg. You have to get out of here yourself.
Now climb up."

Greg's body shook with sobs, and the pain was intense, "I can't." He was too afraid. It was too dark. The snake was too close. It was going to bite him if he moved, and how could he climb in the dark with a broken arm?

"You can do this, Greg."

"I can't see."

"Reach in your pocket."

Greg felt with his left hand, reaching across his body. His fingers wrapped around the book of matches he'd used for the ants. "I can't light one with one hand."

"You can, just try," Eli said, as the snake's rattle became slower and more ominous.

The first three matches wouldn't light as Greg put the matchbook on the ground and ran the match across the lighting strip. The fourth one sparked to life. The faint glow had a blue center and illuminated only a small area. Greg raised the match, trying not to move it too quickly.

The rattlesnake lay coiled right in front of him. The light glinted off its eyes. The rattle was held high, and its head was cocked to strike. The fire singed his fingers, Greg shook his hand. The snake reacted to the motion and struck at Greg's face. The little boy sprang back with a shout. He banged into a rock wall, hitting his head and sending a jolt of pain down his broken arm.

The snake rattled loudly again, the sound echoing in the once again black pit.

"Climb up, Greg. Come on," Eli said, "it's not far."

"But I can't see." Greg wiped his eyes. He wanted to find the matchbook he'd left on the ground, but the snake was right there, waiting for him. He couldn't risk it. He couldn't do anything. He was going to die in the pit once the snake bit him. No one would ever

find him. Bobby and the others wouldn't tell anyone
what had happened. He would disappear forever.
Maybe that was for the best.

"Greg, you have to find a handhold and climb up."

His breath came in short gasps. He couldn't think.
He was trapped with no way out. His knees and arm
hurt so bad.

"Listen to me, Greg." Eli's voice was strong. The
strongest it had ever been. "Feel the rock. Find a
place to climb up. I'm going to help you. I'll always
help you. That's why I'm here."

The tears stopped. His friend was with him. He
wasn't alone. Greg felt the rough wall, realized he was
in a corner. His one good hand traced the rock, found
nothing; then he discovered a little hole smaller than
his fist. He imagined baby rattlesnakes or black widow
spiders in it, just waiting for him to put his hand in
there so they could bite down.

"Climb up, use the corner," Eli said.

Greg gnashed his teeth and put his hand inside the
hole. It was cold and there were soft wispy things in
it, but he used it to lever himself up to his feet. Greg
leaned against the rock, supporting all his weight with
his feet and grit his teeth to endure the pain in his
arm. He took in shuddering breaths as he reached up
with his good hand to find a place to grab onto.

"That's right, come on up," Eli said, sounding much
older than he had before.

The rock was cold and sharp, but Greg held on and
pulled himself upward, then moved his feet higher. He
leaned against the rock again and was shocked to find
the lip of the shallow pit. But there was nowhere to
hold onto. His hand disturbed some small rocks. They
tumbled down and clattered on the stone.

The snake started rattling again, more slowly, louder.

"Eli, help me." Greg couldn't find a handhold. He searched along the edge, and his foot slipped a little. He was going to fall.

A warm wind moved his hand into a crevice just wide enough for his fingers. "Thanks." He grabbed on and pulled himself up and out of the pit. There was no light visible at the entrance tunnel, but he felt along the wall until he bumped into the boards and saw the lights of town below him. He wondered how long he'd been missing as he exited the tunnel. Greg staggered out, feeling the cool night breeze and seeing a massive blanket of stars. Bobby and the other boys were long gone, but his bike was still there.

"Leave it," Eli stood by the bike. "You can't ride it now."

"But . . ." He immediately reconsidered arguing. White, angelic wings protruded from Eli's back.

"You're my . . . " Greg blinked. The wings were still there. "You're an . . ."

"Something like that." Eli smiled as he walked down the road and disappeared.

From now on, Greg decided, he was going to listen to his best friend.

No one was on the street when he stumbled into the town proper. His arm throbbed, and he couldn't seem to walk in a straight line. A cop car was parked outside his house when he staggered to the gate.

"Mr. and Mrs. Lloyd!" The sheriff yelled, "Your son is back!"

Greg's parents burst out of the door. The little boy stood there with dried blood on his skin, torn clothing and a swollen right arm. Mom gasped, then swept him up in her arms, hugging him close and causing Greg a lot of pain. "What happened, Greggy? Are you all right?"

"I . . . fell." A wave of dizziness swept over him. "Mom, I don't feel good . . ."

"Greg, baby?" His mother's voice cracked. "Greg!?" She faded from his consciousness as he blacked out in her arms.

When Greg woke up, his right arm felt like a lead weight. A florescent green cast encased his arm from his elbow all the way down to his fingers. His parents slept on a little cot beside him, snuggling together in the dim hospital room. He barely remembered the ride in the helicopter that had taken him to Vegas.

"Mom, Dad." Greg croaked through a parched throat.

First Mom, then Dad bolted off the cot and knelt at his bedside, nervous smiles on their faces.

"Do you want me to turn on some lights?" Dad asked, ready to flip the switches.

Greg shook his head. The dark didn't bother him that much now. "No, I'm fine."

His parents looked at each other with raised eyebrows.

"I'm so glad you're okay, honey," Mom said, holding his good arm. "I'm so sorry for being a bad Mommy lately. It's been so hard since . . ."

"Since Joe died," Greg said.

She nodded and wiped her eyes. "I haven't been myself. I'm sorry, baby."

He stared at his mother, wanting to tell her about Eli, but he remembered his dad saying not mention him. He figured out what to say. "Mom, you know that little voice in your head that tells you things?"

"Yes, honey. I know it." She looked away, guilt on her face, as if she had not been listening to hers.

"Sometimes I don't listen to mine." Greg sighed, remembering all the times Eli told him stuff and he didn't pay attention. "If I hadn't listened to it when I fell in the pit," Greg touched his mom's hand, "I wouldn't have gotten out."

"I'm so glad you listened, honey," Mom said. "We all need to listen to our inner voice."

"It wasn't just some voice though, Mom. It was like a friend," Greg glanced at his father. "He told me what to do, Mom. He told me how to climb up."

His mother blinked.

"He was there with me in the dark when I was all alone."

Mom's eyes filled with tears again. They hugged him, one parent on each side of his bed. It was the best feeling ever, but Greg had to ask them something else. "Mom?" Greg pulled back a little.

"Yes, honey." She lifted her head off his pillow.

"What does your little voice say about . . . you two getting divorced?" Greg glanced nervously at both of them.

Her lips trembled, and her eyes were moist. She choked up and couldn't speak, but she looked at her husband and squeezed his hand.

Dad said, "No matter what happens, Greg, we'll always love you. You'll always be our son."

They hugged him close, and he figured things were never going to be as good as they had been before. But they loved him. Greg knew they weren't pretending. He always knew.

Greg woke up in the morning when a nurse came into his room. He recognized red-haired Megan from the "I See You" when his mom was there after the accident. She had been his favorite nurse ever since that first night when Joe went to Heaven.

"Hi, Greg." Megan's bright smile made him feel better and he thought her freckles were even cooler in the sunlight. "I just saw your parents in the cafeteria, and I had to see you, sweetie." She sat down at his bedside.

"Do you like my cast?" Greg pointed to his arm and the fluorescent green wrap.

"That's a cool color. Can I sign it?"

"Uh-huh." Greg moved his arm toward Megan as his parents walked in with breakfast trays and broad smiles.

"Hey," Megan touched the cast, "someone already signed it."

Greg's parents nearly dropped their food trays when they saw the letters. Greg twisted his arm to see the signature. He couldn't believe it. The letters were scrawled as if a young child had written them.

"Who's Eli?" Megan asked.

Mom shook her head and sank into a chair as if the wind had been knocked out of her. "It was going to be . . . " She stared at the cast in disbelief.

Dad finished, "Eli was going to be the middle name of our son. Joseph Elijah Lloyd."

Greg touched the signature on his cast. He understood at last about his friend. Greg looked up at his mother and didn't let the tears come. His little voice quavered. "See, Mom, he didn't have to be born to be my brother."

AN ORCHID FOR VALDIS

Russell Davis

"If you forgive me all this,
If I forgive you all that,
We forgive and forget,
And it's all coming back to me now."
—Jim Steinman, *"It's All Coming Back to Me Now"*

Part I: Of Envelopes and Empty Trailers

JAMIE Marsters held the envelope in his hands, studying it with deliberate care and debating what to do with it. The envelope was an odd shade of lavender—not a proper purple, nor a little girl pink—but a washed-out combination of the two that was so singular it both drew the eye and simultaneously repelled it. Larger than a traditional greeting card envelope, but smaller than the usual six by nine that some people liked to use for more significant correspondence. The sender, using the careful penmanship of an old man, had addressed it properly to one Ms. Valdis, and the amount of the postage was fine. Jamie could remember when it had been mailed out, almost three weeks ago now.

He had been a postman for a long time, working the rural areas of his route with almost machinelike precision. He knew the roads, the people, even the dogs and horses that he encountered on his route most every day for the past eleven years. He had believed that there were no mysteries in the postal system for him anymore. Until today when the envelope he was holding in his hands presented several problems.

The first problem was that it had been clearly marked in bold, black, block lettering: **RETURN TO SENDER**.

The second problem, more challenging than the first, was that the sender was dead.

And the third problem, more vexing than anything else, was that he wanted to open it and read what was inside. The envelope was like knowing there was a secret or a mysterious conspiracy, while being denied the details. It reminded him of being a young man, a teenager really, and just *knowing* that beneath all the wrapping, women were a mystery waiting to be revealed.

Jamie sat in his truck, parked near the battered mailbox, and looked the envelope over again, running it through his hands as though by simply touching it, he could somehow discern its contents. From the feel, there was more than a letter inside, but what the envelope contained precisely, he didn't know. All he really knew was that the old man who had lived and died here had sent it out, and now it was back.

The old man had been a strange sort of fellow, moving in to the single-wide trailer at the end of Tumbleweed Road about four or five years ago. He'd brought along a German shepherd with an inky-black coat and an ear that looked as though it had been through a meat grinder. The dog was friendly enough, though, that on those rare occasions Jamie had gotten out of his truck, he'd been able to give him a pat on the head and one of the doggy treats he kept in his pocket for such occasions. The dog was sitting on the porch as usual, looking as though the old man might open the door at any minute and offer him dinner.

Next to the trailer, still in his stall, was a copper-colored Arabian gelding that was getting on in years but that he'd seen the old man riding from time to time. They never looked as though they were going anywhere in particular but were just meandering through the desert to see what they could see.

The trailer itself was a lot like the old man had seemed. Worn down and tired and well past its prime. In the windows, curtains that were bleached from the sun blew lazily in the slight afternoon breeze that always sprang up during the late summer days. The tire tracks from the ambulance he'd called yesterday when he'd found the old man were still visible in the dirt drive of the front yard. The trailer itself was bone white and unremarkable for this part of the world: a swamp cooler on top along with a satellite dish, windows that were too thin to be energy efficient, wooden steps that led to the front door and were no doubt rotting from within. Wood didn't do well in the dry, high desert of northern Nevada.

The old man's real name—and why did he think of him that way? As "the old man"?—was Rhys Dylan, and he was from a Welsh family that had come to the United States three or four generations back. He wasn't particularly talkative, but once in a while, he'd offer Jamie a glass of lemonade, and they'd have a short visit. From what he'd said, Rhys grew up out in the plains and came west when he was in his thirties. He'd been a writer of some sort or another, then gave it up after something he wrote made him a bunch of money. He'd spent most of the rest of his years riding horses and . . . what was it he'd said?

"Writing bad poetry because I can afford to."

That was it, Jamie remembered. So far as he knew, no one ever visited the old man, and he didn't receive much in the way of mail either. A few catalogs, the occasional business correspondence, nothing that stood out in Jamie's mind, anyway. And now one of the very few things he'd ever sent out for him had come back—a day too late for the man to know that whoever Ms. Valdis was, she hadn't received his letter.

Shaking his head, Jamie pulled his truck into the driveway, put it in park, and turned off the engine. It ticked quietly as it began to cool down, and the horse raised its head.

"Hey, old boy," Jamie said, trying for reasons he couldn't explain to keep his voice down. "Has anyone come out and given you water today?"

The dog came off the porch to greet him, and Jamie offered him a treat, which the dog gulped down greedily. "No one has fed you either, have they?" he asked the dog, who looked at him hopefully. Jamie sighed and figured the least he could do—he would still bring the mail out here every day until whoever ended up running the old man's estate showed up to tell him different—was make sure the animals were getting food and water.

Tucking the envelope into his back pocket, Jamie crossed the barren yard (no one in this part of the world with a lick of sense had an actual lawn) to the storage shed. He opened it up and saw a large bag of dog food and several bales of hay. Enough to last quite some time. He peeled off two leaves of hay and carried it out to the horse's stall, tossing it over the railing and into the feeder bin. The horse nickered appreciatively and started before the hay dust even settled.

Inside the stall, the horse's water bucket was full, and Jamie saw that an automatic fill system was in place—the bucket was full—so at least he wouldn't have to track down a hose and haul it across the yard.

Jamie returned to the trailer and picked up the dog's dish and headed back to the shed to fill it. Along the way, he tried to remember if he knew either animal's name and realized that he'd only heard the old man call them either, "damn dog" or "damn horse." If they had names, he didn't know them. Or perhaps those were the names the man had given them. He entered the heat of the shed once again and found a large scooper hanging on a peg over the bag of dog food. He took it down and removed two large scoops, putting them in the dish. Damn Dog—or whatever his name was—tried to control his eagerness and sat nearby wagging his tail with such force that it was banging on the side of the shed and making the whole structure shake slightly.

He took the dish back to the porch and set it down, noting that there was another automatic watering system that filled a bucket for the dog. As the dog set to work on its dinner, Jamie climbed the wooden steps to the porch where he had found the old man yesterday. The rocker was still there; it was now simply empty of its usual occupant.

The paramedics thought he'd probably died of a heart attack.

On a whim, Jamie tried the front door. It opened easily, and he peered into the living room of the trailer. He'd never been inside the place and was a bit surprised that the door was open. Not a lot of folks locked up in this part of the country, but someone from the sheriff's office should have locked the place up and arranged for the animals. Maybe they had and things were just moving slowly. Jamie didn't know, but his curiosity was alive within him, so he stepped across the threshold, wondering what he would find.

The living room was dim and cool, and the walls were lined with books. There was a small television on a stand on one wall and, below it, a small stereo. In one corner, there was a desk and chair; the desk was piled high with papers, and the chair looked as though it had been picked up at a garage sale about ten years earlier. A laptop computer was on top of the desk, its lid closed. Beyond the living room was the kitchen, but something else caught his eye, and Jamie stepped forward to look more closely.

Above the desk was a small painting—a portrait, actually—of a striking woman. Her hair was a fine shade of red, long and flowing past her shoulders in waves and soft curls. Her eyes were the predictable green, but they were lit from within and lighter than he would have expected. Her skin wasn't porcelain pale but lightly tanned, her lips full, her cheeks flushed slightly with color. She was wearing earrings that dropped in a series of hoops almost to the base of her neck. Perhaps most interesting about her attire was her dress, which began with a circle of cloth around her neck, separating into two, thin straps that connected to the bodice. The connecting pieces were rings that matched those in her ears, and the brocade pattern of the dress was almost exactly the same shade as the envelope he carried in his back pocket.

The woman in the portrait was almost sideways, so the whole of her face could not be seen. The shadows of her hair covered part of the image, and her body was turned even more, giving the viewer a glimpse of one uplifted breast.

She was beautiful in every respect, and Jamie wondered who she was until he saw the finely scripted lines at the very bottom of the image. It read: VALDIS WITH BLOOD ORCHIDS.

Jamie looked at the image again and saw the red flowers twined in her hair. This was a portrait of Ms. Valdis, to whom the old man had written.

She wasn't a fanciful person from some painter's imagination, a beauty to stare at while the old man sat at his desk.

She was real.

Jamie sat down in the desk chair and pulled the envelope from his back pocket. Who would know if he opened it and read it? Who would care?

"No one," he said aloud, his voice strange in the confines of the small trailer. "He had no one, and she returned the letter." Besides, he reminded himself, if he left the letter here it would most likely get thrown away at some point, and the old man's last words—as a writer?—would never be read. He deserved that much at least. And even if Jamie returned the letter to the post office, it would simply go to the dead file, to be pulped at some unforeseen point in the future.

Decision made, Jamie leaned back in the chair and carefully opened the flap on the envelope. He felt a tingle of excitement sweep through him, because never once in all his years at the post office had he opened a letter that didn't belong to him. Opening this one was invigorating, freeing, and in some unexplainable way, sitting beneath the portrait and in the old man's rickety chair . . . it seemed right.

Inside were several folded sheets of paper, and as he removed them, Jamie discovered that, as he'd suspected, there was something else. As he unfolded the sheets of paper, the dried petals of a red orchid fell free into the palm of his hands.

One of the flowers from her hair! he thought. *She is real.*

He carefully set the petals on the top of the desk, turned his attention back to the pages in his hand, and began to read:

Part II: The Geography of Memory

Dear Valdis,

Summer is winding down now, and for so long I have wanted to write to you, yet I found myself holding back. I stare at the portrait of you above my desk—do you remember when Sebastian painted it?— and I think that it is best if we remain nothing more than memories of each other. But autumn is coming, and after that winter, and though it does not snow here very often, I suspect that I will be dead long before the first frost.

So I took up my pen and, with some trepidation, I began this long, long overdue letter to you.

Here is something I remember: I am standing on the forty-yard line at the high school stadium in late autumn. The air is cold enough to make each exhaled breath a plume of dissipating white. I'm wearing a black leather jacket and indigo blue jeans with a white turtleneck beneath a black wool sweater. You once told me the outfit made me look like an angry preacher. The stadium is empty. Everyone has gone home except whoever is supposed to shut off the lights.

One by one, the big, white arc lamps go out with an odd, echoing clunking sound, and from where I stand, the announcer's booth fades into the night first, then the bleachers, and finally, inevitably, the field itself. For a moment, I know what it means to be invisible, what it means to stand in an empty place and contemplate the surrounding darkness as a permanent thing. The season is over, and the lights won't go on again until next year, and some other young man may be there for the end, but it won't be me.

I know you cannot back into the future, but what if the dark road looking back is brighter than the empty road looking forward? What if there is no road forward at all, and the past is all you have? What if the arc lights of your life are going out, one by one, and the cold dark is coming? That is where I am now, in the final days of my life, and I cannot help but look back and remember. I rebuild my memories one piece at a time—a word spoken, the color and cut of a shirt, an unseen but familiar sound in the whispering trees— until the memory I am recalling is whole and is true. I remember what I know, and sometimes, I try to forget, too.

I wanted, as you know, to be a poet, and I often ask myself if what I wanted to be was really a seeker of truth, of wisdom. In my years, I have discovered that there is little real wisdom to be found in words, only in the experiences we have over a lifetime. Yet there are some truths even I know; you will have to decide for yourself if the truths I have discovered are a form of wisdom, or just an old man's foolish sentiments. There are moments, times, images I remember; others are gone, like cigarette smoke in a high wind.

I know you cannot trust a first kiss, but I remember the first time I kissed you. I remember it so well that I can still feel your lips—the curve of them, the faint wetness, the "o" of surprise made by the corners of your mouth. I remember it so well that I can tell you with certainty that you tasted of strawberry cotton candy. I remember it so well that I can still feel the texture of your long, red hair in my hands, and the subtle curve of your body pressed to mine.

I do not, however, remember what you were wearing or what I was wearing or the song that was playing on the radio. I do not, sadly, remember what was said just before or just after, nor the precise time except that it was after dark, and in the far distance, the lights but not the sounds of the Hall County Fair could be seen, and not heard.

You and I had been there—that was why you tasted like strawberry cotton candy—and then we drove out, past cornfields high with summer and smelling green and fertile, to a narrow bridge over the Platte River. Below us, the shallow waters were black and smooth like dark mirrors, and above us, the night sky was filled with the silvers and whites of stars, the odd flickers of satellites, and (though I do not remember for sure) perhaps a planet or comet passing through our field of vision.

The geography of memory is strange—a land filled with unknown (and unknowable) terrain.

A number of years ago, I was riding a chestnut Arabian mare in the northern Nevada desert, and she stepped into an unseen (and unseeable) gopher hole. She broke a leg, and as I shot her in the head to end her suffering, the memory of kissing you, my Valdis, for the first time came into my mind, and that is how I know that memory and geography are unreliable sources of information at best.

I had ridden that path in the desert many times. How, then, could I rely on my memories of you?

And the voice of memory inside me says, *Because Valdis was your friend. You don't forget your true friends. You don't forget what happened.*

Is the voice of memory more reliable than memory itself? Than geography?

I do not think so, not really, but I often pray that it is, that dreams and memory and their voices *are* reliable. At least where you are concerned. In the absence of any real language, any effective words or wisdom, I can remember you, hear your voice, and know that as the darkness grows and winter comes on, I am not really alone.

You cannot trust a first kiss, Valdis, you told me that yourself. But I was too young to believe you then, and now . . . now I am too old and too alone to do anything but wish that you had been wrong.

Do you remember how I used to enjoy driving, especially at night? The sound of the tires on the highway, the switching between radio stations, going from one type of music to another to a talk show about UFO's, the sleepy sound of the windshield wipers *swish-swishing* over the glass if it happened to be raining.

Movement. That was the part I enjoyed. It didn't really matter if I was going somewhere in particular, but just knowing I was moving. The mostly empty stretch of Interstate 80, running out of the east and heading west, toward the distant sandhills, was perfect for driving at night. Sometimes, the traffic would be so sparse that it was just me and the stars and a radio station from Hastings or Kearney or Grand Island, bouncing signals off the cornfields and playing music just for me.

I covered a lot of distance in those days, and on some of those long drives, you came along. Do you remember those drives? I didn't really need the company—I liked driving by myself better than anything—but it was sometimes nice. And, to be honest, your voice was a hell of an improvement over Art Bell's anyway. You used to sing along to the radio, especially if you were feeling moody, and you'd tune in some late night show playing nothing but ballads.

Do you remember my telling you that you had a chicken fried steak and mashed potatoes voice? Ha! Valdis, you had a farm girl's voice: sweet, but not too high, and a little rough around the edges, as though you'd been smoking for a few years or had a little prairie grit in your throat.

We would move along, and you'd start to sing, and I'd say, "Valdis, you've got a chicken fried steak and mashed potatoes voice." I don't think you ever really knew exactly what I meant, but I'm old enough now to tell you that for me, your voice sounded a lot like someone singing me home.

Movement. Distance.

Sometimes, I think about you and me and those roads we would travel and how the distance between us slowly grew to be so long and so dark, like walking the rows in the cornfields on a night with no moon. But even the greatest of distances can be traveled, and I know this to be true, too, because after so long and so dark, I believe you are still, must still be my friend, and that somehow, despite the distance between us, you came to find me.

Your voice has returned to me. Sometimes, it is a voice from the past, reminding me of things I have almost forgotten. At other times, it is a voice from the present, calling to me out of the dark shadows of my mind, or a voice from the future, singing of bright light and sunshine on cornfields.

Your voice, Valdis, is a voice of light and shadow, and I know it well, despite the time that has passed since I last heard it.

I said before that you cannot trust a first kiss. It makes promises that are rarely kept. It makes promises in the mind and the heart that are rarely kept. A first kiss is the illusion of warmth in the long, white moments before one freezes to death in a blizzard. But each first kiss we experience creates a memory that lasts, it creates images in the mind that last like handprints in wet concrete.

I shouldn't have kissed you, but even now, I'm glad I did. That one kiss told me that we could never be lovers, but we would always be friends.

I am not a doctor or a psychiatrist to explain to you how or why memories work the way they do. Like oxygen or growing older or taxes, memory is something that simply *is*, existing for each of us so long as we draw breath. I once took the power of memory—its ability to call and be called upon—and that is the road that leads me here, to this moment, this transmission of my thoughts in these waning days of my time. Take it as you will, but I have traveled the dark highway of my memory, traversed the geography of the night it happened, and while I cannot tell you how or why memories work the way they do, I can tell you that some memories are barbed like fishhooks.

Some memories won't let you go, and the more you struggle—to find forgiveness, to forget—the more enmeshed in them you become. Until living with them is all you have, until the memories *are* your life, your existence. It is an unfair exchange, but it happens, and the real world becomes the shadow you see through lenses tinted dark, a place you live in but never touch, taste or feel. It becomes the memory, too.

I shouldn't have kissed you, Valdis, but I did.

And on that particular day in October of each year, when I would drive north, from Las Vegas to Reno, as fast as the car would allow me, and always—*always*—alone . . . I shouldn't have taken you along with me, despite how wonderful it was to see you. But I did.

You see, the memory of that kiss has stayed with me, but it is not nearly so powerful, so barbed, as the memory of the night I killed you.

Running into you after so long a time apart, with no words or letters exchanged, ended in your death and with me trapped here in the dark, waiting for my brain to catch up to my body. Waiting for the last of the stadium lights to go out.

Imagine how thankful, how grateful I must be, that the power of my memories has been able to call you back to me.

I can hear your voice, and the last thing that is left for me to do is to make sure that you can hear mine.

Part III: A Break from the Old Man's Past

Jamie looked up from the letter with a start, his forehead damp with sweat, though the trailer was cool enough. It wasn't from the heat, he knew, but from guilt. Reading the old man's letter to this woman who was dead—and why did he send it anyway?—would be enough to make any man squirm a little. For a man like Jamie, it was enough to make him squirm a lot. This letter was *private* in a way few letters truly are.

He looked at his watch and realized that what he should be doing right now was getting in his truck and driving back down the rutted dirt road, heading for the post office and the end of his day. The sun was fat and heavy in the west. Instead, he stood up and went into the tiny kitchen to find something to drink. On the refrigerator, there was a small note taped to the door. Jamie started in surprise when he saw that it read: *Mr. Marsters, please help yourself to some lemonade. The glasses are in the top cupboard to your left.*

Bemused, Jamie opened the refrigerator to find a large pitcher of the old man's lemonade. He took it out, found the glasses where promised, and poured some for himself. He leaned back against the scarred countertop and stared out the window that looked into the area behind the trailer. It was all empty desert except for one large cottonwood tree that had been there so long, it needed no watering—its roots would run deep, deep into the ground, all the way down to the dark aquifer where water hid in the high desert.

He sipped on the lemonade, savoring the cold, tart-sweet flavor, and wondered how the old man had known to leave him that note. Jamie had never once

been inside the trailer; they weren't friends or even
close acquaintances. He just delivered the mail, shared
an occasional short conversation, and tried to be kind.
He'd felt bad for the old man, living out here with no
one for company and no one that Jamie had ever seen
stopping by. Somehow, though, the man had antici-
pated that he would be here, inside his trailer.

Jamie finished the lemonade and put the glass in
the sink, then looked at his watch. He knew that he
should be going, but he hadn't finished the letter to
Valdis yet, and he wanted to. She had been a real
person, and the old man had killed her . . . and yet
he was writing her a letter and sending it as though
he fully expected it to reach her. He returned to the
living room and the desk chair.

There were too many unanswered questions for him
to walk away now. He had to keep reading, to see if
he could find out what was really going on with the
strange old man who lived in this tiny trailer and had
written a letter to a dead woman.

He picked up the pages once more.

Part IV: The Writer Voice

I know that I have to write about it, Valdis. What
and how it happened. But I have missed you so much
over these years, the secrets I was unable to share with
you, the little things that friends have: comfort in sorrow, laughter at bad jokes, small talk over strong drinks,
an understanding look. These *are* little things, yes, but
they are important. I suspect you know this, and understand why I resist putting it all down on paper.

Friendship and marriage have much in common, but
I look back at my own short-lived marriage and realize

that what makes the marriages work that last a life-time is true friendship. It is friendship—actually liking the person you are married to—that carries you over the dark times that inevitably arise. I tried so hard to save my marriage, but the truth is that during the good times, we were fine . . . the hard times is when things weren't fine. I have learned that real love isn't the water, and that while being in or out of love may be the waves coming in or sliding back to sea . . . real love is the sand. Real love is what lies beneath all the fleeting moments that are passing overhead.

I suppose I should tell you about the Writer Voice. The Story Voice. The voice that I simply cannot shut up despite the fact that all I have written since the last book is (very, *very* bad) poetry and checks. That Voice . . . it wants me to write, Valdis. It wants to turn every bit of my life into a story, as if it could take all the good and the bad and the often ugly times and put them into some sort of blender and make me spit it all out again. As if it wants me to regurgitate my life onto the page. I hate the Voice, and yet . . . I would not know what to do without it.

Even in my sleep, it speaks to me. Out here alone, waiting for the end of my life to come and taking Damn Dog for a walk through the desert or riding Damn Horse for as long as my joints can take it, I want to talk to you. But the Voice . . . it talks to me.

"Do you know what your problem is, boy?" it says to me. It calls me "boy," which I suspect it learned from my father. It wants out, wants me to write, and because I can't, won't . . . it will torment me.

When I don't answer, it says, *"I said, do you know what your problem is, boy?"*

Giving in, I tell it, "No. What is my problem?"

"You think too damn much. Life is never about the now *with you, is it? It's always about the past. You live there like a goddamn ghost. If it weren't for me, you wouldn't have written word one. I am your memory, your conscience (not that you have a huge one), and your parents. I am all you've got left, and ain't that a goddamn shame? I am your best friend."*

This is what angers me the most, Valdis. That it thinks it's my friend, when all it has ever done has brought me misery. "That's not true!" I tell it. "I had a wife, children, a family. I . . . I had Valdis. She is my best friend!"

"Bullshit," the voice says to me. *"You hide out here to avoid the truth. Your wife is your ex-wife and wouldn't spare you the cost of a cup of prison coffee. Your children hate you, hate what you became after the last book hit so big and scared you to death. And Valdis? Valdis is dead. Dead and dust and crunchy bones."*

That's the part that always shuts me up, Valdis. I don't want the Voice to know the truth. That you are dead, but somehow, I can hear *your* voice, too. Sometimes loud, sometimes soft, but I can hear you. I know you are not dead.

"I am you and better than you," the Voice continues. It is relentless. *"I am the you that spoke at conferences, told stories, found the rhythm of the language. I am your best friend, not a pile of bones, because without me, there would be no you. Without me, you'd still be selling cars in Appleton, Wisconsin, and drinking your lunch every day."*

"Yeah, maybe," I admit. "But without you, I wouldn't have written that stupid book that ruined everything, either."

I hate the Voice, Valdis. I hate it because it's always there. When it is quiet, I can think clearly. I can remember you, the past, and feel it for myself without any translation. Without interference. I can think of my wife and my children. I can look at it all and know it for what it was, what it is, and I don't feel compelled to make it into a storyline. Does that make sense to you?

"For you, boy," the Voice once told me, *"everything is a storyline. Remember when your mother died?"* Sometimes the Voice sounds like my mother, more often, my father. Sometimes, it is just my voice, only more resonant, stronger and sure. No matter what it sounds like, however, the Voice is impossible for me to ignore.

"I said, do you remember when your mother died?" it repeated.

I closed my eyes, Valdis, and I swear to you that I could almost picture the Voice. As if it had a body of its own. "Yes," I told it. "I remember. How could I forget?"

"You and I . . . we turned that into a story, didn't we? A hell of a story, in fact. All that pain on the page. That's when it's good, you know. When I can get you to go deep, organ and blood and bone marrow deep, and find some hidden artery that we cut open, and you get to bleed all over the keyboard. That crimson flood is what makes it really work."

I hate the Voice, Valdis, because so often it is right. I hate it because even when I think it isn't listening, it is. It's spent years watching, recording, taking down little details—the way rain sounds on a particular surface, or how a scar on my wife's leg looked, or the feel of silk sheets on a hot summer day. Or . . . or the way those orchids looked in your hair. Anything and everything it could pull inward and use later.

I hate it because it's right, Valdis. You were my best friend, but I killed you. I killed you, and all that was left for such a long time was the Voice. And the sorry, sad, truth is that if I could send the Voice away, never to return, I'd miss it. He's all I thought I had left until I began to hear you, to know that even in death, you'd found a way to reach me.

What I don't understand yet, my dear friend, is how I can hear your voice—I would know its tones anywhere—yet not understand what you are saying. I know it's you, but the words are unclear, as though they were coming through a wet, heavy cotton comforter. I wish I knew what you were saying, that your voice were as clear to me as the Writer Voice. I don't know how a voice, a sound in my head, can be something so hateful to me, and yet . . . so needed. The Voice is me, and I am the Voice, but we are *not* the same, Valdis. We can't be.

"We aren't," the Voice assures me now. *"You're the idea man, but I'm the one who gets the real words on the page. I'm the cutter. You'd never bleed enough on your own. You haven't got the stomach for it."*

"Fuck you," I tell it. I still have my own memory. I know what happened and how it happened. "I've bled plenty."

The Voice just laughs at me, Valdis. It laughs and laughs because it *knows*.

Despite the fact that I can hear you, feel you . . . I was the one who killed you, and it knows my guilt. Ha! Somehow or another, I've wound my way back to it, and I guess it's time for me to put it on the page. We need to talk about what happened, and I can only pray that these words will reach you.

Part V: Where Crazy People Live

Jamie looked up from the pages in his hand and realized that the old man wasn't just some strange guy living in a tiny trailer in the desert. The old man had been crazy. He was writing a letter to a dead woman— a woman he admitted to killing—and talking about the voices in his head. It was little wonder that he lived out here by himself. He probably had to.

He scanned the small living room once again and wondered about the books. Many of them were classics: works by Faulkner, Melville, Hemingway and others. Various other well known writers like Stephen King and Dean Koontz, romance authors like Nora Roberts and Danielle Steele, plenty of science fiction from Frank Herbert and Kevin Anderson. And many more still. He looked closer and saw that the shelves— which went from floor to ceiling—were double or even triple stacked in some places. The books were worn, too. These weren't display copies like he'd seen in some people's houses. The old man *read* the books he owned.

Jamie wondered where he kept his own books and stood up to look at the shelves more closely. He finally found them on the top of one shelf, not displayed prominently or proudly, but stuck up there as if they were afterthoughts. Most of them were paperbacks in various genres—a fantasy novel, a mystery, two science fiction novels. But there was one hardcover, and he pulled that one out and looked at the cover. It read: *Lies We Told: A Fictional Memoir* by Rhys

Dylan. The image on the cover was a strange close-up shot of three faces, the profile of a woman on each side and a man behind. Nothing but their lips and noses were visible and each of them held a finger to their lips in the universal gesture of "be quiet."

On the back, there was praise from a bunch of different reviewers, but the one that caught Jamie's interest was from the *New York Times*; it said, "Dylan's so-called 'fictional memoir' captures effortlessly the words we wrap around our own lives, the lies we tell ourselves and our loved ones. Demanding, scary and deeply emotional, this is a novel that should be shelved under both fiction and nonfiction, if for no other reason than whatever lies it contains are also truths that should be heard."

Jamie made a mental note to try to find the book and was reaching to put it back when a small piece of note paper slipped out of the back cover and drifted to the floor. He picked it up and read it: *Mr. Marsters, go ahead and take this copy, if you like. Though it adds little (if anything) of value, I signed it for you as well.—Rhys Dylan.*

Jamie opened the book and turned to the title page, where he read the inscription left by the old man: *For Mr. Marsters, who stopped by for lemonade and brought a little light into my last days. Best wishes, Rhys Dylan.*

A small shudder wracked through his body. The old man had known he'd come inside, had known he would get lemonade, would read the letter, find the book. He was clearly crazy, and yet . . . how could he have known all of that from a few front-porch conversations?

A quick glance at his watch showed him that he

should already have returned to the post office, but now he had to finish the letter. He had to read the rest of the story and find out what happened. Some mysteries—like the old man's almost preternatural ability to guess what he was going to do—could wait. The letter for Valdis could not.

Still carrying the book, Jamie returned to the desk, set it down, and once more turned his attention to the pages of the letter.

Part VI: The Distances Between Us

My mother died on October the 25th, as you know. Do you remember when I called you? That was during those long years when it seemed that the only times we talked—once every year or two—were to report on some tragedy or another. The loss of someone we knew. A marriage or a birth (tragedies in their own right), or just to make sure that the other was okay.

She died, Valdis, and every year after that, no matter where I was, I spent that day driving. I would get in my car or my truck—these last few years, I've ridden Damn Horse, because I don't drive anymore—and I would just go. As fast as I could, as far as I could. I never put that part in the story I wrote about her death, but it didn't matter. I drove all those miles for me, and I wish I could tell you why, but all I can do is guess. My best guess is that maybe deep down I figured if I drove hard enough, fast enough, one day I'd just . . . vanish. Like the way a beam of sunlight can disappear in an instant when the clouds race overhead.

The distances between us, Valdis . . . we've never been able to overcome them. I left Nebraska all those years ago, burning bridges and shooting flaming arrows behind me as fast as I could. I ran because I couldn't have you as anything more than a friend. I ran because the Voice told me I had to go, to escape, to find some place where the words would flow more easily than they do in that dumpy little town we grew up in. In short, I ran because I was afraid to stay, and in so many ways, I've been running ever since.

But the world is such a small place, you know? You can run and run, and as the pavement blurs beneath you and the wind sings in your ears, sooner or later, you find yourself . . . back where you started. It seems that I could never run far enough to get away from where I came from, never drive fast enough to escape my mother's death. And, finally, I ended up here. In this little trailer, hiding away from everything during my last days and wondering how I could ever get away from my responsibility to you. For what I did to you.

Do you remember the little gas station, Valdis? I can't recall its name, but it was situated across the street from that ugly casino you were staying at for the conference. You'd wanted some fresh air and a walk, and I was leaning against my car, filling it with gasoline. I looked up and . . . there you were. Walking across the concrete parking lot and looking as beautiful as the day I'd last seen you, your hair a bit shorter, but still as red as I remembered.

For a moment, Valdis, I couldn't speak, couldn't breathe. Time slowed down, and I knew that the distances between us had somehow shortened, that we were meant to see each other again. I found my breath, called your name, and you turned, and then that smile of yours, the thousand-watt one that can stop an entire room, was on your face, and in three running steps we were in each other's arms. Hugging and laughing and crying because it had been so long. Too long.

And in those few moments of excitement, Valdis, I forgot everything. I forgot that I was standing at the pump, filing up my car. I forgot that it was October the 25th and I was going to drive that day, as fast as I could, as hard as I could. I forgot my sorrows, forgot about the stupid book, forgot everything.

You said you'd lost track of me, didn't want to bother me now that I was famous. I told you that all of that was over. There weren't going to be any more books, and you asked why, and while I was trying to find the words to explain it, my gas tank overfilled and . . . and just like that . . . we were friends again. We were talking again, and it seemed the most natural thing in the world to ask you if you wanted to go for a drive with me.

I wish you hadn't said yes, Valdis. I wish I had told you to go back to your conference, that the night air in Vegas isn't refreshing but dark and heavy and weighted-down with guilts most people want to forget. Wishes and wishes. But I didn't. I asked you, and you said yes, and we got in the car and headed north.

We took Highway 95, the only real way short of back roads and byways to get between Las Vegas and Reno. I've been to many places in my life, but in many ways Nevada is the "Big Empty." There are massive areas of the state that are nothing more than desert, rocks, abandoned mines and forgotten shacks. The government owns most of it.

It's a long drive between the two places, about sixteen hours round-trip. I didn't set out thinking we would go all the way north. I lost track of time and space, got lost listening to you and seeing you again for the first time in so long, that before I knew it we were winding around Walker Lake. The road there is all curves and hills, and overhead, the stars were racetracks of light.

You asked me about my wife, my children, where they were now. I told you they were gone. She was now my ex-wife, and my children hated me. You laughed, soft, and said, "They'll get over it when they grow up," and just hearing you say it made hope blossom in my chest.

We talked of many things, but by the time we were driving around Walker Lake, the conversation had started to run dry. I made it clear to you, when you asked, that I didn't want to talk about the book or the stories or anything else. What I wanted to talk about was us, and I tried to force it. In my loneliness, I wanted you to tell me that you'd missed me, that you'd been wrong about us.

Instead, you asked me if I remembered kissing you. I said that I did, my eyes leaving the road, searching yours for some sign.

Then you said, "You shouldn't have kissed me, you know. I knew then we'd never be more than friends, and it would have been nice to have that little mystery in my life all these years. Wondering if kissing you would have changed everything."

Before I could reply, before I could find the words to tell you that you were wrong, that the foundation of love and marriage *is* friendship . . . the car left the road on a sharp curve. I remember the sound of the engine revving, the way we catapulted into space, spinning like a top.

I remember the way time slowed down, and for a

moment, I could see the stars overhead, and it crossed
my mind that the meaning of your name, Valdis, was
from the Scandinavian. Your name means "Goddess
of the Dead."

Then you screamed, the car hit the top of a rock
outcropping, and even over the crunching of glass, the
shriek of metal on metal on rock, I could hear the
snap of your neck as it broke, a branch breaking in
winter, cutting off your voice, your smile, your light.

And just as suddenly, it was over. You were dead
and I was alive. There's an old cliché that God pro-
tects children, drunks, and fools. I am a fool, Valdis.
I should have died in that accident, should have been
just as dead as you were. But I lived. I walked away
from it with little more than some minor bumps and
bruises and scrapes. The police blamed me for the
accident, and rightly so, but my punishment was far
less than I deserved.

I should have died, Valdis, and in so many ways, I
did. I have driven that road many times since. I have
raced to that curve, that hill, hoping that somehow the
hand of God would reach out to right the wrong, that
the car would slide, that I would be catapulted over
the rocky edges of Walker Lake to drown or be
crushed against the bottom of the precipice.

But each time, I lived. I lived and survived and finally, when I could take it no more, I moved here, to
this dingy little trailer in the middle of nowhere. I
took Damn Dog and Damn Horse and retreated to
the high desert to wait for death, for absolution, for
understanding.

You were always my best friend, Valdis, despite my
old man's longing for more, despite your knowledge
from that very first kiss that it couldn't be more. You

were my best friend, and when my eyes searched yours for the words I wanted to hear, my attention drifted from the road . . . and I killed you. For that, I cannot be more sorry.

And now, after all this time, I can hear your voice. I hear it dimly and I wonder what you are trying to tell me, my old friend. What words would you give me? Why do I suspect—hope?—that what you are trying to say is that you forgive me?

Why would you do such a thing when I do not deserve your friendship, let alone your forgiveness?

I am tired, Valdis. I am old and tired, and more than anything I want to rest. I hate what I have become, a man searching for forgiveness when none is deserved. I hate the Writer Voice that plagues me constantly, wanting me to write one last book about our friendship and how I killed you. Oh, how it promises to help me bleed, Valdis. It swears to me that I will bleed like never before, and the words will be both crimson and gold. But I have refused and will continue to do so.

I do not know how to pierce the veil between us. I do not know how to answer your voice, and so . . . I wrote you this letter, and I will send it to you at the only address I have. I am also sending along the petals from the red orchid you wore in your hair the day that Sebastian painted your portrait. They have always reminded me of you, and I have kept them with me all these years. I could not explain how it is they have retained so much of their color.

I do not believe this letter will reach you, not really, but maybe it will.

I am glad that you were—and still are—my friend, Valdis. I do not know what the next life holds for me, but I hope to see you there. To be able to tell you in person how sorry I am for my mistakes.

I no longer want to kiss you; I know now that some dreams must always remain dreams. But I would like to hold your hand and walk with you, and we can tell each other stories. And if there is a song, perhaps you will sing it, and I will feel like I have finally, at long last, come home. I suspect that it will be soon, and whatever truth or wisdom lies ahead, I will discover you waiting there for me.

Love Always,
Rhys Dylan

Part VII: Mysteries Solved & Unsolved

Jamie read the final lines of the letter several more times, feeling more than a little let down. Who had Sebastian been? Why did Rhys believe he could hear Valdis' voice but not understand her? Why would he write to her as though she were truly going to read it? Did he really believe the accident was his fault?

Sighing heavily, Jamie picked up the orchid petals and gently placed them back in the envelope. Then he took the pages of the letter and was carefully re-folding them when he noticed something on the back of the last page. Flipping it over, he saw that there was more writing on the back.

The light in the room was rapidly fading, so he switched on the desk lamp. The script was a woman's handwriting, elegant and smooth. It read:

My Dearest Rhys,
You are right, my friend. I have been talking to you, calling for you in the only way I could. You may not

have understood my words, but I believe you felt my intent.

I was singing you home, my old friend. I was singing you home and telling you that it is time for you to take a rest. Friends don't forget what has happened, but true friends always learn to forgive.

Come home now, Rhys, and we will walk and talk and be together once more. Friends in the next world, holding hands, telling stories and sharing secrets.

I read the book you wrote, Rhys. It was beautiful and moving and . . . and you are such a gifted liar. Who knows where your talents will bring you next?

Love,
Valdis

Stunned, Jamie looked over the envelope once more. There was no sign that it had been opened, no touch besides his and the firm writing on the front saying return to sender. And that was when he noticed something else, something that caused a shudder to run through his body. There was no postmark on the letter. Wherever it had been sent, wherever it had gone, no mark had been made on the stamp.

Outside, Damn Dog began to bark, and Jamie hurriedly put the letter back in the envelope and set it on the desk. Then he switched out the lamp and headed for the door. A battered old car was pulling up in the driveway, and a man in a rumpled white shirt and stained blue jeans, looking two parts determined and four parts lost, offered a feeble wave.

"Are you Mr. Marsters?" he asked.

Jamie shut the door carefully behind him, then stepped down off the little porch. "Yes, sir," he said. "I am. How'd you know?"

The man left his car door open and the engine run-

ning. He stepped forward and held out a hand. Jamie
took it and noticed that it was stained in various
shades and hues. "I'm Sebastian Gardner," the man
said. "Rhys told me you'd be here. I thought he was
crazy, but I guess he was right."

"*You're* Sebastian?" Jamie asked. "The painter?"

"Yeah," he said. "Still at it after all these years.
That's part of the reason I'm here."

Jamie shook his head. "I don't understand."

"Can't say as I do either," Sebastian replied. "All
I know is what Rhys told me to do, so I'm doing it."

"What did he tell you to do?" he asked. "Was he
really famous?"

Sebastian laughed, then turned and headed for his
car again. He went around to the back and opened
the trunk, then removed a package wrapped carefully
in brown paper. "Famous?" the painter asked as he
turned back. "No, not really. He wasn't into the promotion side of things, though his book still sells pretty
well. People still talk about it, teach it for memoir
writing classes, that kind of thing. If he'd kept writing,
I think he would have been huge."

Jamie gave a nod to the package. "What have you
got there?" he asked.

"A painting," Sebastian said. "For you."

"For me?" Jamie asked. He shook his head. "I'm
still a little lost."

"Rhys told me you would be, but he was my friend,
so I figure this is the least I can do." He unwrapped
the painting and held it up in the dim evening light.
"It will look better inside, but you can still see well
enough, I suppose."

Jamie peered at the painting and saw that it was a
portrait, too. Of the old man. In it, he wore a faint

smile, as though he knew a secret and was keeping it
from everyone else in the world. It was as striking as
the portrait of Valdis had been, though the work was
a little darker, the lines a little more heavy. In his
lapel, the delicate petals of an orchid were visible.
"When did you paint this?" he asked.

"Last week," Sebastian said. "Do you want me to
take it inside? It's yours now—along with everything
here, including Damn Dog and Damn Horse."

"What?" Jamie asked. "Mine? What do you mean?"

"I'm the executor of Rhys' estate. Other than some
money for his kids, he left everything to you. I figured
you two were close or something." Sebastian was already moving toward the trailer, holding the picture
by its frame.

Jamie followed. "No, no," he said. "Not really. We
talked once in a while is all. What am I going to do
with a place like this? I don't need a dog or a horse!"
He was starting to feel panicked, as if the whole world
were sliding out from beneath him.

Sebastian pulled a plain white envelope from his shirt
pocket and handed it to him. "He told me to give you
this. Said it would explain everything." Then he turned
and took the portrait into the trailer as Jamie followed
along behind, still stunned at the turn of events.

Once inside, he turned on the lamp again. It illuminated the painting of Valdis, but Jamie turned his attention to the envelope Sebastian had handed him.
Inside was a short note:

Mr. Marsters,

*In my life, I have learned much and, sadly, far too
little. One of the things I have learned is that friendship
is rare. Even though we were not close, you extended
a hand in friendship to me, keeping a lonely old man*

*brief but valuable company in his final years. For that,
I am grateful.*

*I have instructed Sebastian to leave most everything
here to you. All I ask is that you hang my portrait next
to the one of Valdis and take care of Damn Dog and
Damn Horse. They make good company when all others fail. Beyond that, mostly they eat a lot.*

*Thank you, Mr. Marsters, for your visits and your
friendship, as short as it was.*

Best wishes,

Rhys Dylan

"I don't understand," Jamie muttered again. "We
just weren't that close."

"I knew him for years," Sebastian said, eyeing the
wall where the portrait of Valdis was hung. "He didn't
let anyone get close."

"Not even Valdis?" Jamie asked.

"Valdis?" Sebastian said. "What do you mean?"

"Her," he replied, pointing to the portrait. "You
knew her, too, right? You painted her."

Sebastian laughed. "Sure, man, I painted her. But
she's not real. I made her up based on an old Scandinavian goddess of death or some damn thing. Rhys
loved the painting, so I gave it to him. Why did you
think she was real?"

Jamie felt his legs grow weak, as the mysteries of
Rhys and Valdis and the letter swirled about him.

"You should sit down," Sebastian said, sliding the
desk chair around and helping him sit down. "You
look like you've seen a ghost or something."

"I think," Jamie gasped. "I think maybe I have."

"What are you talking about, man?" Sebastian said.

His thoughts whirled as he tried to take it all in.
Valdis *was* real. At least for Rhys she had been. His

imaginary friend was a death goddess. Little wonder that his life had been plagued by so much darkness and depression, and yet . . . she wrote back. Or maybe the old man had done it all simply to be perverse.

"Oh, yeah," Sebastian said, leaning the portrait on the bookshelf. "I almost forgot."

"Forgot what?" Jamie asked, dreading the idea of any more surprises.

"Rhys told me to tell you something. He was real specific about it, too. Can't believe it almost slipped my mind."

"What?"

Sebastian's face screwed up in concentration and thought lines crossed his forehead. "He said to tell you that some mysteries weren't meant to be solved, just as some lies were meant to be told." He shrugged his thin shoulders. "Got any idea what that means?"

Jamie leaned back in the chair and looked once more at the portraits, then he nodded, slowly, as he realized that in some way, he did know what that meant. "Yes," he said. "I think I do."

"Good deal," Sebastian said. He sighed, then ran a hand through his dark thatch of hair and said, "I've got to get going, man. Still a long drive back to Reno. I'll get you the paperwork on this place in the next week or two, okay?"

Jamie looked around the tiny trailer and the hundreds of books. He looked at the portraits and the papers. From the doorway, Damn Dog peered inside, his eyes curious, his ear ragged. In his stall, Damn Horse nickered, wanting an apple or simply to have a talk.

"Take your time," Jamie finally said. "I'm not going anywhere for a while."

Sebastian nodded once, then left him to the trailer and the desert night. Somewhere outside a coyote barked and a rabbit screamed, and the stars appeared overhead. Jamie sat in the chair and thought about it all, knowing that whatever mysteries the old man had concocted, whatever lies he had told, most of them had been to himself.

And that was not necessarily a bad thing at all.

—for Ed Gorman

THE BIG EXIT

Bill Fawcett

THE bullet whined off the sand colored wall, but I did not bother to duck. I did look around to make sure that it didn't mean that Jeremy had been seen. But the shooter was already out of sight, so he was safe, for now. There were a lot of random shots being fired around Sadr City that day. A few were actually aimed at the American patrols, but most were what my Jeremy referred to as poor weapon control. I think he just meant that the Iraqis tend to waste a lot of ammunition by firing their AK-47s just to hear the bang. The stone dust that had been chipped away when the bullet hit high on the wall above him settled on my boy's uniform. The dust passed right through me, of course, since I was not real.

Once, a long time ago, we both had liked big noises. Even when little, he was never afraid of firecrackers or sirens. In those days we enjoyed just banging the garbage can lids together to hear them clang. They made a wonderfully silly sound that was almost music and all loud.

Jeremy forced himself lower, staying where he was crouched down behind a large, full garbage container of the type you need a special truck to empty. It was pretty obvious that he did not like loud noises as much anymore. I wanted to tell him I was proud because he was afraid and he wasn't crying. Jeremy was being a big boy. But about then I realized just how long it had been and that he really was all grown up.

I had been gone a very long time. I know I was somewhere when I was not with Jeremy, but it's a funny thing. It had always been this way. When you were with your child that other life seems far away and hard to remember. It had no meaning then, and it wasn't that I could not remember it but that I didn't care to bother. What mattered to me was that I was here, and that was because my special boy needed me again. And that felt right, because just maybe I still needed him as well. The important thing was that he had needed me and I came. Jeremy always called me Thumper, and so Thumper is who I was. If you could have seen me, you might have laughed. I had hoped Jeremy would when I first appeared again, but he didn't. His laugh used to be such music. When I made him laugh, everything seemed right.

You'd have laughed at me mostly because of the uniform. The metallic red coat and tricorn white and yellow hat are both garish and as silly as only the imagination of a two-year-old boy can conjure. I suspect, more than anything else from my red and white striped pants and thick gold lapels, that my image was deeply influenced by some cartoon version of George Washington or Uncle Sam. A picture on a cereal box seems the likely culprit. Though the First President was really kinda stiff necked and would likely neither have seen or approved of the resemblance. Under long white hair that curled at the end, just as Jeremy's mother's hair had way back then, was a wide, friendly face that was not really handsome, but so very safe and open. My eyes were brilliant blue, loving, and really did twinkle when we laughed. I always liked that twinkle.

We used to laugh a lot a long time ago. But that was before he stopped wanting me. We laughed back when Jeremy trusted me with the naiveté and enthusiasm only a child can generate. Those were the good times that make being an imaginary friend worthwhile. I try to remember those and to forget those last days before I was sent away. Things were different at the end, and I could feel myself slipping away. He still needed me, but I no longer fit into his world. It was a terrible helpless feeling made worse because my boy hurt so bad, and I didn't have any way to help him.

But I am back now, and I make an effort to put that time out of my mind. A mortar round screams by overhead. I know, because Jeremy now knows, that it is still rising and is no real threat. Probably someone with an "Eighty" taking advantage of the chaos to throw a "round" at some place known colorfully as the "green zone."

There were lots of new words in Jeremy's head, but not so many laughs. I paused and wondered if my silly dance could make him laugh again? It always did in the days before he sent me away. But this was not the time or place, and I was a little bit reluctant to find out the dance was gone with his youth.

Seeing the fear in my boy's eyes makes me remember those last horrible days. Jeremy cried a lot, but only I noticed. His parents were too wrapped up in learning to hate each other. We were under the blanket that last night, hoping the heavy wool would stop the sounds, or maybe just that the powerful demons that had been his parents would not notice us. They were yelling mean things at each other as had been almost always the case the last few months. Hurtful things about useless burdens and dark, evil secrets. I only understood what Jeremy did, and mostly he knew with certainty that whatever was wrong had to be his fault. He knew his father was big and strong and seemed to know just about everything. And the boy of four was just as aware that his mom was the most loving person in the world and the only one who knew how to make a skinned knee feel better. His parents were, well, his parents, the one thing he could depend on in a world that grew bigger, and more threatening, every day. He was the one who always seemed to do things wrong. So if there was trouble, it had to be his fault too. Mom and Dad were just too special for it to be them. So he hid from the sounds, and the light, and even the air so that no one could see his guilt and despair.

It was hot under the blanket and wet from his tears. I made the face that always made my boy laugh, but Jeremy just buried his head under his pillow and sobbed some more. I stayed there, but he was too deep inside himself to see me any more. Finally the front door slammed, and it got quiet.

Some time later he was brave and came out from under the blanket. The air was cool, and with the quiet Jeremy let himself have just a little hope. Maybe he was forgiven and everything was okay again. But a while later we could hear his mother sobbing, deep wracking sobs that hurt to just listen to. So they both sobbed, Jeremy and his mom, she on the living room couch and Jeremy in his bed, until each had cried themselves to sleep.

The last time Jeremy saw his dad was the next morning. He arrived with the crash of the door opening and a silent glare that froze all three of us over our breakfast.

"Just gettin' my stuff," the man who controlled my boy's world growled and brushed past. What hurt was that Jeremy never took his eyes off of his dad, but the big man never even looked at him.

They were eating Cheerios in chocolate milk. His mother used to make that on some days to make breakfast a little special. This was the last time she ever did that. They ate without tasting the treat to the sounds of drawers opening and muttered curses. It seemed a long time before his father appeared again. The man had changed into his dark suit and carried the big, gray Samsonite bag that smelled of mothballs. They never traveled much and only had that one suitcase. From the way he walked, it must have been heavy. My boy's mom stood up, but his dad gave her such a look that she took a step back and almost fell over her chair. He didn't seem to care and hurried past them both, his head rigid and eyes empty.

"Dad?" Jeremy risked just as his father opened the kitchen door.

The big man turned, and for an instant his expression softened and the pain in his eyes screamed to get out. But then his mother stood again, and the softness went away.

His father slammed the door hard. He left without looking back.

The rest of that day was a blur. I knew better than

to try to make Jeremy happy. He was pretty sure he would not only never be happy again, but also that his mom was going to leave him too as punishment for whatever he had done to drive his father away. So I stood by and waited.

Jeremy waited too. He waited and hurt, but each day just became grayer and less happy than the last. His mother made the food, washed his clothes, but she never said much. She tried a few times to talk and explain what had happened to her four-year-old son, but she lost the words every time, and they just ended up crying and holding each other.

With his dad gone and his mom lost in herself, my boy began to learn to be alone. He got used to being locked inside himself. Eventually he even managed to not want or need anyone at all. The problem was that I, his trusted and ever faithful imaginary friend, was part of that earlier time. The good times just seemed to fade away, as if they belonged to some other, happy child. Finally he had learned to not need me anymore either. Every companion knows that when they are not needed anymore, it is time to go away. Generally that is a happy time because the child has become a real, almost grown-up, person. A man or woman has found enough joy in the world that they do not need an extra push from a conjured companion. This was different. Jeremy didn't grow out or up; my boy just disappeared into himself and hid. Still, the way it is, that's how it always is. There is no fuss when a companion goes. It is not meant to even be noticed. We just fade away. So I did.

Now I realized it had been an incredibly long fifteen years, which was forever for an imaginary friend. But somehow Jeremy not only remembered me. I felt complimented and a little sad to say that his childhood companion was all he had to call on in his need. But in his need I was the one he turned to, and so I was back—his Thumper, the companion of his youth. Now my companion was alone and scared and wishing he were with me again under those blankets that made him feel almost safe. So, to what I suspected was real astonishment on both sides, there I was again. He was bigger, and older, but I was with my boy again.

Finally he looked up after taking a deep breath. He knew he had to do something. From the way his eyes widened, seeing me was a surprise.

"Thumper?" my boy sounded young again.

"Yep!" I tried to put on my most reassuring smile. We always smiled. "Right here."

"What? How?" Jeremy's voice trailed off as he looked past me at the run-down buildings of Sadr City. Seeing no one around, he stood up and then carefully looked all around, him again. Then he just stood there staring at me.

"Are you real?"

This was no time for philosophy. In this world I know I am not something solid or even part of it in any normal sense. So there was no use denying it.

"Nope," I grinned. "Never was. I'm you're imaginary friend, after all." I tried to sound chipper but likely failed.

"You sound different, more grown up," my grown boy half-accused and half-wondered. That took me a few seconds to accept myself. We were in unexplored territory here. Except in rare cases where the human was injured and became a boy again, we companions are rarely able to return.

"Because you are too," I finally explained with my best guess.

The young soldier that had been my child took a few moments to absorb the concept. Then he smiled; it was the old smile I knew from so many happy times. I wanted to do my silly dance, but I resisted.

It felt right to be there, but I was not sure why. Maybe we both just needed closure. Jeremy seemed pretty sure he was going to die soon. I looked around at the dirty street and run-down pastel buildings and felt in him just how far from home the place was.

An automatic weapon chattered in the distance. There were more gunshots, but none close.

I knew from Jeremy that we were in a place much more distant and deadly than the Midwestern home we knew before. This was a place that was even named after a man who hates Americans. That man's orders were to kill every foreign soldier on sight, and we were at least a mile from its edge and safety, and there were patrols of armed men roving all over. The sun was high and hot, not leaving many shadows. The air was dry and still full of grit from the gunshot dust, which was lifted by wind to twist up toward the small, closed windows high on both sides of the alley. There was no place to hide, and Jeremy knew he could not stay there, but he was afraid to move. Every corner he turned might be where he walked into an ambush or a mob.

It seems Jeremy had been on a patrol. He was in some sort of armored vehicle, and it was his job that day to ride on the top of it and man something called a "fifty." There had been a bomb. It had been placed or thrown at the side of his vehicle. The massive, armored beast had been pushed aside, and Jeremy was thrown halfway out of the protected area he had been standing in. Before he could recover, the driver had gunned the engine, and the jerk this caused threw my boy off and into the street. He understood why the man had hurried away. Very often the IED, as he called the bomb, is just the first part of a bigger attack. This time it had not been, but the result was that Jeremy found himself alone, hiding in an alley deep in the middle of a very hostile place.

It was my turn to look around. I could hear the sound of an engine getting louder. Then there was a grind of gears and the sound of something heavy on the road at the end of the alley Jeremy was hiding in.

He ducked, and I started to and then had to laugh. Only my own, personal child, with one exception I was not certainly not ready for yet, could ever see me.

The vehicle turned out to be an old British-made flatbed whose back was packed with men on benches wearing turbans and carrying rifles. It spewed soot from its exhaust while the men filled the air with anger. A few seconds after passing us, the truck turned at the next corner, and the sound and stench faded. Jeremy had just started to stand up when one of the high windows right over his head opened.

I stood frozen, and my soldier had to throw himself against the wall below the window to avoid being seen. Something flew out of the window, and Jeremy thought grenade so hard that even I dived for cover, but then the empty can clanked in the waste bin, and we both just stood there.

"If I stay, someone is going to see me or the curfew

ends. Either way I'm dead," Jeremy explained in a whisper, more to himself than to me.

I saw him reach down and pull out his only weapon, one of the squared-off automatic handguns that the army gives its tank personnel. He checked it and put a round into the chamber before returning it to the covered holster. His actions were very professional, and suddenly the child I knew seemed far away. With a look of grim determination the young soldier straightened and turned toward the empty street visible a dozen steps away.

"Let me check the road," I offered, hurrying ahead of him. I was still learning about this war stuff and had just realized that being invisible to everyone but him meant I could do so safely. We don't see our kids grown up. This whole thing was still new to me, and I suspect it would be to imaginary friends in general. We normally only give emotional support to our child. There were no rules on what to do when in the middle of a war zone.

You could see down the street for a few blocks in either direction. The street wasn't really straight, more gently rambling and winding around the buildings as if it was not planned but just happened. No one at all was in sight. I wondered at that for a second, and then the answer was in Jeremy's knowledge. Both the US and the local militia had declared an all-day curfew. To venture out into the street, or even look out your window, was asking to be shot.

This was good in that otherwise he would have had no chance of sneaking through the crowded streets of a ghetto packed with two million hostile Shiites. But it also meant that by being out he would instantly become everyone's priority target. The words "friendly fire" sounded very unfriendly in his thoughts.

"Clear, come on out," I yelled. I had been almost whispering, but I realized that was silly as only Jeremy could hear me. And then I knew what I could do. "Come on, I'll scout ahead and warn you at every corner."

For a moment Jeremy just stood there looking at me. It had to be a strange sight, me standing there and trying to look reassuring while my faux, spangle-covered Washington uniform stood in contrast to those tan and gray buildings. The yellow and white tricorn may be what finally did it. I doffed it and gestured for him to follow.

"Let's get home," my soldier agreed and almost, but not quite, smiled.

We made it two blocks before anything happened. I was watching everywhere while walking down the middle of the empty road, and Jeremy kept dashing from cover to hiding place along behind me. Twice we had to stop when I saw movement that turned out to be stray dogs. But once another truck of armed militia roared past going very fast. Jeremy dived behind a closed merchant stand just in time after I yelled, and he wasn't spotted. I just stood there as the old Ford pickup with a machine gun bolted to the cab's roof drove right through me. As it passed, I could feel more frustration than anger from the men in it. Those were some seriously unhappy dudes, and they desperately needed imaginary friends too. I wonder if they had companions like me in this part of the world?

We made it another quarter mile before things almost got really bad. The dry wind was picking up, and the air was filled with dust and litter, and Jeremy's eyes were watering. I was some distance ahead, and we were just passing by what appeared to be a small mosque. Jeremy was on the same side and just approaching the ornately carved double doors in a crouch. He was preparing to creep past them when one door began to open. The handgun had been drawn since the second truck had passed, and he raised it and gripped it with both hands.

The door was opening toward Jeremy. All he could see was a slab of carved wood moving just a few feet ahead of him. What I could see was that the door was being opened by a young girl all covered in those strange, black robes.

My soldier had his pistol ready, and I could sense the pressure of his finger on the trigger. To him mosques were a threat. The enemy often hid in them or stored their weapons there. He was ready to shoot at the first glimpse of a target.

"Don't," I yelled with all the force I could summon. "Don't shoot."

He didn't. At the last moment he raised the weapon above his head and ducked between the opening door and the wall.

The little girl took two steps out and looked through me down the street. She was young, barely taller then my chest, and had lovely brown eyes.

Then there was a frantic woman's cry from inside the mosque. The girl turned, and the one woman's pleas were joined by a chorus of feminine admonitions for the girl to get back inside. Frightened, she turned and dashed back inside. The door drifted closed behind her.

I could see Jeremy again. He must have gotten a

glimpse of the young child he had almost shot. He was just leaning there, staring at his pistol and looking slightly ill.

"You have to keep moving," I admonished more to distract him than from any need for haste. "It's dangerous here."

"Yeah, for everyone," he almost laughed back in a sotto whisper.

Twice we had to wait until groups of militia I had spotted moved or dispersed. Those were bad times. I would stand in the middle of the intersection keeping watch and chattering about what was happening to my soldier. He hid as well as he could, and we both hoped nobody else came along. Just like old times, my Jeremy would shake his head at my more absurd comments.

We rounded a corner, and suddenly Jeremy froze and then pressed himself even harder against a pale gray wall. I looked around but saw nothing. I could sense his deep concern but not the reason. Knowing what your boy is thinking and understanding it are two different things. I shrugged in an exaggerated manner to let him know I didn't see anything and then walked over to where he hid.

"This is the bad part," he explained.

I must have still looked confused.

"We are getting close to the edge of Sadr City. There is likely to be a sniper up there somewhere. They spot them all along the entry roads. Sometimes they get lucky and some noob forgets to button up," he continued. "I'll never know if one sees me until it's too late."

I looked at the three-story buildings that lined the

last five hundred yards before safety. In the distance there was a roadblock. Unless the Shiite militias were now using M1 Abrams main battle tanks, it meant safety for my companion. We were just beyond the effective range of small arms fire from the soldiers there. Close but not close enough. Those tanks looked a long way off.

We both stood and worried. It wasn't as if Jeremy had a choice. He had to try. But we both knew it was a bad idea. I could not just walk ahead and scout as I had. Any snipers were hidden on the top floors of the buildings.

Then it hit me. There was no reason I could not try to find the sniper. Then I could at least warn Jeremy where he was. Then my soldier could slip down the street on the same side as the sniper under the window where he watched and never be seen. I was quite proud of myself. But then I am sorta, kinda meant to look like a general after all.

Explaining my plan in a few words, I got my soldier to agree. He would stay put and wait for me to lean out a window and yell. Then he would hurry along the wall under whereever I yelled from. Jeremy agreed, though there was a sense of better than nothing in his tone.

I hurried. The longer it took for me to find the sniper, the more danger. There was always the slight chance that even this close to the edge of the ghetto a militia patrol could pass by and spot him. That or some desperate civilians breaking the curfew could raise an alarm. So I hurried from building, to building, slipping through locked doors and walls as needed. Mostly what I saw were miserable, frightened people

wishing the whole war would go away. Lots of women
and children keeping carefully away from windows
whose curtains were closed.

I found the sniper in the fifth building on the left.
He was set up on the top floor as expected. The militia
gunman was small, maybe no more than five feet tall
and slightly built. He was dressed in what might have
been an attempt at a uniform. Both his skin and the
uniform were stained. He sat there at an open window
reading from a small book and occasionally glancing
up and down the street looking for a target. His rifle
was Russian, with a French-made scope. I wasn't sure
how I knew about rifles, but I guess Jeremy knew,
and so I did too. Funny, but even this close the sniper
did not feel evil, just determined. I was equally determined that he was not going to get a shot.

I watched for some time. The man would study his
book for a minute or more before looking up again.
Finally I was ready to lean out the window. He had
just started studying that book again. It was time.

"One here, but you can get past!" I yelled down
the empty Sadr City street. "He is reading. Koran,
maybe. You can slip past when he reads. Half minute
bursts. Wait for the word each time."

I could see Jeremy get ready to slip down this side
of the road. If he could go right under the sniper's
perch, there was a good chance he would not be seen
even if the shooter looked up unexpectedly.

Twice I gave the word to run, and he hurried from
doorway to doorway. I had just seen him duck into
one when I was startled as the sniper leaned right
through me and out the window.

For a horrible moment I though he had seen Jeremy. That wasn't it, but it was almost as bad. He

yelled something I could not understand, and a man appeared in another window across from the sniper's on the far side of the road. He also had a long rifle with a scope.

I had almost sent Jeremy to his death.

"Jeremy, hide! Two snipers!" There was a touch of panic in my voice. I was not sure what the fate was for a companion whose mistake caused his child to be killed, but part of me wanted it to be horrible, and the rest was afraid I was about to find out. I could see my soldier press deeper into the shadow of the doorway he was in and freeze.

I could sense Jeremy's concern and frustration. So close to safety and yet no way past two snipers. Worse yet, I could hear the roar of another badly tuned engine and abused gear changes that marked one those militia trucks, and the sound was getting louder. He couldn't move without being shot, but if my boy didn't act soon, it would be too late.

I was proud and sad at having my second idea that day. Proud for thinking of a way to help my childhood companion to safety and sad at the price. I hurried down to where Jeremy hid and warned him to get ready.

"I'm going to provide a distraction," I promised. "You need to just get going, and don't look back." I paused and looked at the approaching truck. Jeremy seemed about to argue. "They won't be watching you," I insisted.

Jeremy seemed confused, but the sound of that truck was getting louder, and there was no time to explain further.

"Can you just trust me?" I finally asked.

His old smile came back. I could almost feel the ability to trust coming back to him.

"Okay, Thumper, let's do it . . . and thanks," he agreed, nodding.

There is, you see, one time that everyone can see an imaginary friend. It isn't used often because it can cause more problems that it prevents. Sometimes to save a child from being condemned for his friendship, we companions can become visible in your world. We can be seen not only by our child but by everyone.

It does not last very long and the strain of it means we can never, ever return.

We call it the Big Exit.

So with Jeremy perched to run, I made my Big Exit.

It must have been quite a shock to both snipers and the truckload of men just bailing out of the truck in the intersection behind us when a six-foot-three George Washington in a star-spangled jacket with gold trim appeared suddenly, high-stepping down the center of that Sadr City street.

I was the very image of the enemy. The cliché version of that which they had been ordered to destroy. The first few rounds passed through me within seconds, and then everyone opened up.

The street was filled with the sounds of weapons firing and confused shouts. Dust rose where dozens of bullets hit the street. As I expected, everyone looked at me, and no one even noticed a lone, camo-clad soldier who crept hurriedly along one side.

I just hoped Jeremy would not get clipped by a stray bullet or ricochet.

Me? I just kept strutting and high stepping along. I even waved at one of the snipers. He was so shocked he stopped firing.

My soldier, my boy, was past now and running down the street toward the roadblock. Men in uniforms like his poured out, weapons ready, but the bad guys were still concentrating on me. They swarmed around Jeremy, and the tank's guns rotated to point down the street.

When I saw he was safe, I began to let go. It was getting hard to stay in this world now. I had been visible much longer than even most exits called for. Then I saw him stop and turn just short of the sand bags.

I think he knew I would not be back. Jeremy waved, and even from so far away I could see that smile. He was smiling his smile, and it felt good. I waved back.

Then, knowing Jeremy was safe again, I could not resist any more. Even as I began to disappear, there was one last thing I wanted to share again. I started doing our silly dance.

Dancing, I said my last good bye to the fading sound of my boy's laughter.

WHETHER 'TIS NOBLER IN THE MIND

Fiona Patton

THE unopened government envelope lay accusingly in the center of the dining room table. The large and expensive gift basket sat no less accusingly beside it. George Prescott stood, studiously ignoring them both as he watched the driver of the red minivan that had just delivered the gift basket back up his driveway, trying to avoid the fence posts and cedar trees to either side. The unexpected early December snowstorm that had blown in the night before had hidden most of the potholes, and George winced as the van dropped into the largest of them with a heavy thud. He'd meant to get a load of gravel brought in since he'd moved to the county nearly two years ago, but it'd kept slipping his mind.

"Oh, well, as we seem to be here to stay, there's always next spring, eh, Lucky?"

The tiny, brown chihuahua tucked in the crook of George's arm sneezed at the sound of his name, then lifted itself up, propping one tiny paw on his shoulder so that it could see out the window.

"Of course," George added, eyeing the gift basket with a resentful expression, "there'll be just as many opportunities to forget it. Maybe I can ask Brandon and Fred to see to it."

Outside, as if on cue, the minivan screeched to a sudden halt as a dark blue Buick shot into the driveway, narrowly missing its side view mirror. George heard the van's driver shout a profanity as the Buick swerved around the pothole and stopped beside his dilapidated drive shed with a spray of snow and gravel.

His young cousins, Brandon and Fred Geoffries, emerged from the car a moment later. Each lit a cigarette, Fred answered the driver's gesture with one of his own, then both men ambled up the crumbling concrete steps of George's 19th-century farmhouse.

George watched them approach with a certain amount of grudging admiration.

Both men had the Geoffries' lean, rangy build and dark blond hair and wore ball caps, lineman's jackets, and jeans paled almost white stuffed into scuffed old work boots. They carried themselves with a confidence and an air of competence that made it easy to forget that neither brother was over the age of twenty-four.

Lucky began to bark an hysterical welcome, and George quickly set him down before he leaped out of his arms.

"Go on, then," he said with an indulgent smile. "Go and meet them."

The dog took off like a shot, and George eyed his laptop sadly.

"So much for my quiet day of writing," he noted.

Moments later, Fred appeared, the still smoldering cigarette stub tucked behind his left ear and Lucky tucked under one arm. Brandon paused a moment to toss his own cigarette into a snowbank and bang his boots on the side of the house before entering behind him. After setting Lucky onto the floor, Fred glared out the window.

"Hey George, why the hell hasn't Jesse come by to plow you out yet?"

"My paper sent it."

George waved in the general direction of the dining room table as the two men whistled at the sight of the gift basket.

"Your Torawna tabloid, you mean," Fred snickered.

"Yes, my Toronto tabloid. They must have received my letter of resignation."

Brandon glanced over at the card affixed to the handle with a gold and burgundy ribbon that read *"Happy Retirement! Good luck in your new life!"* "Looks like," he said in a neutral voice, "bout time you left that piece-a-shit rag, anyway."

"I suppose."

Fred tipped the brim of his orange Mill Valley Propane cap up to peer through the bright polka-dot wrapping paper. "Whoa. There's a whole lot of fancy shit in here, George. Aren't you gonna open it?"

"I was going to do it later."

"Why later?"

"Well, I . . ." George sighed. "No reason, really." He reached for a pair of scissors with a resigned expression as Fred headed for the kitchen to get them each a beer.

*   *   *

"What the hell is all this shit anyway, George?" Fred demanded once the contents of the basket had been spread out across the table. Lifting a jar of brownish paste up to the light, he peered at it suspiciously. "Onion jam? You gotta be kidding."

"It's caramelized onion comfit," George answered primly, lifting it from Fred's hand. "And no one invited you to comment. Or to try it either for that matter."

"I'll try the maple beer whatever-it-is," Brandon offered.

"Pate. And don't give me that look," George snapped. "I know very well that you know what pate is. And I hadn't planned on opening any of it right now."

Brandon glanced over at the government envelope still laying on the table. "That's not all you haven't opened," he observed.

George's face grew pink. "Yes, well, not as such, no, not yet."

"Your birthday was last week."

"I'm fully aware of when my birthday was, thank you."

"When'd it come?"

"The day before yesterday."

Fred glanced from the envelope to George's expression and back again. "So what's the big problem," he demanded, popping a strawberry-wine bonbon into his mouth. "It's money, ain't it?"

"It's a check, yes," George allowed. "An *old age pension* check."

Fred let out a loud bark of laughter. "Right. The Holy Grail of governments handouts. Can I touch it, George? Please. Is it made of gold?"

"No you can't touch it, and it's not a handout," George snarled at him. "I earned every penny of that in fifty years of hard work and sacrifice."

Fred laughed again. "Yeah, yeah, I know, that's what all the old timers say."

"Them that don't throw stuff at you for making the joke," Brand added.

"Only Auntie Maude." Fred cracked the lid on the jar of pate and offered a bit to Lucky on the tip of his finger. "It's money," he said bluntly, jerking his head at the envelope. "Money's money. Fuckin' cash it and go buy a Stairmaster or something if you're worried about getting old. Hey, pup, the food, not the finger!"

Lucky licked his chops unrepentantly and stared up at Fred, pointedly waiting for more.

"I'm not worried about *getting* old," George answered, lifting the dog out of reach. "I'm just having a little trouble with the idea of *being* old."

"Beats the alternative."

"I'm sure it does. Still . . ."

"You talked to Art an' Lloyd at yer birthday party, didn't you?" Brandon asked, opening a box of English crackers and retrieving the heavy silver plated cheese knife from the depths of the basket.

"Yes . . ."

"Well, maybe you should talk to 'em again. Pass the . . ." He glanced around the table with the air of a connoisseur. "Danish brie, will ya?"

George handed it over with a querulous expression. "What are you doing here, anyway?" he asked.

Fred grinned at him through a mouthful of hazelnut paste and crackers. "Saw yer cousin Jerrold in town. He sent us."

"Oh."

Ever since he'd been welcomed back into the south county's sprawling four-family community he was related to, George Prescott had struggled to come to some kind of logical terms with their unique abilities and their nonchalant acceptance of them without any proper explanation. Brandon, Fred and the rest of the Geoffries could cast illusions so powerful that even they couldn't see through them; Frawst, like Brandon's girlfriend Cheryl, could levitate people, beer cans, or even the heaviest farm machinery; Akormans could make any engine stand up and do tricks without a drop of gasoline to power them; and Mynakers, like George's grandmother, Dorothy, and his cousin, Jerrold, had the Sight.

"So Jerrold told you to come over and mooch off my gift basket?" he demanded.

Brandon shrugged. "More'r less."

"Remind me to thank him."

As the sound of Jesse Frawst's four-wheeler announced the arrival of their young cousin to plow out the driveway, Lucky began to bark again, and George just shook his head.

Most of the less exotic items in the basket had been polished off when their meal was interrupted by the sound of another car navigating the driveway's potholes. Lucky began to bark at once, nearly throwing himself from George's lap as a battered, old, white Pontiac pulled up behind Brandon's Buick.

"I seem to be very popular today," George groused. "I'm never going to get any writing done at this rate."

"It's Danny," Brandon answered. Then, as two six-year-old girls spilled out from the back seat, he nodded. "An' Rose an' Molly. It's chocolate buyin' time. They touched me up yesterday."

"Touched you up?"

"To the tune of ten bars. They're like a swarm of locusts all on their own, them two."

"They hit me an' Lisa up for six," Fred added. "Looks like it's your turn to eat shitty chocolate for the cause, George."

"Oh, dear."

"Count yerself lucky," Brandon continued, then rolled his eyes as Lucky turned to yap at him indignantly. "Last year it was Christmas cakes, an' I nearly went broke before they were done."

George glanced back at the chipped chihuahua mug sitting by his laptop where he kept his *money for when the families' children come selling things* with another sigh and went to open the door before Lucky barked himself into a seizure.

Daniel Geoffries was a tall, lean man in his late forties, thick, dark hair peppered with grey. He shook George's hand around the huge cardboard box he was carrying, accepted the offer of a beer from Fred, then dropped onto the couch beside the dining room table with a tired sigh. Lucky had already thrown himself into the arms of the quieter of the two girls and was now snuggled down into the crook of her elbow while the other girl launched into her sales pitch.

"It's high-quality chocolate with only the finest almond bits made right here in Canada, and all the proceeds go to supporting our local soccer club. How many can I interest you in, Uncle George?"

The girl gave George a penetrating stare, and he was surprised to see that her wide, blue eyes did not go dark the way the rest of the families' usually did when they wanted to emphasis a point with one meta-physical ability or another.

Daniel chuckled at George's nonplussed expression. "That there's Molly," he said. "An' this here's Rose," he added, indicating the other girl who had perched herself on the edge of the couch, Lucky still held gently in her arms. The dog looked as if he'd fallen asleep, and George smiled at him fondly.

"You don't really have to buy any if you don't want to," Daniel continued, "but to be honest, the sooner we get 'em sold the sooner I can get home to my own supper."

"And it's for a very good cause," Molly added emphatically. "Soccer promotes team work, physical fitness, and settling disputes peacefully. And every bar is wrapped in a seasonal, decorative sleeve that makes it an excellent Christmas present for those hard to buy relatives on your list."

"Well, I suppose I could buy a bar or two," George offered, wilting under the pressure of both her and Rose's expectant expressions. "How many do you have left?"

Once Daniel and the girls had left, George eyed the two dozen bars of chocolate with a glum look. "Well, I suppose I can always take them to Wanda's bingo night," he said morosely.

Brandon snorted. "She won't thank you," he observed. "That girlfriend of yours told me she was trying to lose weight before Christmas. Better just throw 'em in the freezer; they'll keep."

"Hell, stuff each one in a candle holder," Fred added sarcastically, "there's enough wax mixed in to that *high-quality chocolate* to light up a room."

"Hm." Unwrapping one absently, George sat down before his laptop and, opening a file marked *Family Tree,* began to scroll down. "That little Molly is certainly a pistol," he noted. "Let's see, Daniel Geoffries. I don't seem to have him listed."

"He's one of Uncle Albert's," Fred supplied, opening another bar. "He and Tanya married right outta high school. They work together up at the cement plant."

"Tanya . . . ?"

"Geoffries. Lloyd's daughter."

"That would make them first cousins, yes?"

"Yep. Sammy was born right after the wedding."

George was typing madly. "Sammy?"

"Samuel Albert, their first."

"Right after?"

"Damn near right after."

"You know how it goes," Brandon supplied.

"Slowed down a bit after that," Fred continued. "They had Baby-Danny about three years later. Course, he don't care much for the baby name these days, but he's gonna be stuck with it forever. Old people've got memories like steel traps for that sorta thing. Don'tcha, George?"

"Shut up."

"Rose now, she was kind of a surprise," Brandon added, glancing at the screen over George's shoulder. "Tanya thought she was all done with babying. That's Mackenzie Rose Geoffries," he expanded. "She's a quiet kid; kinda lonely, I guess, with both her brothers already grown up and gone an' no kids her age livin' nearby. That was, until Molly came along about a year ago."

"So Molly's a cousin?"

"Not exactly," Fred laughed.

George sighed, expecting another tale of complicated family genetics and relationships to muddle up his filing system. A number of the four families' children had been conceived while their parents had been *on a break* from each other—at least two in every generation from what he could sort out—and more had been born either out of wedlock or very nearly out. His friend and cousin Art Akorman had once said that the families only married when the oldest was able to serve as flower girl or ring bearer. But somehow they all knew how they were related, and so George paused, fingers hovering over the keyboard expectantly, as the two brothers exchanged a glance.

"Molly's imaginary, George," Brandon said solemnly. "Rose is a Geoffries after all."

The phone rang the next morning just as George had managed to almost sort out how he was going to input this latest surprise into the family tree file. With a faint groan, he stood, lifted Lucky out of the dog bed beside his laptop, and headed for the kitchen. He had planned to have a phone jack put into the dining room but had somehow never gotten around to it. Like the load of gravel, he supposed.

"Yes, it's official," he sighed. "I am old and dotty."

Pulling the ancient rotary phone from the top of the fridge, he winced as it crackled loudly in his ear—technology was very uncertain in this end of the county. On most days he counted himself lucky that his laptop worked.

"Hello?"

"Hey George." Thanks to the Geoffries ability, Fred's voice came through loud and clear. "I need you to do me a favor."

"Thanks for taking us around selling, Uncle George," Molly said brightly as she and Rose settled into the back of his SUV with Lucky, dressed in a tiny, red Santa suit for the season, seated on Rose's lap. "Dad's on double shift today, an' we're real close to selling out."

As George maneuvered out of Daniel and Tanya's narrow driveway, he eyed the three large boxes looming over the back cargo area with alarm. "You're very welcome, Molly. Um, how many boxes have you sold already?"

"Ten an' a half. Whoever sells the most bars wins a bike, an' we're just two bars behind Caitlin Frawst, an' she cheats 'cause her mom takes 'em to work with her."

"I see. So, who haven't you sold any to yet?"

Rose pulled a piece of paper from the pocket of her overlarge ski jacket, and the two girls and Lucky bent over it while George tried hard not to stare through Molly. He'd thought he'd gotten used to the Geoffries illusions, but this was the first time he'd ever had a conversation with one. That a child as young as Rose could maintain such a high level of clarity was amazing.

"There's Grandpa Art an' Gramma Janet," Molly read out loud. "Great Auntie Maude, Uncle Kevin an' Auntie Bev, an' Great Uncle Charlie an' Great Auntie Peggy. Oh, an' Grandpa Albert says he'll buy a couple more if we come by after *Jeopardy*. We woulda had Uncle Randy an' Aunt Carol, but Cody's sellin' too. But those should do for today."

"Yes, I'm sure they will," George allowed. Most of

the people on Molly's list were either middle aged or elderly and all of them would be expecting them to *visit* for a time. They'd be lucky to be finished by midnight.

"Let's try Grandpa Art an' Gramma Janet first," Molly said, breaking into his mournful reverie. "Gramma Janet always makes oatmeal cookies on Saturday mornings."

"Oh." George brightened at once. "That's right, she does."

Art and Janet Akorman lived on the outskirts of Mill Valley in a small yellow bungalow, festooned with Christmas lights that didn't plug into anything. Their short driveway was plowed halfway across the front and side lawns, revealing a dozen cars, trucks and pieces of farm machinery in various states of repair lined up beside a quonset-hut style garage three times bigger than the house. Two black labs and four shih-tzus greeted them noisily when they pulled up and Lucky leaped into the passenger seat at once, barking furiously and paddling his tiny paws on the dashboard until George was afraid he would set off the air bag.

"All right, all right, just a moment."

He caught the diminutive dog around the middle with one hand and, opening the driver's side door, set him carefully down on the ground. Art and Janet's dogs were all friendly, and George no longer worried about Lucky getting eaten, stepped on, or bitten. Led astray into some hideous dead skunk or raccoon was another matter however, and he eyed the pack of dogs sternly before exiting the car behind Lucky.

"*Don't* roll in anything," he warned them. "That's a new dog coat."

Labs, shih-tzus and chihuahua all ignored him.

*   *   *

Art Akorman was a heavy-set man in his mid sixties, his brown hair long ago gone to white. Of an age, he and George had become good friends in the last two years, and he could always be counted on to dredge up an old story about the families or offer a bit of practical advice on how to survive in the country.

As Molly launched into her sales pitch, George settled into the large, blue sectional that Art and Janet's kids had bought them for their fiftieth wedding anniversary with a contented sigh. By his calculations, after the girls had finished selling their chocolate bars and he and Art had finished catching up on the latest news out of Mill Valley and Greenville, it would be just about noon, and Janet would invite them to stay for lunch. Friday was meatloaf night at the Akorman house, and Saturday noon was meatloaf sandwich day. George loved Janet's meatloaf.

Removing Lucky's coat, he accepted a coffee and a plate of warm oatmeal cookies and settled back with the dog on one knee and the cookies on the other. He supposed he could get used to selling chocolate door to door, he mused as Lucky began to stare intently at the plate. If he had to.

Events played out exactly as he'd expected. Seated around the kitchen table, George surreptitiously watched Molly eat lunch with the rest of them—meatloaf sandwich, carrots from Art's garden, and nine day pickles that Janet and her daughter Lisa had laid down last summer—and wondered if her food was imaginary as well. He supposed it would have to be. Assuming that both Art and Janet knew that Molly herself was imaginary, he marveled at how easily they interacted with her as if she were just another one of their dozen or more grandchildren.

Every now and then, he would take a peek at Rose. The girl sat eating quietly, seemingly engaged in the conversation, but her eyes were wide and dark, and George realized that he had never actually seen their true color since he'd met her.

Two hours later, lighter by half a box and with Lucky's belly tight and round from too much meatloaf, they pulled out of the Akorman's driveway.

Rose carefully tucked their money into a ziplock bag, then glanced expectantly at Molly.

"Great Auntie Maude's in Mill Valley," Molly answered thoughtfully. "But she'll be down for her nap right now, an' Uncle Kevin won't be home from cuttin' wood with Uncle Brandon an' Uncle Fred yet."

"Yes, but your Auntie Bev should be home," George supplied. "She doesn't baby-sit on Saturdays."

Both girls gave him an identical look of calculated greed.

"Auntie Bev'll only buy two bars," Molly explained patiently. "Uncle Kevin'll buy at least six."

"I see."

"And the sooner we sell out . . ."

"The sooner we go home, yes, I understand."

"Great Uncle Charlie's place is up Greenbush Road. We could go there first an' then swing around to Great Auntie Maude's, an' after that Uncle Kevin should be home."

George nodded. "Great Uncle Charlie's it is then."

Greenbush Road was more of an isolated dirt lane than an actual road. Large, mature maple trees loomed over the car, creating a soft, thick canopy despite their lack of leaves. The flat sides of the road had been plowed back to the edge of the well-cared-for cedar rail fence that separated the verge from the fields beyond, and George nodded approvingly.

"It seems the plow has been by," he noted.

Molly shook her head. "No, that's Great Uncle Charlie," she explained. "He has a plow on the front of his lawn tractor. In the summer he keeps it all mowed down."

"Ah." George had noticed this before. Half the ditches in the county were kept to golf-course height by old, retired men on lawn tractors.

Wondering absently when he was going to find himself half a mile down his own road on a brand new John Deere, George turned into a well-plowed driveway beside a green mailbox painted with flowers that read: *"Charles and Peggy Geoffries."*

As at Art and Janet's house, half a dozen dogs gave them a noisy greeting when they pulled up to the old, brick farmhouse at the end of the drive. They parked beside a long line of trucks and old cars, some of which were up on blocks while others showed the signs of more current use, the dogs swirling around them like a swarm of furry bees.

Unfamiliar with these dogs, George held Lucky high up by his shoulder as he left the car, but both Molly and Rose greeted them happily. Rose fished a dozen chocolate bars from the back, and together, they made their way through the muddy, snow-filled farmyard as a pair of cats peered suspiciously at them from the top of the neatly stacked woodpile. The stone and timber barn and half a dozen outbuildings and silos were much closer to the house than was legal in this day and age, and George guessed their age at more than a hundred years.

The man who met them at the door was close to that age himself.

Charles Geoffries was a thin, white-haired man of ninety, his lean frame bent and his large hands gnarled and swollen from arthritis, but his blue eyes sparkled as he spotted the girls. Accepting a kiss from each of them, he listened gravely as they introduced George and explained quickly how he fit in to the family tree, then ushered them into the covered porch.

The cloying aromas that always lingered in old, old farmhouses enveloped them at once: damp stone, wool rugs, moth balls, furniture polish, and woodsmoke overlaid by baking bread and just a hint of kerosene. George breathed it in with pleasure as he removed his boots, then followed the girls into the huge county kitchen.

As at Brandon's farmhouse, the kitchen was the main center of activity. A woodstove sat in one corner with a wood-burning cooking stove at the other and a more modern kerosene heater peeking out from beside the fridge. A large harvest table dominated the middle of the room, with a dozen mismatched chairs covered in hand-crocheted seat-covers around it. A wooden china cabinet and sideboard covered in lace doilies and figurines stood against one wall, and a well-worn couch draped in a brilliantly colorful afghan sat along the other. Charlie's wife, Peggy, a round woman with pale gray eyes and a warm smile, paused long enough to say hello before returning her attention to the dough she was kneading. Half a dozen children

ran about from the kitchen to the dining room and
back, while the sound of a television filtered in from
somewhere in the depths of the house.

Peggy shook her head. "That's our two boys, Doug
and Vernon," she explained. "They do the milking for
their dad these days, but you won't get them in here,
not with the game on." She turned with a frown as
the sound of angry lowing joined the sounds of barking outside. "Tyler, go tell them dogs to shut up, will
you? They're upsettin' the cows."

"Ok, Gran!"

A boy of about ten pounded out the door, yelling
the names of various dogs at the top of his lungs.

"Now," she said as Charles gestured at George to
make himself comfortable on the couch before plug-
ging an ancient kettle into a wall outlet that seemed
just as ancient. "Why don't you help me here, Mackenzie Rose, while Molly tells us about those candy
bars of yours."

Time passed quickly in the warm kitchen. Children
came and went, fetching beers for their fathers in the
sitting room or eggs from the hen house for their
grandmother. George joined Charles for a cup of tea
and a scone, listening to Molly's now familiar speech
and quizzing his hosts on their place in the family.
Charles had been born in 1912 and Peggy in 1914, and
between them they had a wealth of stories and lore
that made his head spin.

Finally, as the winter sun began to set, sending strips
of sunlight and shadow across the room, the old, mahogany clock on the sideboard began to chime half
past four, and he stood with an expression of real
regret.

"We should be getting on," he said shaking hands with Charles. "But this has been wonderful. I very much hope I can come by again with my notebooks. I'm writing a personal history of the families, and I would love to hear more, if you wouldn't mind."

Charles nodded. "You're always welcome."

"What's your phone number?"

The old man just laughed. "Never had no phone," he said. "Didn't want the 'lectricity neither, but the boys insisted about, oh, goin' on twennie years ago now. No, you just drop by whenever. We're usually home. We've got years of old photos that nobody's touched for a decade or more. You're welcome to go through 'em. There's some of your grandmother as a girl. Her an' her sister Elsie used to pick strawberries in our north field every summer. Thought I might marry Dorothy myself, but she went and fell for a city feller," he said with a mischievous grin. "Course, I'd already tipped my cap at the prettiest girl in the county by then."

Peggy cast him a fond look tinged with mock severity. "Best keep to that story, Charles Douglas Geoffries, if you want your supper tonight," she warned him. "Now, Mackenzie Rose, I'll think we'll be having . . ." she glanced at Charles a moment. "Two bars. One for the children and one for the adults. No arguments, old man," she admonished as Charles opened his mouth to protest. "You're not supposed to have candy at all with your diabetes. Be thankful I'm letting you have any."

Charles stood with a sigh. "Come on, I'll walk you out," he said. "An' just maybe I might have a coin or two in my pocket to buy a couple more bars," he whispered, winking at the girls.

*   *   *

The farmyard seemed dark and cold after the warm kitchen. The cats had disappeared, and even the dogs seemed less interested in barking at them as they made their way back to George's SUV. Handing Lucky to Rose, George buckled in, then headed back up the long farm drive.

"It's getting late," he noted. "Perhaps we should call it a night."

Daniel was able to take the girls out selling the next day, so George spent Sunday catching up on the bits of freelance writing he had contracted for the local paper and getting as much of what Charles and Peggy had told him into his computer as he could remember.

Monday morning dawned cold and damp, the cloudy sky threatening another storm. He'd just finished jotting down a dozen or so questions he wanted to ask Charles and Peggy when a knock at the door made him jump. He glanced worriedly down at Lucky curled up in the dog bed beside him, and the chihuahua opened one eye with a uninterested expression.

"Some guard dog you are," George admonished as he pushed his chair back and stood with a groan. "You usually bark at bumblebees and hummingbirds."

The dog yawned impudently at him, then tucked his nose under his paws and went back to sleep. Wondering at this unusual behavior, George went to the door.

His Cousin Jerrold stood on the step, and George blinked at him in surprise. Of all the Mynakers, Jerrold's gift was the strongest. He'd never been out to George's before, and, although George was not surprised that he knew where to find him, he was surprised that he had. Jerrold rarely went farther than the A&P parking lot, where he spoke prophecy and sold rope out of the back of his truck.

Now Jerrold shook his head, his long white beard waving across his faded, black coveralls, when George invited him inside.

"I was just up to Art's place for a brake line," he explained, jerking one large, grubby thumb in the direction of his old half-ton Ford. "Just thought you might like to know; Charlie Geoffries died early this mornin'."

The funeral was held at the tiny, funeral home in Mill Valley. As was the case in rural communities, most of the families came to the visitation held the day before. As he made his way through the small viewing room, George spoke briefly with Art and Lloyd and Albert, nodded to Brandon and Fred, standing with their families at the open back door, where they could talk and smoke at the same time, then stopped before the open casket surrounded by flowers.

Charles Douglas Geoffries lay on the white satin dressed in a black wool suit some decades out of date, his gnarled hands placed across his chest and his Legion tie pin and World War II medals prominently displayed. George stood, staring down at him for a long time, mulling over lost opportunities, when he heard a harsh cough beside him.

"He was a fine man."

He turned to see Brandon and Fred's grandmother, Grace Geoffries, standing, leaning on her cane, beside him. "We were at school together," she continued, looking down at Charles with a fond expression. "Him an' me and Peggy, Clifford Mynaker an' yer Grandma Dorothy, Willie an' Eula-May Frawst, an' a few others. They're all gone now. I'm the last of 'em."

George felt a sudden, cold, tingle run up his spine as the Mynaker gift, so diluted within him after a full generation away from the county that the Sight barely even colored his dreams, began to stir.

"But surly not Peggy," he said in a small voice, somehow knowing the answer even before he asked it. "I met her last Saturday. Didn't I?"

"Did you?"

He nodded weakly.

Grace gave a slight, one-shouldered shrug. "Charlie was a Geoffries," she said simply. "An' one of the strongest I ever knew."

"And Peggy?"

"Died of the cancer in 1973."

"But she seemed so real," he protested, feeling as if his head were wrapped in gauze. "How do their sons feel about . . . no wait," George paused as he saw Grace's expression. "The boys too?" he asked.

"Yep. Dougie died in Korea. Vernon rolled his tractor a few years later. Charlie quit farming after that. Didn't have the heart to keep goin' with nobody to leave it too, I guess."

"So Douglas and Vernon never had any children either?"

"Nope."

George shook his head with a wondering expression. "I met them all," he said. "Peggy, Douglas, Vernon, their children, cats and dogs and . . . cows and chickens. It was. . . . nice. It was . . . comfortable."

"I dare say it was. Old Charlie had years to perfect

it while the farm fell to ruins all around him. Kevin tried to get him move in with him an' Bev, but he wouldn't have any of it. You can understand it, I suppose. Why leave the life you want if you can make it seem as real as if you were really livin' it."

George stared down at Charlie, his lips pursed in thought. "He had blue eyes," he said after a time.

"Hm-hm."

"No, I mean all through our visit, his eyes never went dark. Your eyes, the families' eyes, they always go dark. Even Rose's." He turned to see Rose and Molly standing quietly beside their parents. No, beside Rose's parents, he amended.

Grace shrugged again. "Like I said, he was strong. Likely, he carried the illusion over to his eyes so he wouldn't ever be reminded that Peggy an' the boys were really gone, not even in his mirror when he shaved in the morning."

She turned. "I saw him Sunday, took a pie over an' had a nice visit with him an' Peggy."

She cast him a sharp glance when he stared at her. "Don't you look at me like that, George William Prescott. Peggy Geoffries was one of my best friends. I was maid of honor at her wedding, an' she was matron of honor at mine. I missed her. I still do. An' like you said, it was comforting. Charlie had a gift. A strong gift."

George shook his head, unsure of what to say as Grace turned away. "Now I'm headin' home," she continued. "I'm an' old woman an' I'm wore out. I've buried too many friends an' family over the years." She jerked her head in the direction of a wooden box sitting on a side table. "Charlie wanted you to have

those," she said. "They're all his old photos. Said he
was glad he had someone to leave 'em too. It gave
him some peace at the end. You take care of 'em."

She hobbled away, and after a moment, George
made for the table.

The box, an old apple crate, held about a dozen
cracked and faded leather and cardboard photo al-
bums, neatly labeled by month and year. On the top
was a single black and white picture of two young girls
in calico print dresses and straw hats standing in front
of Charlie's stone and timber barn. The writing on the
back read: *"Dorothy and Elsie, 1928."*

The visitation began to break up about an hour
later. Charles would be interred until spring in the
small mausoleum on Blind Duck Island where most
of the family had been buried since the first of their
line had settled there in the seventeen hundreds.

As the sun began to set, George followed Brandon
and Fred outside, blinking in the cold, December air.
Daniel and Tanya were standing by their Pontiac, talking to Kevin and Bev while Rose and Molly drew
pictures in the snow with dried teasels a few yards
away, and he wandered over to them, smiling as a pair
of blue eyes and a pair of black eyes looked up at him.

"Hello, Uncle George," Molly said solemnly.

"Hello, Molly; hello Rose." George turned to the
quieter of the two girls with an earnest expression.
"You know, Molly is a very good illusion, Rose," he
said gently. "One of the best I've ever seen."

She nodded.

"I tell you what," he continued, "if you come by,
say . . . after *Jeopardy*," he added with a smile, "I'll
buy another dozen bars. But will you do me a favor?

Will you give the sales pitch yourself, because I've never heard you speak and I'd like to."

The two girls exchanged a glance, then Rose nodded again.

"Rose, Molly! Come on, we're going!"

At the sound of Tanya's voice, the two girls gave him identical waves of farewell, then headed for the Pontiac at a dead run. George watched Daniel open the back door for them, then close it once again after both girls were safely inside.

He found Brandon and Fred leaning against the funeral home's front door railing having a cigarette. He frowned at both of them, and Fred grinned back at him.

"You cashed that check yet?" the younger man demanded.

George shook his head absently, watching the Pontiac pull out of the funeral parlor's gravel driveway with a frown.

"All of Charlie's life was an illusion," he observed quietly.

Fred gave a careless one-shouldered shrug much like his grandmother's, and George shook his head at him.

"You don't think that it was a little unhealthy?" he demanded.

"Nope."

"He lived all alone for years and years with no one in his life, living an illusion, living a lie, pretending his wife and sons had never died, and you don't think that was unhealthy?"

Now it was Brandon's turn to shrug. "Made him happy," he said simply.

"But it wasn't real." George shivered slightly as the Mynaker Sight prompted another thought to occur to him. "How much of the life the families live is actually real, Brandon?" he asked suddenly.

"How do you mean?"

"You know what I mean. How much is real, and how much is a powerfully crafted Geoffries' illusion? How many of the people listed in the family tree on my computer, or the people that came to George's visitation for that matter, are actually real?"

Brandon took a long draw on his cigarette before answering. "I could tell you they're all real," he said. "Or at least most of 'em were real once."

"How many are imaginary?" George pressed.

"A few here and there over the years. A kid dies too young or a kid's never born. Someone goes to some war an' never comes home. Someone else rolls a tractor or crashes a car or swamps a boat. The people left behind can't cope, so they bring 'em back. It happens. It's the way. It's our way."

"I need to know who," George insisted. "It's one thing for the families to use their abilities to cheat at bingo or levitate their cars into tight parking spaces; it's quite another to use them to deny reality."

Brandon tipped his ball cap up to scratch at a faint scar on his forehead. "Okay, George," he said. "I'll make you a deal. You cash that old age pension check, an' I'll tell you who's been imaginary down through the generations all the way to the beginning. Deal?"

George glared at him.

"Hey, you can't expect us to accept the reality of death and loss if you can't even accept the reality of bein' sixty-five."

"Good point. Very well, deal."

"Good." Brandon tossed his cigarette to the ground, gesturing at Cheryl, standing by the Buick with their daughter Kaley in her arms. "Now we should all get back; it looks like it's gonna snow again."

Together, the brothers headed for the parking lot and their own families, and, after a long moment, George followed them.

IMAGES OF DEATH

Jim C. Hines

DEATH reminded Dierdre of Gonzo from The Muppet Show. She moved her hand to block the sun's glare as she peered more closely at the framed sketch within the dusty display case.

Most of the characters were as familiar as her own pale reflection, though she hadn't seen them in years: Libon, the green three-tailed philosopher; Seeblu, the waterbound clown with rippling fins; Dorg the trickster, a furry blob whose crossed eyes gave him away no matter what shape he assumed.

They were family, conceived in her father's studio in this very house and birthed through the tip of his gold-trimmed mahogany fountain pen.

And then there was Death, who was always smiling. Death with his round head, bulging eyes, and potato nose. Disheveled blue fur covered his body. His arms were long swirls, branching and splitting into fractal shapes that poofed around him like dandelion fluff.

Death, who had found her little boy.

She grabbed her cigarettes from her purse, tapped the pack, and slid one into her mouth. "What are you?" she whispered.

An older woman behind the desk cleared her throat. "You know you're not allowed to smoke here?" Her disapproving voice carried clearly through the empty museum.

"He did," Dierdre said, jabbing her cigarette at a self-portrait of her father. When she was growing up, peeling sunflower wallpaper had covered the living room walls. Today, those walls had been stripped and repainted a neutral beige. Her father would have hated it, just as he would have hated the pale wood floors and fluorescent lights. "He smoked in his office upstairs. He set fire to his desk at least twice when I was growing up."

Bill Hammerberg had drawn the Sunday strip "Dreamscapes" for almost thirty years. His work had been described as a bizarre hybrid of Seuss and Picasso, mixed with the smallest pinch of Schulz. It was as good a description as any for the rubbery landscapes and the strange Wonderland creatures who populated them.

Dierdre stepped through the arched doorway into what had once been the dining room. Beneath a sign pointing to the restrooms, a large print showed twenty-four years worth of characters crowded together on an island of purple cliffs and blood-red whirlpools. Death floated above them on a blocky green cloud as he stuffed Coylee the spider into a burlap sack.

An unfinished companion piece showed Death carrying the bulging sack off of a blank page. The uninked drawing had a sad, empty feel. Dierdre shivered as the image triggered memories of childhood nightmares.

The grandfather clock in the far corner chimed three, each ring driving guilt deeper into her chest. She was already late picking Paul up from the sitter. If she didn't leave soon, they would miss his doctor's appointment.

But instead of moving toward the door, Dierdre walked to the stairs and sat on the bottom step. After checking to make sure the receptionist wasn't looking, she pulled a folded piece of yellow construction paper from her purse.

She had found the drawing two days earlier, while changing Paul's bed. He had stuffed it into his pillow-case, along with a Spider-Man action figure and a Canadian two-dollar coin he kept for good luck.

Dierdre had never taken Paul to the museum. He was too young to understand his grandfather's work, and she had never bought any of his collections, unwilling to reawaken old nightmares. When she asked Paul if he had ever seen "Dreamscapes," he had simply stared at her.

Yet the marker-drawn figure, with its oversized nose and blue wing arms, was a crude twin to her father's Death.

"I remember you," she whispered, blowing a stream of smoke at the drawing. She pulled out a pen and began to sketch a crude chain-link fence. The pen tore through the paper before she could finish.

"I won't let you take my son." She jammed the pen back into her purse, then pressed the tip of her cigarette onto the paper.

The ashes crumbled away and the cigarette died, leaving Death untouched.

Paul's drawing was like a glowing coal, burning Dierdre's leg through the worn leather of her purse as she dragged her son through the endless hospital corridors. The walls of the children's wing were covered in bright handprints, with photos of recovered patients smiling from the bulletin boards. The cheerful decor was a sharp contrast to the smell of vomit and disinfectant.

Dierdre dodged past a girl in a wheelchair and pulled Paul into the waiting room. "I'm sorry I'm late," she said as she dug out her license and Medicaid card.

Paul sat down in a chair and began to play with his battered, bald Superman action figure. He had used sandpaper to scrape away the toy's painted hair after his first round of chemotherapy. "I don't understand. I thought the leukemia was in remission." The words were far too adult for an eight-year-old boy. "I'm not supposed to see the doctor until next month."

Dierdre forced a smile. "I thought it would be better to get it over with before school starts."

"But I wanted to—" Paul cocked his head, his eyes briefly focusing on something beyond her. "You're still scared I'm going to die."

"No!" The waiting room went silent. Face burning, Dierdre stepped away from the receptionist and lowered her voice. "You're not going to die."

"Whatever."

She reached out to squeeze his shoulder, but he pulled away. That was how most of their conversations ended these days.

He looked so thin. His Transformers T-shirt hung loose on his shoulders, like a sheet on a clothesline. He wore his Detroit Tigers cap with the brim pulled low over his eyes.

"Paul?" A young nurse smiled as he spotted them. After the past year, most of the staff recognized them both on sight.

Dierdre tried not to fidget as she waited for the nurse to weigh her son—only forty-four pounds—and check his vitals before escorting them to an exam room.

"Doctor McCarthy will be right with you," the nurse said, leaving Paul and Dierdre to wait in silence.

Paul's symptoms had begun when he missed a few days of school with a fever and sore throat. His doctor prescribed antibiotics and Children's Tylenol and sent them home.

Two weeks later, Dierdre was carrying her sweat-soaked son into the emergency room. If she closed her eyes, she could still feel his fingers digging into her arms as he groaned and begged her to make it stop. His heart had been pounding so hard she could see his chest trembling beneath his shirt.

Leukemia had driven his white blood cell count to eighty thousand, four times the healthy range. His bone marrow had been full of leukemia blasts: immature, abnormal cells that ravaged his system.

After months of transfusions and chemotherapy, Paul slowly began to recover. His white blood count improved, and Dierdre dared to believe she and her son might finally get their lives back.

She squeezed her purse, hearing Paul's drawing crinkle within. The clock on the wall showed that only seven minutes had passed since the nurse left. She clenched her fists and forced herself to wait, mentally bracing herself for the news she knew was coming.

Paul lay back, and his sneakers tore the paper rolled out over the exam table. He mumbled to himself as he stared at the ceiling. No, not at the ceiling, but—it.

An unwanted memory forced its way to the forefront of Dierdre's mind. She saw her father as he had been during the last years of his life. He sat staring at the blank paper on his desk. His hand trembled, and the fountain pen clutched between his fingers peppered his sleeve with ink.

Looking at her son, Dierdre saw her father's vacant gaze. What did he see?

Footsteps approached. Dierdre held her breath as the door opened and Doctor McCarthy stepped inside. She braced herself, the drawing in her purse burning hotter than ever.

When he smiled—a real smile, not the expression of sad sympathy she had come to know so well—her relief was so great she nearly collapsed.

"Your labwork looks good, buddy. Your white blood cell count is almost normal." He tossed the thick green folder with Paul's paperwork onto the counter and pulled up a stool. "How's your stomach? Any more diarrhea?"

Paul rolled his eyes. "It's fine. My mouth has been hurting a little, but that's all."

Dierdre bit her lip. Paul hadn't mentioned any mouth pain. But then, why would he tell her? Every time he complained, the result was another trip to the hospital, another round of exams and shots and worse.

Doctor McCarthy checked the inside of Paul's

mouth, then palpated his throat. "Swallow for me." He grunted, then glanced at Dierdre. "Have you noticed anything unusual?"

My son has been drawing Death.

"You're sure . . . all of his tests were okay?"

"At the rate he's improving, he'll be healthier than either of us." He gave his gut a rueful slap. "I don't see any reason he can't go back to school." He double-checked the catheter in Paul's chest for signs of infection. "If all goes well, we should be able to yank this sucker out by the end of the year."

It took all Dierdre's strength to keep from crying. That catheter had haunted her for months. Without it, medicating her son would have required countless injections, leading to massive bruising and blown veins. But every time she saw that alien bit of rubber and plastic protruding from her son's chest, she wanted to rip it out with her bare hands.

She twisted her purse strap around her hands. If Paul was okay, then why had he drawn Death? "Are there any other tests we could run? To be sure?"

"I understand why you'd be afraid," Doctor McCarthy said gently. "We checked his results twice to be safe. He's getting better." He hesitated. "If you insist, I suppose we could repeat the tests again. It's only been a few days since the last blood draw, so the results would be the same, but—"

Paul's tired sigh was so quiet she barely heard. A year ago, he would have whined and argued at the thought of more bloodwork and doctor's visits. Now he just seemed to shrink a bit more.

"No." Dierdre pulled the purse strap so tightly her fingers began to throb, but the relief on Paul's face was worth it. And Doctor McCarthy had checked twice. Paul's drawing was wrong. He was getting better. "Thank you."

On the way out, as Dierdre stopped to give the receptionist her copayment, Paul's hand darted into her purse.

"Why did you take this?" he asked. His Superman toy dropped to the floor, and he clutched the drawing with both hands. "You ripped it!"

Neither her aborted scribbles nor the smear of cigarette ash obscured that too-cheerful grin or the golf ball eyes that followed you no matter how you looked at the picture. "I'm sorry about that," Dierdre said. "I found it when I was cleaning."

Paul crumpled the drawing into his pocket.

"Does he have a name?" Dierdre asked, fighting to keep her voice casual. Her father had never named Death in his strip. Only after his death had she realized who the strange creature was.

But she had been wrong. This was nothing but another of Bill Hammerberg's mad sketches, and Paul was going to be okay.

"I dunno." Something in Paul's tone chilled her in a way she hadn't felt since her father died. "He hasn't said."

Three weeks passed before Dierdre found the next drawing piled with Paul's coloring books. Long enough for her to truly begin to believe the worst was behind them.

Paul had drawn a battle between small, blocky tanks and triangular jets. Death floated down from the clouds, using his oversized arms as a parachute.

She held the drawing in both hands as she moved through her father's museum, searching. Her sneakers slapped the wooden floor as she moved into what had once been the kitchen, now cleared of cabinets and appliances.

Bill Hammerberg's very first illustration of Death had been done in black marker on the back of an orange hospital tray. The hospital had displayed it in their lobby for several months after he recovered from his first stroke. Four screws now secured it to the wall next to the kitchen window.

Seeblu the fish-man took center stage. He wore an obscenely immodest hospital gown as he munched on a stethoscope. Dorg was dressed as a nurse. He carried a long, rubbery thermometer that looped about like a garden hose. Seeblu's thought-bubble read: You want to put that *where?*

Behind Dorg and Seeblu, a crudely drawn door swung inward. Only one of Death's featherlike arms was visible, but it was definitely him.

Dierdre stared at the drawing. Her father had survived Death's initial visit, recovering from that first stroke with minimal damage. In fact, he had spent more time drawing after that first stroke, until he was working nearly six months ahead of his deadlines.

Only Dierdre had seen her father's final drawing, years later. He had sketched it on a napkin. When she closed her eyes, she could still see the jagged pencil lines, a result of stiff fingers and useless nerves. The tip of the pencil had torn the napkin in several places.

A shaky caricature of her father lay on a bed, eyes closed. Instead of a blanket, Death's infinite arms reached out to cocoon her father's body, squeezing the life out of him.

Even back then, before she had named Death, the strange character and his moronic smile had frightened her. She remembered tearing the napkin from her sleeping father's hand and flushing it down the toilet.

Destroying the drawing had done nothing to stop Death. Bill Hammerberg had died the following morning.

She stared at Paul's drawing, then looked back up at the tray. His grandfather had died before he was born. Paul still insisted he had never seen another picture of Death, and he was too poor a liar to fool her. So how could he draw these things? What did they mean? Doctor McCarthy said he was getting better.

Death floated above the earth in Paul's picture. He hadn't yet landed. Just as he hadn't entered the room in her father's first drawing. Paul still had time.

She tore the picture to pieces and tossed them in the trash as she hurried out of the museum.

"I don't understand," Paul said for the third time as he crossed the parking lot with Dierdre, heading for the playground. Just one year earlier, he would have been holding her hand. "Why can't I draw anymore?"

"Because I told you not to!" Guilt made her cringe. What kind of mother shouted at her sick child? In a way, she was relieved to see him energetic enough to argue. But why did he have to choose *this* to argue about? "You're getting better, remember? You should be outside getting some exercise, not hunched in your room."

"It's him, isn't it? That funny-looking guy with the big nose and the arms." He stopped talking long enough to try to blow a bubble with his gum. One small bubble popped, but then he blew too hard, and the gum flew from his mouth. He scowled. "Why does he scare you?"

"Why did you start drawing him?" Dierdre countered, refusing to be drawn in. Damn eight-year-old insight, anyway.

Paul shrugged. He could be as stubborn as his father had been. As Dierdre was too, she admitted. That was part of the reason Paul's father had left. Minor squabbles turned into huge fights, with neither one able or willing to let go.

"I dunno." His gaze slipped past her, and he cocked his head as though he were listening to something. "I'll stop drawing him if you promise me I don't have to go back to the hospital. I want to go to school on Monday."

"Of course you're going to school on Monday," Dierdre said. Her shoulders slumped as the tension in her neck and back began to loosen. "Now go play."

She pulled out a cigarette as she watched him explore the playground, walking from the swing set to the monkeybars to the slide, touching each one but never actually playing. Before the leukemia, he had run everywhere.

"How are you feeling?" she shouted.

"I'm *fine*, Mom." He moved like a sleepwalker, feet dragging through the grass. He hesitated when he reached the teeter-totters.

The teeter-totters had always been Paul's favorite. One of his proudest moments had been the day he learned to balance on the middle of the board, bending his legs and shifting his weight to tilt it from one side to the other.

Arms spread, Paul took a tentative step onto the

old yellow board. Dierdre was too far away to see his face, but she could imagine his expression. His eyes and forehead wrinkled when he concentrated. No doubt he was biting his tongue, as he did when he practiced his handwriting.

He reached the midpoint and bent his knees, leaning to one side, but the board didn't move. The equipment was old and stiff. Paul stepped past the midpoint and stomped his foot.

The board squealed into motion, and Paul's foot slipped. His shin scraped the board, and he tumbled backward onto the ground.

Dierdre was there in an instant, helping him sit up as she rolled up his pants and examined his leg. Pinpricks of blood bloomed along the skin.

"I'm okay." Paul shoved her away. His face was red. He wouldn't look at her.

She reached out to help him stand, but he twisted out of her grasp. As he did, Dierdre glimpsed the back of his leg. Red spots dotted the back of Paul's thigh, above the knee. There was no blood. These hadn't come from the teeter-totter.

"What's wrong?" Paul tugged his pantlegs back into place.

"Nothing." The spots might not mean anything. They could be a rash, a reaction to the new pants, or to the cheap detergent she bought at the laundromat. Doctor McCarthy said he was okay.

Paul clearly wasn't buying it. "You promised I could go to school." He looked close to tears. The last time he had come so close to breaking down was at one of his earliest blood draws, and he had fought and kicked like an animal the entire time.

School was only two days away. She could take him

to the emergency room now, or she could schedule an appointment for Monday afternoon, after his first day back. Deep inside, she was screaming.

"Come on," she said. "Let's get you back home before it gets too late."

The relapse hit Paul on Monday morning, only a few hours after Dierdre dropped him off at school. His teacher took him down to the nurse's office when he started shivering and couldn't stop. The nurse took one look at Paul's records and called Dierdre. By the time she arrived, Paul was wrapped in two wool blankets, his teeth chattering.

He threw up halfway to the hospital, splashing half-digested Froot Loops all over the back seat. The smell made Dierdre's stomach rebel, but she couldn't open the windows without chilling Paul worse.

An eternity later, she was back in the children's care unit, pleading with Paul to take another sip of broth, another spoonful of lemon Jello.

Doctor McCarthy stepped softly into the room. "We've got his lab results."

The gentleness in his voice made Dierdre want to hit him. Instead, she turned up the television mounted on the wall and stepped away.

"You don't have to leave," Paul yelled. "I know what he's going to say."

Dierdre couldn't answer. Paul sank back into his pillows and stared blearily at the television screen.

For an instant, Dierdre imagined she could see Death dancing and grinning next to SpongeBob SquarePants.

Doctor McCarthy waited for her to follow, then

gently closed the door behind her. "His white blood cell count is almost seventy thousand."

So fast. Her skin felt like ice. "What about his blasts?"

His eyes were sad, but his voice didn't falter. "Around eighty percent."

Dierdre collapsed against the wall. Paul's bone marrow was packed with undeveloped, *useless* cells. "You told us he was getting better."

"I know. But sometimes—"

"Don't say it! Don't tell me things *happen*." She should have dragged Paul in the instant she found the second drawing. Death had known, even if the doctors hadn't.

"We're waiting on a few more tests," he said. He reached out to squeeze her arm. "Sometimes there are setbacks. We're going to beat this thing. Paul's a strong boy. You should—"

Dierdre pulled away. By the end of the day, they would be starting Paul on yet another round of chemo. Paul said the medicine was like liquid fire pumping through his body. Or would it be bone marrow transplants this time, and with them the immunosuppressants that would leave him weak and vulnerable to every germ that floated through the air?

No. Death would *not* take her son. She turned her back on Doctor McCarthy without another word and hurried into Paul's room.

Paul rolled over as she entered. He looked so helpless, tangled in a spider's web of tubes and wires. An IV tube ran past his neck, disappearing down his hospital gown into the catheter in his chest. A blood pressure cuff engulfed one arm. Other wires monitored his heart rate and blood oxygen.

His complexion matched the pale walls behind him.
Dierdre sat down and ran her fingers over the downy
brown fuzz on his scalp.

Paul squirmed away. His arms were stretched awk-
wardly to one side, his hands tucked beneath the
pillow.

On a hunch, Dierdre grabbed beneath the pillow.
Her fingers touched paper, and she pulled the drawing
free before he could stop her.

"That's mine!"

It was another portrait of Death. Her hands began
to shake. "When did you draw this?"

"At school today." He untangled his IV tube, then
sat up to glare at her. "When I started feeling cold."

A crude stick-figure wearing a baseball cap sat on
one side of a teeter-totter, with Death on the other.
There was no ground, only a vast black plain. Wavy
motion lines showed Death rising as the stick figure
descended toward the darkness.

"Why do you keep ruining them?" Paul asked.

Because I don't know how else to fight him.

But destroying the pictures wasn't enough. Death
still found him. "You promised you wouldn't—"

"I'm dying!" Paul said. His frustration and fatigue
hit her like a physical blow. "Who cares about a stupid picture?"

She stood and backed away from the bed. "Did you
see him yesterday?" The paper crumpled in her hand.
"Is he here now? Here in the room?"

"No." His gaunt face was full of anger, but she saw
confusion there as well. Confusion and fear. His forehead wrinkled. "You know what that thing is, don't
you?"

"I . . . I don't know." She moved toward the door, still holding his picture. She *didn't* know.

"Mom, wait! I'm sorry." He sounded frightened. "Where are you going?"

She stopped in the doorway, searching for an answer that would make sense. But how could she explain what she didn't understand? She couldn't help him. Not here. She bowed her head and said, "I'll be back as soon as I can."

The museum was dark, save for a small spotlight illuminating the front sign next to the porch. The old house was more familiar in the darkness, making Dierdre feel like a child again.

Climbing the old pine tree in the side yard was harder than she remembered. The branches were thicker and harder to grasp. Her muscles and joints protested the unfamiliar strain. But she made it to the roof without falling. There, she clung to the dormer shingles while she regained her breath. She picked pine needles from her hair with her free hand. Gummy sap covered her sleeves.

The security system would sense if she opened her old window. She could just make out the wires in the middle where the two panes came together. It was an old system, but effective.

Her father had used a simpler system with a board, some twine, and an old mason jar. Opening the window tilted the board, sending the jar rolling down the roof to shatter in the driveway. When her father was working, anything quieter than shattering glass would go unnoticed.

Squirrels had occasionally smashed a jar, but the

makeshift alarm had stopped Dierdre from sneaking out her window at night.

Instead, she had gone through the attic.

She doubted the museum would have bothered to wire the gable vent on the north end of the house. Nor were they likely to have noticed the missing screws where a young Dierdre had prepared an alternate way in and out of the house. She made her way to the end of the roof, then stepped out to balance on another tree branch as she worked the vent loose. Her body was thicker than it had been in those days, but she managed to squeeze inside, her feet automatically finding the beams beneath the fiberglass insulation.

The hinges squealed like a wounded animal as she lowered the attic ladder into the house. She froze, half expecting her father to come thundering out of his office. Back then, Dierdre had oiled the hinges regularly.

She used the tiny LED flashlight in her cellphone to make her way toward her father's office. Framed comics decorated the wall where Dierdre's memory still expected to find family photos. Dierdre. stopped as a familiar figure caught her attention.

Bill Hammerberg liked to experiment with new characters, often introducing a new one into the strip for a few weeks, then discarding it before anyone even knew its name. Kind of like his relationships with women, after Dierdre's mother left him.

Perhaps that was why nobody ever noticed the significance of Death. He was one more experiment, like the feathered bowling ball with long chicken legs in the single-panel strip titled "The Nursing Home."

Bowling Ball wore a dirty butcher's apron. Clawlike

fingers clutched an oversized vacuum cleaner that sucked elderly, twig-limbed men and women from a brick building. Death, dressed like a garbage man, was pulling people from the vacuum and tossing them into a riveted steel dumpster.

Standing in the empty house where she and her father had lived for so many years, it was all she could do to keep from screaming. "What is he, Dad?" What was this thing her father had brought into her son's life?

Sweat dripped down her face as she moved from one strip to the next, searching for answers. Her throat was dry and dusty from her trip through the attic.

Dierdre opened the door to her father's office and stepped inside. Green velvet ropes surrounded the ink-stained desk. Drawing paper sat stacked to one side, far neater than it ever had been in her father's life.

Paul had drawn Death, but Dierdre's father had created him. Death lived *here* on the walls, and in this office. She could almost see that horrible Cheshire smile floating in the darkness. She could smell him, an oily scent barely noticeable over the too-strong floral tang of the plug-in air freshener.

Setting her cellphone on the desk, she picked up one of the old fountain pens. The ink had long since dried, and the inkwell on the desk was empty, but Dierdre had come prepared. Tossing the fountain pen aside, she pulled a ballpoint from her purse and grabbed the top sheet of paper. And then Dierdre sat in her father's chair and drew Death.

Destroying Paul's pictures hadn't helped, any more than it had when she tore up her father's final sketch. She had ruined paper, nothing more.

At first, she drew Death trapped. Tied to railroad

tracks like an old cartoon villain, crushed beneath a heavy safe, sinking to the bottom of the ocean in chains. Even as she drew, she knew her pictures were somehow *wrong*. Paul's sketches, crude as they were, captured the essence of Death. But when Dierdre drew him, it was merely a drawing. Death was ignoring her.

After trying and failing yet again, Dierdre stood up so fast the chair toppled backward. She stormed out of the office and retrieved "The Nursing Home" from the hallway. Back at the desk, she flipped over the print and ripped it from the frame.

This Death was real. Unlike her poor drawings, even more than Paul's, her father's Death watched her and laughed. For an instant as she studied the brittle paper, one of the discarded bodies appeared to be wearing a T-shirt and baseball cap.

This time, Dierdre didn't bother with neatness. Her scribbles were like a child's, looping a thread of ink around Death again and again. If she had to, she would tie up every last image of Death in the museum.

Her pen dried after only a few seconds.

"Dammit!" She flung the pen away and dug in her purse for another. Finding none, she hurried out of the office and down the stairs. A small guestbook sat on a pedestal by the front door. She grabbed the pen and ripped it free, breaking the chain that secured it to the book.

On her way back, she stopped as a black and white photograph caught her eye, illuminated by the light through the front window. The photo showed her father receiving an award from the city council. His face was wrinkled as a prune. He looked uncomfortable in his suit and tie. According to the caption, this would have been less than a year before his death.

"You knew what he was," Dierdre whispered. "You must have known. But you kept drawing him. You drew *more*." She stared at the pen in her hand. "Why didn't you stop him?"

Those last years had been his most productive. Knowing Death was near, Bill Hammerberg hadn't tried to fight. He had simply drawn faster.

The broken pen chain tickled her wrist as she returned to the office. She sat down and stared at the comic. She had crossed out the lower part of Death's body, along with his vacuum cleaner, before her pen went dry.

Dierdre set the tip of the guestbook pen against the page. Her hand trembled, leaving a small black streak next to Death's arm. The space around Death was mostly empty. With the vacuum scribbled away, the whole thing appeared incomplete.

"Why didn't you fight?" she whispered.

Slowly, the pen began to move.

Back at the hospital, Dierdre was stopped twice by well-meaning staff who told her visiting hours were over, and that if she wanted to bring a gift to a patient, she should come back in the morning.

"It's for my son. He has leukemia." She barely managed to get the words out without breaking down. Both times, the staff stepped aside with that *look*, that sad, sympathetic, pitying expression that made her want to scream, *He's not dead yet, damn you!*

Paul was sleeping when she arrived at his room. The lights were out, but the door was open. The hall lights provided more than enough illumination for her to make her way to the bed.

He had his thumb in his mouth, and his knees were

pressed against the bedrail. Dierdre tried to be quiet, but Paul stirred before she reached the chair beside the bed. He never slept deeply, even with drugs to soothe his pain.

"Mom?"

She reached over to turn on the fluorescent lamp above the head of the bed. Then she lowered the bedrail and sat down beside him. "I'm sorry I left you."

"You look horrible," he said.

Dierdre ran one hand through her hair, grimacing at the tangles and pine debris.

"Where did you go?" Paul rubbed his eyes, then tugged his IV tube to give himself a bit more slack. "What's that?"

Dierdre unrolled the print she had taken from the museum and spread it on the bed.

Paul's index finger nearly tore a hole through Death. "Who drew this?"

"Your grandfather." Dierdre's throat tightened. She wiped her hands on her pants, fighting the urge to yank the picture away and destroy it. "I did the part in the middle."

"That's terrible, Mom."

She snorted. "I know."

"Grandpa Hammerberg liked to draw?" he asked, still studying the picture.

"He had a comic strip in the newspapers for a while," Dierdre said. She pointed to Death. "He started to draw this character a few years before—." She swallowed, then forced herself to continue. "Before he died."

"Oh." The flatness in his voice made her want to pull him out of bed and rock him in her arms.

He ran a finger over the freshly inked swirls. Dierdre's pen had looped around and around, but she hadn't scribbled through Death himself this time. Instead, she had expanded his arms until they were like tiny tornadoes spinning from his body. Each arm cocooned a struggling figure. On one side, a line through a protruding oval formed a baseball cap. On the other side, a single arm reached through Death's grip. The fingers appeared to be clutching a pen.

"That's me, right?" Paul asked, pointing to the capped figure. "Then who—"

"Me," said Dierdre.

"I don't understand."

"Do you remember when your father and I were still married?" Dierdre asked. "How he and I were always fighting, and we never had any time for you?"

Paul nodded.

"Ever since you got sick, I've been so focused on trying to fight this. On fighting *him*."

"Does that mean you're giving up?"

She swallowed, then said, "It means I won't let him take me away from you."

"Oh." Paul studied the picture more closely. "Grandpa was really good."

"Yes, he was." Dierdre forced herself to look at the picture. "I think Grandpa knew he was going to die. Just like you knew you were going to get sick again."

Paul stared at his hands. "So what did he do?"

"He concentrated on what was important to him." Dierdre had to try three times to get the words out. "Is he going to take you away from me?"

He stared past her, and his face tightened. "He says he doesn't know yet."

Dierdre grabbed his hand. Small fingers clung to hers.

"I don't want to die, Mom."

"You—" *You won't.* But even Death didn't know what would happen. "I don't want you to die either."

After a while, Paul pointed to Death again. "He looks like a muppet."

Dierdre's startled laugh sounded more like a hiccup. She reached down to retrieve the second item she had brought, a copy of *The Complete Dreamscapes, 1972–1976.* She had taken it from the museum gift shop. The cover was bent and grass stained from being tossed out of the attic, but that didn't matter. She would leave an anonymous donation to cover the book and the damage she had done, but that could wait.

Paul opened the cover and flipped past the introduction until he found the first page of comics. He cocked his head before pronouncing, "Grandpa was weird."

"Yes, he was." She sat down on the bed and carefully pulled Paul onto her lap. The book went on the small table, next to the Kleenex box and an unused bedpan. "Would you like me to tell you about him?"

Paul started snoring before she had said more than a few words. She reached back with one hand, adjusting the pillows to support her back. Her leg brushed the stolen picture of Death.

Could she change the picture now? A part of her longed to blot out those arms, to free herself and her son from Death's grip, if only for tonight.

She kissed the top of Paul's head and closed her eyes. A twitch of her foot knocked the print of Death to the floor.

About the Authors

Rick Hautala has had more than thirty books published under his own name and the pseudonym A. J. Mathews, including the million-copy, international bestseller *Nightstone*, and *Bedbugs*, *Little Brothers*, *Cold Whisper*, *Four Octobers*, *The White Room*, *Looking Glass*, *Follow*, and *Unbroken*. More than sixty of his short stories have appeared in a variety of national and international anthologies and magazines. His screenplay *Chills* was recently optioned by Chesapeake Films. Born and raised in Rockport, Mass., he is a graduate of the University of Maine in Orono with a M.A. in English Literature. He lives in southern Maine with author Holly Newstein and Kiera, the Wonder Dog. Visit him at www.rickhautala.com.

Anne Bishop lives in upstate New York where she enjoys gardening, music, and writing dark, romantic stories. She is the author of eleven novels, including the award-winning Black Jewels novels. Her most recent novel is *Tangled Webs*, a story set in the Black

Jewels world. Please visit her website at www.annebishop.com.

Jean Rabe is the author of more than twenty novels and more than forty short stories. In addition, she has edited several DAW anthologies. When she's not writing (which isn't often), she delights in the company of her two aging dogs, dangles her feet in her backyard goldfish pond, and pretends to garden. She loves museums, books, boardgames, role-playing games, wargames, and movies that "blow up real good." Visit her web site at: www.jeanrabe.com.

Juliet E. McKenna has always been fascinated by myth and history, other worlds and other peoples. This ultimately led to her studying Greek and Roman history and literature at St Hilda's College, Oxford, as well as to a lifetime love of SF and fantasy fiction. She is the author of the acclaimed *Tales of Einarinn* series, currently translated into more than a dozen languages, as well as the highly praised *The Aldabreshin Compass* sequence. Her current project, *The Lescari Revolution*, is a trilogy exploring divided states, personal conflict and the rights and responsibilities of power. She is one of the leading lights of The Write Fantastic, a UK authors' initiative promoting the breadth and depth of current fantasy fiction. Living in Oxfordshire, England, with her sons and husband, she fits in her writing around her family and vice versa.

Kristine Kathryn Rusch has sold novels in several different genres under many different names. The most current Rusch novel is *The Recovery Man: A Retrieval Artist Novel*. The Retrieval Artist novels are stand-alone mysteries set in a science fiction world. She's won the Endeavor Award for that series. Her writing has received dozens of award nominations, as well as several actual awards from science fiction's Hugo to the Prix Imagainare, a French fantasy award for best short fiction. She lives and works on the Oregon Coast.

Kristen Britain is the author of the bestselling fantasy novels, *Green Rider*, *First Rider's Call*, and *The High King's Tomb*. She grew up in the Finger Lakes region of New York. After earning a BS in film production with a writing minor from Ithaca College, she served for several years as a national park ranger, working in a variety of natural and historical settings, from high on the Continental Divide, to 300 feet below the surface of the Earth. Currently she lives in Maine with a cat, a dog, and her imaginary friends, Ian and Sven, where she continues to work on the next book in the *Green Rider* series.

Donald J. Bingle has had a wide variety of short fiction published, primarily in DAW themed anthologies, but also in tie-in anthologies for the *Dragonlance* and *Transformers* universes and in popular role-playing gaming materials. Recently, he has had stories published in *Fellowship Fantastic*, *Front Lines*, *Pandora's Closet*, *If I Were an Evil Overlord*, and *Time Twisters*. His first novel, *Forced Conversion*, is set in the near future, when anyone can have heaven, any heaven they want, but some people don't want to go. His most recent novel, *GREENSWORD*, is a darkly comedic thriller about a group of environmentalists who decide to end global warming . . . immediately. Now they're about to save the world; they just don't

want to get caught doing it. Don can be reached at
and his novels purchased through www.orphyte.com/
donaldjbingle.

Tim Waggoner's novels include *Pandora Drive*,
Thieves of Blood, the *Godfire* duology, and *Like
Death*. He's published close to eighty short stories,
some of them collected in *All Too Surreal*. His articles
on writing have appeared in Writer's Digest, Writers
Journal, and other publications. He teaches creative
writing at Sinclair Community College in Dayton,
Ohio. Visit him on the web at www.timwaggoner.com.

Paul Genesse told his mother he was going to be a
writer when he was four years old, and has been creating fantasy stories ever since. He loved his English
classes in college but pursued his other passion by
earning a bachelor's degree in nursing science in 1996.
He is a registered nurse on a cardiac unit in Salt Lake
City, Utah, where he works the night shift keeping
the forces of darkness away from his patients. Paul
lives with his incredibly supportive wife Tammy and
their collection of frogs. He spends endless hours in
his basement writing fantasy novels, short stories,
and crafting maps of fantastical realms. His novel
*The Golden Cord: Book 1 of The Iron Dragon Tril-
ogy* was released in 2008, but his current project is
Medusa's Daughter, a fantasy set in ancient Greece.
He encourages you to contact him online at www.paul
genesse.com.

Russell Davis has written numerous short stories and
novels in a variety of genres under several different
names. Some of his most recent work can be seen in

Fellowship Fantastic, *Man Vs. Machine*, and *Under Cover of Darkness*. He lives in Nevada, where he writes, rides horses and spends time with his family.

Bill Fawcett has been a professor, teacher, corporate executive, and college dean. He is one of the founders of Mayfair Games, a board and role playing gaming company. Bill began his own novel writing with a juvenile series, *Swordquest*, for Ace SF. Anticipating cats, he wrote and edited the four novels, beginning with the *Lord of Cragsclaw* featuring the Mrem, which appear in *Shattered Light* as a hero class (all rights owned by Bill). The *Fleet* series he created with David Drake has become a classic of military science fiction. He has collaborated on several novels, including mysteries such as the *Authorized Mycroft Holmes* novels, the *Madame Vernet Investigates* series, and edited *Making Contact, a UFO Contact* handbook. As an anthologist, Bill has edited or coedited over fifty anthologies. Bill Fawcett & Associates has packaged well over two hundred and fifty novels and anthologies for every major publisher. Bill is the editor of *Hunters and Shooters* and *The Teams*, two oral histories of the SEALs in Vietnam. His most recently published work is as coauthor of *It Seemed Like a Good Idea: Great Historical Fiascos*; *You Did What?*; *How To Lose A Battle* and *It Looked Good on Paper*, all fun and informative looks at bad decisions in history and the folks who made them.

Fiona Patton was born in Calgary, Alberta, Canada, and, grew up in the United States. In 1975 she returned to Canada and now lives on 75 acres of scrubland in rural Ontario with her partner, Tanya

Huff, six and a half cats and a tiny little chihuahua that thinks he's a great dane. She has written six fantasy novels for DAW Books, the latest being *The Golden Tower*. She has also written more than two dozen short stories, most of them for Tekno Books DAW anthologies.

Jim C. Hines began writing more than a decade ago, but he tries not to think about that. He is the author of three humorous fantasy novels, *Goblin Quest*, *Goblin Hero*, and *Goblin War*, all from DAW Books. His next novel, *The Stepsister Scheme*, will start a new series from DAW in January 2009. Jim lives in Michigan with his wife and children, all of whom have been amazingly supportive and tolerant of his writing career. He has never been all that fond of writing author bios, so he asked his children to help finish this one. From his six-year-old daughter: "Daddy likes Snoopy, and I just lost a tooth." From his one-year-old son: ",po ;l[;=[pl,8yu8 thh bbbbbbbbb V$# v Ecv"

Kristen Britain

The **GREEN RIDER** series

"Wonderfully captivating...a truly
enjoyable read." —Terry Goodkind

"A fresh, well-organized fantasy debut,
with a spirited heroine and a reliable
supporting cast." —*Kirkus*

"The author's skill at world building and her feel
for dramatic storytelling make this first-rate
fantasy a good choice." —*Library Journal*

"Britain keeps the excitement high from beginning to end, balancing epic magical battles with
the humor and camaraderie of Karigan and her
fellow Riders." —*Publishers Weekly*

GREEN RIDER	0-88677-858-1
FIRST RIDER'S CALL	0-7564-0209-3

and now available in hardcover:
THE HIGH KING'S TOMB 0-7564-0209-3

To Order Call: 1-800-788-6262
www.dawbooks.com